NO ISLAND OF SALVATION

Peter is spending his holidays at his grandfather's manor-house in Eastern Poland. He loves his cousin Catherine and the place has always stood in his imagination for security and happiness; but since he was last there, war has come, the Russians have occupied the region and been followed by the Germans. Now bands of Ukrainians are savagely working off old grudges and Polish patriots are fighting to protect the peasants.

The old house and its way of life are surprisingly unchanged, but its inhabitants seem uneasy and unreal and Peter soon senses that much is being hidden from him and also that something unexpressed is being demanded of him.

With a part of himself he wants to know the truth; with another, he fears it. What eventually he learns, the decision he takes, are the facts upon which this very moving novel is built.

Against a background in which rape, arson and murder stand in contrast to first and last love, a sensitive boy leaves childhood behind, and, recognising that mere survival is not enough, tries to find that solidarity from which a common future for all of them may spring.

by the same author

THE DYING DAY

NO ISLAND OF SALVATION

by

Wlodzimierz Odojewski

translated from the Polish by
David Welsh

HARVILL PRESS
LONDON

Printed in Great Britain
by Collins Clear-Type Press
London and Glasgow
for the publishers
Harvill Press Limited
23 Lower Belgrave Street
London, S.W.1.

Originally published in Polish under the title
'Wyspa Ocalenia'

PUBLISHER'S NOTE

Poland's unhappy history provides the background and the motivations for Wlodzimierz Odojewski's novel. Partitioned between Russia, Austria and Prussia in the early nineteenth century, Poland had been reunited as a national state after World War I. Russia, which had held its eastern borderlands from Lithuania to the Ukraine, renounced all claims to Poland in 1919. When the German army invaded Poland in 1939, the Soviet Union—then Germany's ally—reoccupied the eastern areas, only to be pushed out again by the Germans in June 1941.

In the province which is the locale of *No Island of Salvation*, things are further complicated by another national group, the Ukrainians. These, under their leader Stefan Bandera, formed the Organization of Ukrainian Nationalists and agitated for a separate Ukrainian State. We have, then, in Eastern Poland in the summer of 1942, the Germans as occupying power; the Poles, who consider the country their national territory; and the Ukrainians fighting the Poles in the name of their own national aspirations.

At the end of the war, all Poland became a 'people's republic'; the Polish officers, representatives of the Polish ruling class, who had been taken prisoners by Soviet Russia in 1939, were found murdered in the mass graves in Katyn wood near Smolensk.

I

NOT A SCRAP OF SHADOW. THE LIGHT-BROWN slope glowed with reflected sun, infinitely empty, proscribing by its very appearance any suspicion that it ever had anything to do with life. The burning breath of an east wind died among the rocks and ceased troubling the silence in which there was total oblivion. Closer, almost suspended on the brink, two chestnut trees, incongruous here, scattered with whiteness, seemed to glow rather than flower, although the rainy season had not long passed, and the newly tarred road leading down into the valley was so black that when Peter closed his eyes, which were scorched with heat, he retained it for a long time under his eyelids, like a deep ravine of shadow eroded in a sea of fire.

'So you're from over there . . .' the old countrywoman repeated his question and, without looking at Peter, 'over there, there, over there . . .' she mumbled the words persistently so that they'd have become meaningless even to him, had he not recalled that he himself had uttered them only a moment ago; although already he wasn't entirely certain of that either. But then, before she stiffened entirely into immobility, her clasped hands drooping helplessly between thin knees that projected sharply under the material of her black skirt, plunging totally into her own thoughts, into that which was for her an obscure, insoluble riddle or perhaps a dream, for she closed her eyes and sat in this white cruel sun under the white, half-ruined wall of an inn, which gave no shade at all, even the coping over the porch gave none, nor the two roughly hewed beams supporting the coping, nothing at all gave any shade; she sat on as if elsewhere, as though she were present merely in her frail, old, unimportant body, while in reality she'd gone to another, more distant end of the earth (as though this one wasn't distant enough, and lost on the world's rim); only the handkerchief with which she had wrapped her head, and under which it was hard to suspect the presence of any hair, protected her from the glow; drawing it down over her face, she muttered something about salvation, just before she passed into complete immobility.

Peter said nothing; leaning against the wall, which seemed to him to retain some vestiges of coolness despite the sun, he thought that his departure from over there and his taking refuge here, in this deserted and mutilated region, was too unbelievable and uncertain to be called salvation with any genuine conviction; still, this refuge had to be accepted, even if it were to prove only temporary, just as a gift from Heaven has to be accepted, and he must swear to himself once and for all that this threshold of a mountain inn, where he sat, would be now and in future the most easterly point in his wanderings over the world's surface, and that he would never cross this frontier he'd already established for himself.

When he closed his eyes, the crevice in the flames under his eyelids slowly contracted, and it was as though he were on the point of dying. So he hastily opened them wider and wider, as wide as he could, until it hurt, to protect himself from this insanity, and then the broad black line of the road was cutting across the slope as before, everything motionless and yet shimmering, but in its proper place and real, while only the smouldering tar kept giving off fountains of air that agitated the leaves of two chestnut trees, Peter—no longer aware of any of the peculiar desires and insane urges which had been driving him on from place to place, nor of anything except faint though equally insane desires, totally at odds with common sense, to return once more if only in a dream to the home of his youth, the only desire capable of inspiring him—gazed at the slope below his feet, at the road running down to the valley deserted from end to end, at the trail winding along its bottom which wasn't a stream, nor a shepherd's path nor a railway embankment, at the roof of some building rising in a clump of trees, close to that trail which stood out with an ashy gleam from the slope (he hadn't noticed that roof before, and asked the woman what it was, but she didn't reply or didn't hear or didn't want to answer), and also at the trees encircling that roof which were green and yet somehow parched, and as he gazed he couldn't accept the notion that they might only be the product of his febrile imagination; and he waited patiently for the day to cool and for the light finally to diminish and change the day into a dusk full of the thunder of a rising storm; and he even had a vague hope that the dazzling haze caused perhaps by the sunbeams, or which perhaps was only the product of his own exhaustion, veiling everything from him in an indistinct mist, so that nearby objects were hazy while the distance acquired clarity, like a mirage, this troubling haze would (he hoped) open up a little when the daylight faded, and the time which was the present would pass, without significance, reluctantly filtering all those distant echoes, and that he would suddenly remember it all:

and he thought that, of course, soon the time would come for him to start remembering it all again, before the image of those years faded entirely, soon, from one incident to the next, choosing those dearest to him, for soon dusk would spread over the valley, perhaps a storm would roar up, he could feel it, so that soon all this would painlessly liberate him, as always, soon it would, he thought, yes and: I was then a little more than fifteen, well, perhaps that age or a little older, never mind, the same light was in my eyes, and at once it seemed to him he could sense the stifling, hot weather, and that heat weighing down upon the world from noon onwards, the sensation which drifted in a burning breath from the valley plain out of the deepest shadows of a long dead world.

And then, though he'd vowed that the threshold of the inn where he now sat at rest would be, now and in future, the most easterly point of the globe where he could remain unpunished, though he'd vowed many times, he rose and, without saying good-bye to the woman in black leaning against the wall, not even saying the slightest word to her, though he ought to have done so, he walked on, overcoming his own fatigue, towards the road. However, before he reached it, before he decided on the direction to take, perhaps not even realizing very clearly where he was going, he looked back, briefly surveyed the half-ruined inn and the cross-roads, dissolving in the light, and the woman who, from a few paces away, looked as though she had long been dead; she was not even animated by her breathing, and looked like the daughter, wife, and mother mourning all the men of this region shot and tortured to death. But then he finally realized where he was going, chose his direction, so, despite his fatigue which had not decreased, he decisively avoided the stone foundations of a burned-down wall, skirted a dusty dog which lay asleep, paws outstretched, by a ditch, motionless as carrion, and walked on to the asphalt of the road in the direction of the valley.

The road was bordered by heaps formed of fallen lumps of chalk cliffs: tightly matted clumps of grass sprouted around them, shrivelled and looking as if they too had been turned to rock. The misty haze which came from the glare of the light or perhaps from his own exhaustion thinned out, it had risen upwards, had even dissolved here and there into long, fine strands fading away into the rocky ravines, and the place in the valley for which he was making, that clump of parched trees (or so they seemed when he looked at them), above which rose the top of a red roof, soon became clearly visible. He thought that in a different state he'd have been able to reach it quickly and easily, without tiring himself at all, but now he wasn't sure he'd ever reach it, for suddenly he felt worse than before, and he might even have thought that he had a fever again if he hadn't noticed that it was only another slight, burning breath of wind that had risen from the mountains. However, this breath entirely dispelled the misty haze in the valley and reassured him that the clump of trees with a roof in the middle wasn't the product of a state bordering on illness, but as real as it possibly could be, and soon he saw that the trail standing out from the rocks, which at first had given the impression of a pathway, then of the course of some dried-up stream, then again of a railway line, was, in fact, a railway line set on a low embankment; then the exhaustion which had been confusing his thoughts from the very start by erasing the proportions between things and by confusing time past with time present and the chronology of events too, this weariness and exhaustion which he had no longer even hoped to rid himself of suddenly yielded. Perhaps he forgot it, for a moment later he didn't even remember that it had ever troubled him, and when this happened, he quickly and easily succeeded in crossing the last section of the road and approaching the clump of trees.

There was a smell of damp pine needles, of leaves, of freshness; when he passed the first trees he felt as though he were in a completely new dimension of reality, but when the trees thinned and revealed a small open space, not quite a clearing but not a cutting either, he realized he hadn't set eyes on such a good place for a long time, and it hadn't even occurred to him before that he might find one in such a sombre region; but then, after going around the edge of that clearing or rather small lawn, for he noticed a flower bed in the grass, so as to reach the far side, and when he was on the far side, and saw the building of which he'd previously seen only a roof emerging from treetops, he realized again that this place was strangely familiar to him from some other time, as if it had been brought here from somewhere different, or at least it reminded him of something familiar and close. Then he heard an impatient cry: 'Pete! Pete! Do I have to wait much longer?'

No one had called him by that name, well hardly a name but more of a pet name (which only a few people in the world said in precisely that way), for years now; for several years, for a long time, since forgotten times, so it seemed to him, but now someone was calling impatiently, clearly, and in a voice well known to him; and he'd have thought (for it was so improbable) that he'd misheard or that his imagination was playing another trick, had not the call been repeated again a moment later: 'Pete!' impatiently now. He thought confusedly that during the years he'd grown used to all kinds of names which acquaintances and strangers, friends and enemies, had called him by, names given him in the streets and highways, during marriage ceremonies and funerals, in everyday life and on holidays, in dark apartments and under the open sky, during interrogations, in sombre buildings, and under the blaze of arc lamps glaring brilliantly into his eyes, also in reports, protocols, on passes and identity papers, he'd grown so used to all these names written or spoken with the most varied emotional colouring, that in the end he'd forgotten he might ever have had another name, although sometimes he'd had a faint hope that it wasn't entirely lost and that in future someone would again call him by this name; and now, when he heard it and realized that his imagination hadn't deceived him, he had to pause a moment, catch the air vibrating in his lungs, had to cool down after the first shock, to prepare himself inwardly, as it were, to accept this name again, and this lasted some time, perhaps a minute or two, perhaps whole years, but when it finally happened and he gained enough courage to take a stand face to face with what awaited him, he moved on to confront whatever it was, unknown and yet exciting in its proximity. He went into the door of the building, passed a row of ticket offices screened by thick glass, saw maps and schedules hanging crowded on the walls, and went out by a door on the opposite side.

This is what he saw, black and white and blurred at the same time, as if in a dream, then clear, precise, taking on colours: on the freshly gravelled platform, by suitcases and a bulging trunk, stood Demoiselle Spang, his sister Constance's governess, wiping her sweating and sun-reddened face with a handkerchief and glancing impatiently towards the door in which he, Peter, had just appeared.

For a moment longer he was filled with the amazement caused by the sound of his own pet name, then the amazement began changing into a sorrowful awareness that the natural order of events had, perhaps as a result of his own state of mind, of that tendency of his memory to plunge into chaos, become confused and started arranging itself in a way that didn't conform to the rules of logic, but he soon forgot all this, yes, he even forgot what he'd once heard about Demoiselle Spang, about her death in a concentration camp heaped with the snows of the Far North, when she had been hanged along with his uncle Theodore years ago, and everything which he himself had earlier seen or heard now seemed totally impossible to him; the sight which appeared before him, as soon as he emerged from the door, the sunlit platform and Demoiselle standing amidst suitcases and trunks at once took on a still greater clarity.

She glanced at him in silent reproach, then, without hiding her vexation, said: 'You are a naughty boy to go away for so long just before we leave. . . . The train will soon be here, and you might have missed it,' to which he replied he'd gone out for a moment to the front of the station to look once more at the little town, that they had at least three minutes or so before the train arrived, but despite what he'd just said, a metallic hum came along the railway line, which suddenly yielded in its ties, and an engine rushed rattling and hissing up to the station, pulling a line of carriages after it. The usual confusion that accompanies all arrivals and departures started, then someone had to help him load the baggage, and in a moment they were sitting face to face in a compartment, the train was rushing on, and outside the window Peter again saw a strange, silver and sparkling haze which gleamed and thickened into a compressed layer like cotton wool, so that the onrush of the train inside this misty haze gave Peter the impression of travelling through a long tunnel of sleep; perhaps it lasted long, perhaps not, anyway after some time the veiling haze parted, fell into two, changed into a wall of trees on both sides of the track, and soon wild flowers were glowing here and there in the rich grass amidst thread-like vestiges of the haze, then later still the forest gave way to cornfields, the haze disappeared entirely, and here and there knapweed and poppies rose out of the corn. But this landscape too yielded to another, more familiar, and Peter felt as if he'd woken or, more precisely, as if he'd returned from non-existence, and he already knew his destination.

Now and again the train slowed down, a solitary stop appeared to Peter: two or three poplar trees with a stork's nest in the highest, a small kitchen garden farther off, in which stood the stationmaster's house, built of pine logs on a stone base, with a small room on the upper floor where gilly flowers blossomed in the window and from which the stationmaster's wife, drawing apart the stalks, watched the train arrive and depart, along with a few of what seemed to him to be the same country women running along the platform stirring up the dust with their feet, calling: 'Berries! Berries!' or 'Yoghurt, young sir, buy my cold yoghurt!' Then, later, the almost limitless steppe and greyness of fields, which it was difficult to differentiate from the steppe, with only an occasional and distantly darkening smudge of forest.

Peter sat pressed into the corner of the compartment, elbow on the frame of the wide-open window, chin in hand, fighting his utmost against the insistent sleepiness which everything seemed to encourage: the monotony of the journey, the heat, the uniformity of the landscape. Demoiselle Spang was dozing. Her face had relaxed a little, that shade of severity which he once feared so much had vanished (though she'd been a sort of second mother to him since he'd grown out of her charge and she only took care of his sister Constance; even so, she had yielded no less than his mother to his often peculiar fancies), but another shadow had come to the drooping corners of her lips, a trace certainly of bitterness left by incidents with the occupying authorities and, generally speaking, by the ambiguity of the situation in which she, a German woman, had been placed after 1939, not prepared to yield to the terror inherent in this situation. Now tiny streams of sweat were running down her full but still quite fresh face, disappearing into the lace of the old-fashioned bodice fastened high under her chin, and she sighed heavily in her sleep until Peter, touched by an almost filial reaction, quickly leaned over and stroked her hand: she smiled without opening her eyes. It was hot in the compartment, and smelled disagreeably of old, dirty plush; clearly this single second-class carriage hadn't been cleaned since the outbreak of the war, so Peter murmured consolingly that the journey wasn't long, an hour, or an hour and a half at the most, and Demoiselle, as before, without opening her eyes, smiled in silent thankfulness.

He was unhappy but felt reassured; besides, he always felt the same way whenever he returned to Chupryn, perhaps because of a sensation of all-embracing order: everything that happened there, even the strangest things, soon became comprehensible when he thought of them, dark or evil things could be explained as soon as he reflected more deeply on them, although usually he didn't need to do this at all, since he felt their meaning, whereas the house of his mother's relatives at K. held too many troubling puzzles he could never get to the bottom of; and, besides, that house at K. had become almost hostile to him without his father, although earlier he hadn't cared for him, because of jealousy for his mother, so that sometimes he'd have preferred not to have a father at all. It was difficult for him to endure his father's baffling, extremely changeable moods, his attacks of homesickness during which he would sit for days at a time staring out of the window, without saying a word to anyone, or drinking brandy and singing monotonous Russian songs, the tunes of which always sounded like weeping, or else reciting Blok's verses to himself; and his lack of will power, which made his father basically an alien to him, he tormented himself just as he tormented the people he lived with, and Peter's mother: and all those futile attempts he'd made to take roots in a country not his at all, to attach himself to where he was living—all those intolerable facts which, however, Peter let slide into forgetfulness when his father was away, so that the house had become hostile to him, for it was full of his father although in fact he wasn't present and his father there was different from what he was in reality.

Watching the landscape moving past the window, he recalled one of those far-off days. He was standing at a window and looking into the rain-drenched garden. The sky, damp with mist, looked like a gleaming highway millions of vehicles had driven across, and the sun, if it had already appeared, was pink and white like the underside of a huge carp ripped open. The last cloudy drops of water from a recent shower dripped from triangular gables over the windows, down the icicles of tar. When he caught sight of his father and mother walking along a path he opened the window to call them, but then he heard them speaking to each other in raised voices, gesticulating strangely, and although he soon realized they weren't quarrelling, nevertheless there was an inner complaint in their voices, as if they wanted to tell each other a great deal (important things, they must be, as they weren't able to control themselves), but they couldn't express it, or had already gone too far from one another and couldn't find suitable words. He saw his father's pale face changed out of recognition, and his mother's chest heaving with quick, gasping breaths, while her lips were parting as if for a shriek; he didn't want to hear it, he stopped up his ears with his fingers and fearful thoughts rushed through the rumbling silence in his head; but perhaps in the end that shriek of his mother's which would have rent his heart didn't happen, perhaps he himself prevented it by this desperate gesture, for suddenly it was as though the picture changed. They were standing face to face in sunlight which came from a space in the sky, it coloured them with pink light, it was fragmented in his mother's tears when she burst out crying, while his father stroked her hair and whispered something quietly which he couldn't catch because they were too far away; but soon the sun went down into the raininess of a dying day, it grew almost dark and they stood like that for quite a long time; his father and mother, silent now, and still face to face, as if engraved in stone and all this darkness standing between them, dividing them sharply. And soon his father was no longer at K. at all.

But those were far off times, and he didn't like going back to them in his thoughts. The years he spent later in the little town passed as alike as drops of water, and stretched interminably, as if ten had passed, though in reality there had only been three. They passed without school, for which at first he didn't long, but when suddenly it was ruled out by the outbreak of war, he began to feel the lack of it; without school friends, for he was too attached to his former crowd of friends in town, and in K., that small, boring hole, he wasn't able to find any suitable new ones: most often with a book or at the great globe from Hamburg in his aunt Dominique's room, where he would sit chin in hand staring at the red lines of steamer routes across all the oceans and seas. Then again he saw his father (it would seem as though he was specially attached to him, but on the contrary he bored him, irritated him; it was merely that tendency of his imagination to attach itself to what no longer existed), or rather he heard the characteristic hoarse voice behind his back, for he saw only the hand and finger running along the red lines, and when his father spoke he heard: 'Hong Kong, the Equator, Osaka, Puri, Colombo, Karachi,' and these names were like large glass balls in which, when the sun falls on them, all the distant worlds sparkle with light, or 'Odessa, Constantinople,' these meant defeat, but they opened up deep chasms into the past before he, Peter, had been born, as if the earth had suddenly opened up to show him all its dark interior. And at once he felt the dark sorrow of his father's words as they emerged from a memory enriched by vestiges of the bitterness of the years which divided him from these words, but robbed of its boyish innocence, sometimes letting him accept his father's words simply, without any need to penetrate into all their meaning; and he also felt the sorrow of his own helplessly flickering thoughts when he understood all this, as a result of those years which experience had built up in him, but then at once he felt shivers shake his body as though he were cold, but he wasn't at all cold. Later, he told his mother he must be sick, that he'd go and lie down, and she said, Yes, surely, you didn't put on your thick socks again, or you got wet outdoors, but indeed it wasn't that, as though she didn't understand anything at all about this, even if he'd told her the whole truth; and still later, lying in bed in his room, following the regular motion of the pendulum in the wooden clock-case, listening to its ticking which usually took the place of counting up to a hundred, and warming himself in the cool, bitter-scented blankets (but before he'd plunged entirely into warm sleep, before he fell into it as into an abyss where everything grows smooth, is deprived of sharp edges and even moves into the distance and—the most agreeable of all—that slow falling away of the bonds with surrounding things; with the lamp in its green shade with varicoloured beads round it, with the miniature of his great-grandmother in a white cap tied with blue ribbon on her head, hanging between the windows, with the clock in a corner by the door, and with the heroic picture of King John the Third in a huge splendid frame carved with captured Turkish insignia from the Battle of Vienna: though later he felt a sort of half-awareness of the existence of these objects and felt that when he opened his eyes they would be just as before and nothing in the vicinity would have changed either, it would all be just so, just as before he crossed that imperceptible frontier between sleeping and waking); he recalled a windy day, so cold that it pinched the flesh, when he was walking with his father through the park after school, though maybe that was in K. after all, and they hadn't been walking through the park but beside a lake, yes it had certainly been in K. for there was no lake in that other little town, and in K. there was the Garch lake, constantly animated, gleaming like mercury, anyway never mind where, the sky had been overcast, rising high like a balloon, so there was no place for the eyes to rest on, and his father was talking very excitedly about something Peter no longer remembered what, his words had been disjointed, something about life being exciting but that at times the price one paid for it was out of all proportion to what it was worth, this was what was left, this and a feeling of something indescribably fleeting, distant, but his eyes had been bright and sharp, and he looked as if he knew everything, as if in some strange way his eyes had taken the measure of and penetrated the whole world; and Peter thought, perhaps at that moment, as he was walking arm in arm with his father, aware of his breathing or perhaps it hadn't been until he was lying in bed a few months after his father's departure, as he was plunging into the warmth of sleep—then he thought it wasn't true that he hadn't loved his father or had wished him ill and hadn't understood his father at all, for he understood him and pretty well too, and was only defending himself subconsciously from accepting his father's attitude towards the world; the attitude of an alien who wants to rid himself of his foreignness, but was at the same time incapable of surrendering that which prevented him from discarding the foreignness. Peter didn't feel alien, what was alien to him was everything which attracted him to his father, that world of his, which—if it engulfed Peter—would make him fight against himself, as his father had done, and still more vainly.

In those days Peter had been a completely carefree boy, and often saw the world through rose-coloured spectacles, though later as he grew older they got broken one day, well perhaps they got broken on several occasions and for days at a time, and then he'd looked at everything through the cracks and holes in the magic lenses, seeing nothing that wasn't flawed, particularly because the clarity of recollections of his father had grown confused in his mother's family, and he was afraid the same thing might happen in his memory, which he didn't want. Letters started coming from Chupryn again, which he often re-read in solitude, more and more eagerly, and it seemed to him that the figure of his father lived on in memory there, at his grandfather's house, as he had really been (meaning in the reality which Peter had created in himself for his father), and besides other memories linked him with Chupryn; there was a misty recollection of something indefinably sad yet sweet, which was associated with Catherine, his grandfather's foster child, later wife of the elder of his two Woynovich cousins, Alexei, who disappeared in the first days of the war.

The thought of her brought a warm flush to his face, and even shamed him, although in time Catherine's face had been overlaid by the faces of numerous girls he'd known as a boy; the face, for instance, of Julia the Second, the daughter of his former nurse, also called Julia, but of others too, although he no longer remembered their names. However, Catherine's face—for the details of her figure had been erased, had become difficult to visualize—this face, seen as late as the first month of the war, emerged again now as he closed his eyelids tightly and concentrated on her alone so that the image of this face came to the surface, emerged from beneath layers of other faces and he was able to keep it there under his closed eyelids for a short while; but just then another surge of sorrow washed over his entire body: he surrendered to it passively, for although it was unspeakably troubling, it at once brought about another sensation, one of excited delight, although this too lasted for only a moment, then he felt as though a living flame of burning lava had engulfed his inside entirely and had left him bleached as white as bones in a wilderness. He also saw the house at Chupryn somewhat mistily, though not so long had passed since that other time when he'd left it with his grandfather and grandmother to escape from the approaching Soviet troops. Then, however, the Bolsheviks had soon quarrelled with their Nazi allies, military operations shifted into the depths of the Red empire, and his grandparents had gone back home, evidently anxious to wait there and nowhere else for the end of all the upheavals, and later they'd written more and more insistent letters to his, Peter's, mother at K., urging her to bring her son and daughter to them for the summer: 'It's so peaceful here,' they'd written, and in the end his mother yielded.

It had been a Saturday evening, immediately after a May day service, from which she returned excited and gay with Demoiselle Spang, evidently she'd met someone she knew (Peter didn't like these sudden outbursts of piety in his mother, he always suspected they concealed something which he couldn't even think of without rage and humiliation), and as she threw her wrap and hat into a chair, she'd laughed somehow inwardly, as if not directing her laugh to him at all, and then she'd said: 'Well, you shall go. I've just been discussing it with Demoiselle,' and although he already knew where, he'd asked—still conscious of that laugh of hers and how falsely it had sounded: 'Where? Where am I going?' and she: 'What do you mean? To your grandparents. You yourself wanted to go, after all,' and he, briefly: 'So I did.' 'But now you don't?' she asked, and he'd said: 'I do,' for the infuriating sound of her laugh had already died down in him, and it was a matter of indifference to him or rather, yes, he wanted to be off as soon as possible, so as not to know about anything, and this was why he'd repeated once again, firmly: 'I do.' Then at once all the tedious packing and preparations for a journey started, which he awaited impatiently, and at the last moment it was decided that Demoiselle would go too. Not, of course, that she was to give him lessons, for after all it was the holidays, nor that he needed her to look after him, indeed he had long since considered the roles reversed, but Demoiselle had already been a bitter pill for the local Germans in the little town to swallow, a German woman in a Polish household. Finally, on the Tuesday, a telegram came from Chupryn to say horses would be waiting at the station—as he now recalled with that pleasurable sensation of order which he always experienced whenever he came back east, and he also felt that he'd be at home there (he even called the ride to Chupryn a 'return,' though in reality it was only the home of his father's parents but actually he considered it as his own home and didn't have to seek any justification for this feeling, either earlier or at present, as he gazed at the landscape moving past the compartment window), meditating on all this as it flowed farther and farther away from him and gave way to scenes from still earlier memories, when he'd been at the place he was now approaching.

Demoiselle Spang sat immersed in a newspaper, then his gaze caught her attention and she asked whether he was hungry: '*Wenn ja, dann sag. Wir haben noch ein Stück Huhn, und ein wenig Kuchen ist vorhanden,*' but no, he wasn't at all hungry, '*Nein, danke,*' he replied turning back to the window, where dust clouds had thickened along the horizon meanwhile, the sky was beginning to glow with a livid light which the earth, grass, undergrowth, the single trees here and there and the blackthorn bushes and even the brown, blotchy walls of the compartment were reflecting—it all turned bluish and he thought a storm will certainly catch up with us, already feeling how the shuddering of the storm in the air would affect him.

Soon he began recognizing the district: to the right, submerged in its valley, was the county town, Krzysztopol. Only the towers of the Basilian church rose out of the low-lying site, and a few dark smudges of smoke rose close by them from the chimneys of local factories. Farther to the left, the Motren Forest appeared on the horizon, then they passed the pitch-burners' settlement of Sydonovka, and when the train had left the Smily stop behind he saw close at hand the lazy flow of the Sert as it wound away into the flatness of the steppe, forming a ravine of winding turns, and he knew that soon the parish convent of Nikorycha would appear, gently enfolded in an arm of the river, but a good fifteen minutes elapsed before the train drew up at a little station where it hissed and stopped, then a little man in a faded uniform and peaked cap without a badge came running along the train and began shouting out the name Nikorycha in a preoccupied tone of voice.

Demoiselle fretted a moment as she looked to see whether anyone was coming to get their suitcases; no one came. Peter quickly got them down from the rack, pushed them to the door, and, when she had got out, dragged them off the step; apart from a few country women, a thin priest in a shabby soutane, the railway official agitated by the imminent departure, running along with his little flag, and another man dragging some boxes on a little cart to the last of the carriages, he saw no one else in the vicinity until, after a moment, rather surprised that the train wasn't moving off, he saw five Jews in long dusty gaberdines with bands marked by a star around their arms come shambling from behind the station, a German soldier with a rifle in one hand following, and he watched them get in, first the Jews, afterwards the soldier who slammed the door with a bang, then the train at once moved off and the platform emptied. The railway official, his flag folded, came over to them and helped without speaking to carry their cases to the exit marked Nikorycha, from where the little town could be seen, and, immediately in front, a black mongrel snuffling for fleas in the dust in the middle of the road. Farther away stood a solitary two-horse carriage which could only be from Chupryn, with an army truck nearer: as they passed it a soldier who had been fumbling under the hood turned to look attentively at them, and he suddenly asked: '*Wohin gehen Sie?*' and, to Demoiselle: '*Sind Sie eine Deutsche?*' but Demoiselle replied stiffly, in a rounded phrase as if repeating a lesson learned by heart: '*Nein, ich bin keine Deutsche, ich bin Polin,*' and without stopping she drew Peter towards the waiting carriage, the soldier shrugged and stopped watching them.

A sleepy youth scrambled from under a horsecloth, reached for their luggage, pushed it under the front seat then put one hand under his shirt and scratched until Demoiselle and Peter had got into the back and, after a poke from her parasol, he started up the horses. They set off at a fairly brisk trot, and as they passed the truck still standing in front of the station Demoiselle sighed deeply and with evident relief. Peter glanced at her and said: 'He only wanted to give us a lift.' 'Perhaps,' Demoiselle replied, to which he countered that they ought not to talk German, and Demoiselle said, 'Yes, goodness me yes, we must take care.'

Sometime later, the thought of the first moment of his arrival, which he'd previously pictured to himself as completely different (a member of the family on the platform, embraces and greetings, loud talk), but no, nothing of the sort had happened, he felt cheated; this thought and its accompanying images produced a resentful echo in Peter: the almost deserted station, those dark figures in frayed robes stumbling into the train, the hard crunch of the soldier's boots, but fortunately these pictures soon faded and presently it seemed to him they'd only been visions of some kind, brought about by some menacing dispensation of Fate in the stuffy, electric, dry air which hung motionless over the district, so that as they drove along no movement was to be felt on their faces, not the slightest breeze touched their hair, and even the fluffy fringe on Demoiselle's forehead looked as if it were glued down, so that for a moment he wondered whether he were still dreaming in the train, but he wasn't. The horses trotted along, harness rattling, they sweated and smelled, and the carriage only emphasized the real, almost tangible silence with a trickling of sand dislodged by its wheels. Nikorycha was soon left behind, slowly they climbed a long slope, then again began to descend, then passed a crossing with a field path where women were kneeling offering up a last prayer to the darkening sky at an old-fashioned, primitive shrine with a figure enveloped in a flaxen tunic, and they turned their heads as they passed to watch that rustic picture fading into the obscurity, then a forked flash of lightning cut across the sky above the Sert, plunging with a crash into the tarry waters, but the storm didn't follow them, then a thick cloud of warm rain drowsily enveloped them all.

Peter closed his eyes and was soon dreaming: a silver samovar bubbled on the table, it smelled sharply of boiling tea, Uncle Theodore was leaning over it, blinking his penetrating eyes in a face like that of a Byzantine saint, and was mysteriously telling him, as he'd done long ago when Peter had been a little boy, that a flotilla of Spanish galleons commanded by Admiral Diego de Mollo y Savieroso had sailed to the northern coast of the Balearics and been attacked by pirate ships of the Bey of Algiers ('three thousand five hundred barrels of gold they were bringing from the West Indies for the Escurial, you see. Listen, you won't learn this from anyone else. And as many barrels of silver. It all went to the bottom of the sea, three miles or so off the coast, d'you see?' said his uncle, 'if you would like to help me we could retrieve it'), and his grandmother was setting out patience by a lamp of glimmering aquamarine light, counting the court cards in an undertone, then suddenly the monotonous clatter of the horses' hoofs stopped, the carriage wheels stopped dead, and the curtain of rain parted above Peter's head to reveal a lowering sky.

Somewhere close at hand water was dripping from a gutter into the surface of a puddle. Some dog or other barked once, then fell silent as though crestfallen. A door squeaked open, the old servant Fedka Cherkvas appeared, like the good spirit of light, in a brightening oblong under the porch and came down the steps, lifting his lantern high overhead. Later on there really was the drawing-room, full to overflowing with aquamarine light, the thin figure of Uncle Theodore in his black, gleaming jacket raptly brewing tea in the samovar, the pleasant drowsy bubbling of the boiling water, that acrid smell of brown tea leaves unfolding in the boiling water, which he so much liked and remembered, mingling with the smell of a cigarette as his grandfather took a cigarette paper packed with tobacco from his little machine and lit it, his grandmother was stooping over her last game of patience at a side table, the porcelain clock above the extinguished hearth was chiming midnight and playing a little tune to a rococo pair under their rose-gilt parasol, and the figure of Catherine was in the door to the next room.

He saw her once, or twice maybe, in any case for a moment in that door, or rather in the obscurity of the shadows filling the door's black outline, already in her night attire, equally shadowy, yawning, briefly, for only a fraction of a second, as she appeared in order to say to them: 'Ah, you're here at last. I'm so glad,' and perhaps a few words more, but nothing of any particular significance, and in that fraction of a second she grew motionless in the black outline, holding her robe around her shoulders and looking sleepily into the depths of the drawing-room as if the light bothered her and she wasn't at all sure whether she saw him, Peter, there among these people and at once she faded away into that shadowiness. Then again there was the purring of his grandmother's Siamese cat which scrambled onto Peter's knees, warm as toast, and all at once, as if everything had been suddenly transformed, the talking voices fused into one quiet murmuring, into a tinkling timeless melody, then the walls revolved slowly, blurring the light and shade, and it was as though the black bird of night had soundlessly fluttered towards him on the sofa, maybe it really did, for he saw an ink-black outline on the raised surface of the plush, standing with outstretched wings and he felt it fan him gently with its feathers, and then there was nothing more.

The close-packed level of darkness finally diminished. The nightmares flowed from the left to the right side of his chest. His heart expanded and began beating regularly, pumping the blood more easily into his swelling arteries. The black bird spread its wings again, and sang. Its neck grew taut, it swelled, it stretched up, its throat gurgled as it swallowed, it was entirely filled with sounds which it uttered in one long phrase, and perhaps it was with them that it awoke the light which had been hidden deeply until just now in the recesses of sleep, for its feathers slowly coloured and soon it reminded him, by its delicate pink mingled with white, of the miraculous flamingo (in the coloured illustrations to Hippolite Lafourierre's *Natural History,* which Uncle Theodore had once given Peter on his birthday), and then it dissolved entirely in the sunlight and only its song didn't die away even for a moment, very strangely spanning Peter's head like a dense spider web, so that even when he opened his eyes he could still hear it unchanged for some time. Then he realized it was broad daylight, he was lying in his old room on the second floor, the windows were wide open, and it was only the park resounding with the choir of bird song, and the room, despite his first impression, was the quietest corner in the whole world, to which sounds from outside penetrated only as echoes of the wind from the walls, like a rather stifled echo, dallying as they came in the curtain folds, and he then recollected all the previous day, especially the nocturnal hour when he and Demoiselle had arrived, and how his uncle Theodore had afterwards helped him clamber up the stairs and took him half asleep to his room, and no doubt helped him undress and put him to bed; he felt confused and embarrassed. Straight away I made a fool of myself, that's not bad going, he thought, reaching for a little mirror in his trouser pocket; his face was puffy with sleep, his eyes haggard but bright. He drew one hand over his unshaven chin, still pale and soft from sleep, and considered his tongue, soon he'd have to start shaving, he thought angrily, in fact the journey had been tiring, the dry heat before the storm had made itself felt everywhere, but that was no reason for him to behave like a puppy and fall asleep just anywhere, hardly even managing to say hello. Then, trying to remember whether it happened in the presence of Catherine (but no, he couldn't remember anything), he rose from the bed and pulled on his trousers which had been thrown on a nearby chair. The room smelled of recently polished floorboards and fresh bed linen, in a word like a place long uninhabited and hastily set in order. He stretched tried a few exercises, and shuffled to the window.

Down below he caught sight of Fedka Cherkvas's bent shoulders and the rusty fur cap which the old man wore on his bald skull on holidays and Fridays, year in year out, no matter what the season. He was cutting the grass around a flower bed, but when Peter leaned out of the window he was leaning on the handle of the scythe and sombrely staring after a black Adler car gleaming in the sun as it moved away down the drive. When the sound of the car finally faded into the distance, there appeared Julia, Peter's former nurse who had ruled in the kitchen for a long time now, on the path leading from the home farm; carrying a basket of eggs, she went up to the old man: 'Them again?' she asked, stopping, and he, irritably: 'Why shouldn't they be here? None of your business, woman,' to which she replied: 'So long as nothing bad comes of it for the family,' and he: 'Hold your tongue, woman, do. They're on our side, mind. Well, at least they're not foreigners. The old gentleman knows what he's doing. No matter what happens they'll help us against Gavryluk's riff-raff.' 'They're no better than the others,' she said crossly and, picking up her basket, she went quickly round to the back of the house. Cherkvas gazed understandingly after her, sighed faintly, then when Peter leaned still farther out of the window and called to him, he looked up rather embarrassed and said 'Good morning'. Peter asked about the Adler, for he guessed the earlier exchange between Julia and the old man had in fact been connected with it, but Cherkvas, as though he hadn't heard, asked: 'Well now, did you sleep well on your first night at home after all these years? You ought to have remembered your dreams. Dreams in a new bed may come true, sir,' then, throwing back his head, he trumpeted: 'Shall we take a trip? Weather's right,' and blinking his yellow cat's eyes he expected, as had always happened before the war, Peter to respond with an outburst of enthusiasm, but he only asked once more: 'Whose was it?' and then Cherkvas at once, reluctantly: 'The R.O.A.'s,' he explained, and seeing that Peter didn't understand, added in an ordinary voice: 'Our people, Russians. Well, the ones who're against the Reds.' 'With the Germans?' Peter asked in surprise. 'With the Germans or without them, who knows, sir? One'll stick to this, the other to that, but what he has in his soul is another matter. Against the Reds,' the old man said quite sharply, and he clearly didn't like Peter's question, for he went back busily to his interrupted work. Not until after some time did he say in the direction of the window, though without raising his head: 'When you've rested, sir, we could go after partridge. They've done well this year,' and after another pause, 'There's no one left to shoot them. People are so busy shooting one another now that there's no one left to go shooting animals, that's the truth,' but he said not a word concerning the previous matter, as though he had nothing more to say. Peter didn't speak again either; he was a bit uneasy and surprised, but didn't feel like questioning Cherkvas. The park was enveloped in the whitish, easily dispelled light which usually comes just before noon. The sky was the colour of milk in which a trace of ultramarine had been dissolved, without a single cloud, indescribably vast, so that a hawk hovering motionless in the air was the only point on which the eye could rest; soon it dropped like a stone into the course of a stream, the sky again became unnervingly blank, so that his eyes watered. In one of the *allées*, the linden trees were beginning to flower, a perfume sweet with sap came from them. A vine against the wall outside the windows rustled quietly, though the day was completely windless, and the trees held their branches stiffly, lifelessly.

Goodness knows what time it is, Peter thought, it's late anyhow. His watch, which hadn't been wound up the night before, had stopped at ten minutes past five, he put it to his ear, shook it, and wound it automatically, then remembered what his mother had said about a change of air always being good for you, and he laughed aloud without knowing why. Hearing his own laugh he felt his body grow lighter, that was precisely how he felt. He turned and looked at the room more attentively for the first time. Since he and his family had left Chupryn in mid-September 1939, he had seen these beloved walls and corners only in his dreams. In dreams he had been used to hearing the characteristic sounds of these things, the familiar creak of wood giving way to the woodworms which inhabited the old furniture, the creak of floorboards even when no one was walking on them, as though shadows were ceaselessly passing through the rooms, the shadows of people who had once inhabited the house, who had died there and, although now buried in the upstanding family tombs in the adjacent cemetery, were yet so attached to the place that they could not leave it; also he kept on hearing those strange voices which were everywhere, even in the scented dust and ashes of the air that filled the interior, but only in his dreams, for when he was awake, it was only occasionally, just before finally waking, when sleep slowly thins out but is still holding the body and its thoughts fast in pleasurable stupefaction; now, however, he was seeing it in reality, and he walked across the room, touched the objects as if to convince himself that he wasn't dreaming, and he smiled to himself.

Not much had changed, or at least so it appeared to him. In a corner stood the little marble-topped table with its old-fashioned blue border, with a cavity for the wash-basin in the top, adorned with a similar border, and on the lower shelf, a matching jug. The rest of the space beside it was occupied by a cupboard for clothes, and a Louis the Fourteenth white bed, with garlands of little carved rosebuds, stood against the opposite wall. Perhaps only the armchairs near the window hadn't been there before, they'd replaced other objects which he couldn't recollect, but on reflection they too seemed familiar to him, somehow, no doubt he'd seen them sometime in another room; but the pictures and clock on the wall, even the blackened engraving and a hunting knife, given to him by his friend Nick, hanging between the windows from a nail, all were the same, which made him realize that although the house had come under Soviet occupation, according to his grandfather's letters, it had by some miracle escaped damage, though most of the neighbouring manor-houses had been wrecked. Still smiling that smile which held delight at the immutability of things he had once reluctantly abandoned in hasty confusion, he went straight to the desk, so as to look through his boyish possessions, but then a rustling outside the door, which he'd heard several times already repeated at short intervals, changed into a delicate tapping. He turned, said, 'Come in,' and she entered.

It wasn't Catherine after all. The blood, which had flowed to his head and stopped, slowly began ebbing, yielding to discomfiture, though he still felt his face burning and his heart beating faster than usual, but at once he smiled, 'Good morning, Julia the Second,' and looked curiously at the woman as she entered (they'd always called her that to distinguish her from Julia, her mother). She seemed the same, although a little larger, perhaps in consequence of the passage of time when he hadn't been here; she was a girl no longer, but a woman, yet after all he too had changed; so the changes in her didn't surprise him much, and he quickly said 'Good morning' again, unsure whether or not she'd heard; she nodded but said nothing. As she was pouring water into the jug and basin, he drew his jacket around his bare shoulders and went closer: 'Why don't you say something?' he asked, they'd been friends once after all, and later on, too, he'd often thought of her. 'Good morning,' she replied quietly. 'I thought you didn't recognize me,' said he, to which she: 'Why not? You haven't changed much, sir,' so he said: 'Aren't you going to call me Peter as you used to?' with a teasing note of reproach in his voice, she replied: 'No.' He wondered: 'Why not, for goodness' sake?' and she: 'You've grown up into a man,' she said, and somehow captiously, significantly, she looked at him without a smile; he again grew embarrassed.

He turned to the window and looked out, rapidly regaining his equanimity. When he turned back to her: 'I overslept. It must be noon,' he said, to break the silence, for she was still standing uncertainly with the empty water-jug in her hand, looking at him attentively, as if she wanted to see how much of the old Peter remained in him (as if she were seeking some resemblance or other, it was hard to discover any now, or perhaps she had something important to say). Suddenly she said with unnatural vivacity: 'The mistress told me not to wake you. For she says that the young master should have his sleep after such a long journey. That's why I didn't bring the water earlier,' but it was as though she hadn't said what she meant to say at all. Her eyes were still motionless and only her face, or rather its outer covering, came alive for a moment; perhaps it was only reflected light and nothing more? At this precise moment he realized with an odd sensation the fact that after all she was entirely different from the previous Julia the Second, the companion of his wonderful, secret childhood games (all her gestures were economical, even constrained, and although they didn't lack charm, they irritated and unnerved him because of some lurking tension in them, as if too much life were coursing through her strong body and she were trying to repress it, they were even careless, though she needn't know that, neither need she be aware of her moderate beauty), and at once, embarrassed again, he thought that if she had changed so much, then so had everything else he would find in this house, all the more so, and he felt a slight tingling around his heart, as this thought grew more clearly defined in him, and he at once pushed it away. Then: 'I haven't seen you for several years,' he said, 'surely something must have happened since then? My grandfather wrote to me that nothing had been burned down, yet there are changes, though fortunately not big ones,' and he stopped, startled by the triviality of his own words, but still, he had no illusions.

She sat down on a chair, with the jug between her feet and her hands on her knees, and looked at him in silence, as if inwardly relaxing, then: 'Well, yes, under the Soviets they turned the house into a hotel for high officials from town, so nothing much was disturbed. Except what the peasants from the nearby villages took away, at the beginning,' she said, however he felt yet again that this wasn't what she had meant to say, but even so . . . neither had he said what he had wanted to say to her. He asked superfluous questions about matters well known to him, his grandfather had described them in letters many times; now he tried for a moment to imagine to himself Chupryn as a collective farm and the house at the time when it had been a Soviet boarding house for Commissars, people among these walls and objects, but he couldn't. He felt they had nothing to do with him and that it was even incredible that they should so suddenly have nothing at all to do with him, for earlier the very idea that Chupryn was inhabited by strangers had been outrageous, had summoned up a positive storm of vindictive ideas and stupefaction that the walls he had grown up in and loved had not collapsed on the heads of those people and buried them, but of course he grew up and realized that they'd been merely childish curses, for after all it was precisely for this reason that the walls had survived the outrage and why he was able to be here again: and now here he was, and suddenly that past meant nothing to him, he didn't want to think of it, or to hear what Julia the Second was saying, as she recalled this and that, no doubt under the impression that it mattered to him, but he only gazed at her, seeking a way back to the other past, the older past, when he and she had been friends, riding together to the market at Nikorycha, playing with a crowd of their contemporaries in the neighbouring fields, taking long trips into the steppe and forest (for Julia the Second had been like a boy and refused to yield to them, the boys, in any way), but she, as if unaware of what was happening to him, talked on insistently and precisely about the topic he had incautiously hooked his question to. She was inwardly thrilled, even delighted, to be able to speak, to have found something to interest him, although she certainly wasn't saying what she meant to say, and his replies were not those he wanted to make, but merely to prevent that embarrassing silence from falling as it had fallen when she entered the room and he hadn't known how to hit upon that living chord somewhere within her, vibrating in himself too, the chord of friendship, of shared remembrances of childhood, of intimacy, which would let him erase from his memory the years during which they had not met, and let him leap over them. All he felt was that this was depressing her too, this feeling of evasiveness in what they were saying, although she wasn't making it easy for him, she was behaving rather as though she were an ordinary servant, despite the fact that she had always been an indoor servant, someone who almost belonged to the family, but she emphasized this distance still more by sometimes calling him 'sir'; no, he didn't know how to strike that chord, what they were saying meant nothing, and in fact she was behaving as though she didn't want to help him break down the strangeness that had arisen between them, and then, when she fell silent and sat motionless with her hands placed on her knees like a countrywoman, perhaps not seeing him, staring out of the window somewhere as if she were staring at that distant point in the past when they'd both been close to one another still, and he too was silent; then, perhaps on account of his expectant silence, she stirred and jumped up in alarm from the chair, as if it were somehow unsuitable for her to be seated in his presence, she said hastily but quietly: 'The young master isn't in the least like him,' in a tone that was, despite herself, full of significance.

A moment must have passed, perhaps more than a moment, before he realized he hadn't understood her, and not until then did he ask: 'Like whom?' but she immediately became alarmed and: 'Oh nothing, I was only saying that. . .'; probably at once regretting the comment which had escaped her, for he must have looked surprised and something within her thawed for an instant; the shadow of something like a smile crossed her face. Then: 'The young master comes and goes, but we and our misfortunes remain. Here. It's a good thing that you don't resemble anyone, sir. But please don't ask, I'm talking nonsense,' she said too loudly, but she had already withdrawn into herself again, had closed down, and when he wanted to ask—perhaps already had, aware of his own embarrassment and of that nervous alarm which he shared with her, but perhaps he only had the question in his eyes, and she caught it in his gaze—she turned quickly away, snatched up the jug from the floor, and hurried out of the room.

He stood uncertain a moment, agitated by contradictory feelings among which uneasiness dominated, and then thinking (with that strange shiver which contact with the 'unknown' always evokes) that after all the day had started with riddles, he realized that something had certainly happened, yes, something must have happened here for her to have met him with a greeting so very enigmatic, but as he still hadn't found out what it was, perhaps the right time hadn't come yet, this is what the meaning of that thought of his was, more or less.

He found no one in his grandfather's study, and the room next to it, which in his childhood had always seemed to him an alchemist's mysterious workshop, was empty. While he had wandered along a corridor which crossed almost the entire house, listening intently, he thought he could hear the sound of a machine for gilding the spines of books coming from this room, a hobby of his grandfather's, who always put on rubber cuffs and a leather apron before starting up the complicated old-fashioned machinery consisting of type, wheels, belts, and little pans in which the binding glue melted, after he'd finely bound a book in cloth or leather, also by his own hands, but no, the machine was motionless: certainly Peter had been expecting to hear its familiar rattling noise, or wished to hear it, for he needed it to complete the general picture of the house at Chupryn, and above all to confirm, to seal as it were, the immutability of the house. When he looked more closely at the motionless apparatus he noticed dust in the cogs and on the calender, and aware of a certain disappointment, he thought it looked as if his grandfather had lost interest in his hobby, and hadn't done anything for a long time. At a sound behind the door he'd left open, he went back into the study again and came face to face with Demoiselle Spang. She was glad to see him: 'I've been looking for you, because I didn't find you in your room. I thought you'd gone off somewhere as you used to. Have you had breakfast yet?' 'No.' 'I'm going fishing in the stream, won't you come with me?' 'Oh no, not today, forgive me, Demoiselle.' 'Well, don't go too far away, will you? It would be best if you didn't go outside the park.' 'And why not? Surely you don't think I still need you to look after me?' he smiled, to which she said: 'Peter, I'm serious. There are Ukrainian bandits prowling in the district. The times are not what you think. No one has had the opportunity yet to speak to you about this, but you'll soon find out. You must look after yourself. Will you be careful?' 'All right, all right, I understand,' he replied, looking at her with an effort, although he still didn't understand very well, and when she went out he stood in troubled silence, trying to rid himself of the disagreeable sensation caused by that strangely worded warning; it seemed to him a riddle not to be solved on the spot. Then he slowly began to realize something which he didn't in the least want to admit, something which made him uneasy and was also hard to accept. The fact was that he would have to start everything in this house from scratch, that there was no link with the time he had hoped to return to, the slender bonds had been broken though they'd still existed yesterday, the day before, they had seemed eternal, but now they had been broken, perhaps last night, perhaps just a moment ago, it didn't matter when, for the meaning was the same anyway. With this premonition he approached the window which looked out from his grandfather's study over the same stretch of park as his room, and indeed as he gazed out, the park didn't seem as radiant as it had done before. The dissolving whiteness of the sun drifted between the trees, it dimmed the greenery, the silence whistled in his ears with a long-drawn cry, and he felt unhappy. Earlier, he'd still been only a boy, or had deluded himself he still was, despite the hair on his face, but now he was grown-up.

When he found himself in the dining-room on the first floor it was nearly noon. Soon the clocks throughout the whole house struck, then silence prevailed again, unbroken, as if all of a sudden everyone had moved away. But he found on the table the food he had always had for lunch at Chupryn before the war: his favourite long crusty rolls were already waiting for him in a wicker basket, fresh-smelling butter in a porcelain dish, and next to it someone had placed his favourite cherry jam, also quince jam. He ate, drank cold milk, and listened to the murmuring of the house, which had gone on as long as the old house existed; to the soft rustle of curtains, the whispering of breezes drifting down corridors and through half-open doors, and the unhappiness, just now so powerful, began slowly to dissolve: again he tried to feel at home, and in the end he succeeded.

Once more his thoughts returned to the previous evening, and he tried to remember whether his seeing Catherine in the doorway for a moment had been only an illusion or a reality, because when he thought about it he could find no reason for her to be at Chupryn on a weekday which wasn't a family feast of some kind; before leaving he'd supposed he wouldn't see her until he himself paid a neighbourly visit to Gleb, but as he now thought about yesterday he wasn't able to eliminate her from it. She had been standing in the door, had nodded her head, and with her hand somehow clutched at her throat, she'd said 'Good day,' or 'Good evening,' or something of the sort, and it seemed to him that he hadn't been asleep then, or perhaps he had, but not so fast asleep that his mind could create images of non-existent things, but at present he simply didn't know. The house gave the impression of being empty, as it had done when the family were alone (his grandfather mostly in his study among his books, his grandmother perhaps down at the farm talking to the manager, and his uncle Theodore surrounded as always by maps, globes, and those assorted old memoirs he'd unearthed in the library in the right wing: of course there was Demoiselle too, but she was certainly sitting with a fishing line by the stream, he thought), as if there had been no one apart from the established family group, so if Catherine . . . No, it was impossible, if she were staying at Chupryn she would certainly have appeared by now; but then his doubts increased still more, because before he finished eating, his grandmother appeared in the door of the passage that led to the kitchen.

She gave him her cheek to kiss in greeting, and looking at Peter critically she said: 'I've an idea you won't find much to amuse you in this isolation, my boy. You'll get bored if you don't find yourself some suitable occupation . . . ' and presently with a sigh: 'Well, there's a war on, after all. Everyone has some trouble or other, some matter or other he doesn't speak of . . . As you'll see for yourself, social life is disappearing. Even the Woynoviches from Gleb hardly ever call on us,' and he, to avoid asking about Catherine directly, said: 'What's Paul doing?' referring to his cousin, Catherine's brother-in-law, and his grandmother said: 'Paul is grown-up now. Well, I don't mean to say that you haven't changed too, on the contrary, you've changed a great deal, you've become manly. But you'll scarcely recognize Paul. You must understand that he has had to take over the farm. Because so many Polish families were deported by the Soviets. The women in the house couldn't cope with it all,' but not a single word, literally, about Catherine.

Then his grandmother, obviously misconstruing his silence, began telling him who of the local gentry had returned to their estates and who hadn't, and it was evident from what she said that although many of the neighbouring manor-houses had been burned down or looted, either during the Soviet occupation or during the first Nationalists'[1] attacks, yet their owners had, apart from a few, come back to their old family seats, were rebuilding them, ploughing the land, farming, in a word trying to live as if nothing had happened. But 'God knows how anyone could really believe that nothing happened after what did happen,' said his grandmother, as if thinking aloud, looking at Peter with barely concealed reproach in her eyes. 'Fires, murder, looting.

[1] Ukrainians fighting for their own national aspirations.

And to think that all this repeats itself as regularly as the seasons of the year. Then the return, a new start, tilling the land, the peasants go about mildly sleepy, smiling, bowing with cap in hand, coming to ask advice on family matters, they're frank and honest until there's another explosion, and they come running to put a torch to our roof. It's terrible, my boy, evidently we aren't needed here at all,' then, rubbing her forehead as though to dispel a nightmare, she added emphatically: 'Don't speak to your grandfather about these matters, please. He must be spared, you see, at his age . . .' so he said: 'Yes, of course, Grandmother, although yesterday he looked so hale and hearty that nothing special can be ailing him,' then all at once, something in the way she fell silent struck him, something which far exceeded the almost unimportant words she had spoken, but which was indeed the very same linking of the present day to the past, of his return to that earlier departure, the linking which was what he'd been searching the whole house for since morning, well perhaps no, it really wasn't this he'd sought and desired, but rather that exciting taste of poetry which he remembered from childhood, he couldn't think of another name for it; the taste of poetry, and suddenly he found the link (that bridge between a distant yesterday and the present today), he found it in the bitter veneer of resignation over her words and gestures, though she was sitting there, tired, not even looking at him now, and he found it too in her gaze, which was clear, seeing too much.

He felt his forehead and neck begin to sweat copiously under the burden of that gaze, and without meaning to he recalled that disastrous day in September 1939, even though he didn't want to, and had decided earlier not to think about it any more, although he could recollect it clearly and accurately, and it was as though a light had been turned too brightly into his eyes, blinding him, with everything around him going dark. This moment persisted, exploded into images, and he saw, as though on a screen, the house piled up with bundles and trunks, all the antlike yet disorganized fuss, then the trunks and bundles wedged tightly into carts and the carts moving off. The dust had already started to rise in front of the column as it moved out into the road, but his grandfather couldn't cope with his body, suddenly it was too heavy, he couldn't get into the carriage, he staggered, but then he got in and sat down breathless in a corner, almost as if he weren't there physically, not speaking to anyone; and still later he saw them drive into the frantic crowd on the highroad, yes, they'd literally driven into it, and the column of carts from Chupryn wedged in among thousands of similar carts, all full to overflowing with refugees perched on bundles, the columns had driven east but later, when it became apparent that they wouldn't find safety there, they'd turned from east back to west, and also the first air raid they'd survived in the open air in a flat region completely exposed to view, when his grandfather hadn't budged from the carriage, though the highway emptied of people, leaving only the horses crowding together, rattling their harnesses insanely, but he went on sitting there, without looking at the sky even once; and how, after five days and nights of wandering under the bombs and devastating fire of machine guns from the aircraft attacking the human ants, they'd reached Przemysl, pursued from the other side by the invading Soviet armies; and how his grandfather one of those days had said, not to his grandmother, nor yet to Peter's mother, but somehow into the air, that 'This time the old world is surely falling into ruins, my dears, I feel it in my bones,' so now, as he suddenly recalled this and many other things too, he looked inquiringly at his grandmother and softly repeated: 'Surely nothing special can be ailing him?' and his grandmother replied: 'Thank God, all is well,' but he asked: 'How old is Grandfather?' getting up from the table to open the door to the terrace (an enervating wave of heat burst in, as if a stove had been opened, he felt a pulse beating in his temple, his grandmother's voice was now far-off and not very clear), and he asked again: 'How old?' 'He'll be ninety in three months' time,' her voice in reply came flowing from a distance, so then, overcoming his momentary weakness and trying to be at ease, quite sincerely, as he thought: 'That really is an age to be,' he said, 'I remember him on horseback in the summer before the war,' and his grandmother, not without pride: 'Even now he'll mount a horse if someone holds the stirrup,' though already her voice barely penetrated to him through the wave of heated air, or rather it didn't penetrate clearly, but was lost, so that he wasn't sure whether it was her real voice, or simply his idea of his grandmother's voice. I'm glad he's keeping so fit and well, he thought, and all at once the *Tales of Baron Munchausen* came to his mind, and it was as though he'd left his grandmother and gone away, so attractive was the memory of this book, which he'd read once in winter, and then seen a film about the eternally young baron, packed with colourful adventures, which set free the following memories: how they'd practised witchcraft in an old shed behind the vicarage at K., calling their meetings sessions of the Secret Masonic Lodge, to which new members (well-dressed boys who knew how to keep their mouths shut) were ceremonially received; the Grand Master was sitting wrapped in a black blanket representing a toga, on an empty cucumber barrel, and the entrant into the mysteries was brought before him blindfold, half naked. The Master touched the novice's chest with the point of a sword (a wire fixed into a tin handle), and gave him a light slap on the face. This was all part of a complicated ritual. They uttered long spells supposed to make them bullet-proof, to ensure the indestructibility of their bodies, and eternal youth as well. At this precise moment his grandfather was transformed in his imagination into the picturesque figure of Munchausen. He was galloping on a black steed through a valley strewn with the corpses of his enemies, and bullets did not touch him. He felt excited. But now his grandmother had stopped behind him and, pointing towards the depths of the park, she said: 'You must have noticed that the orangery has been destroyed. Look.' The spell burst, and he returned to reality.

Obedient to her command, he turned his gaze in that direction, and confessed that he hadn't noticed it before. Moreover, even now that he knew, he still couldn't discern any changes, obviously the abundant vegetation had long since healed the wound, covered the breach. The tangle of overhanging weeping willows and acacias shedding their flowers was dense, close, interwoven with an underlayer of laurels and garden greenwood, while ivy and bindweed, creeping up the trees, had formed fantastically shaped garlands. The paths there looked like tunnels made by wild animals, full of sombre shadows, and the place where once the orangery had stood was now screened by a dense wall of greenery, so he said: 'No. It's all so grown over that one can't see anything,' and his grandmother: 'It had happened by the time we got back. We weren't at home that day, we'd gone over to the Woynoviches. It was a Sunday. The band was led, apparently, by Gavryluk . . . he seems to have been . . . looking for someone. Yes, that's what he was doing. Do you remember Madame Irène?' 'Yes,' he replied. 'Of course you do, she taught you French.' 'What had she to do with this?' 'She was the only person here, except for the servants. On that unlucky Sunday. She hid in the orangery, but they found her and tortured her to death. Although she wasn't the person they'd been looking for.' 'Who was it, then?' Silence, so he asked firmly: 'Who's this Gavryluk?' 'Come, don't you remember?' his grandmother was surprised, 'well, of course, you were little . . . He's one of the local Ukrainians,' and she stopped again, lifting her head suddenly as if listening for some distant rustle in the depths of the house, her eyes clouded. After a time she said: 'Madame Irène was a beautiful woman. Your uncle Theodore was in love with her, and we were thinking they'd marry once she had got over her husband's death, he died in September. She had a favourite place in the orangery. She liked to sit among the flowers and read. One day I'll show you the book she was reading at the end. Your uncle now never walks in that direction, and the window in his room overlooking the orangery is covered up. We haven't rebuilt the pavilion . . . Why should we, after all?'

She was talking quietly all the time, with a sort of inner resistance and as though to herself, but in the end she relaxed, her face reminded him again of a dried-up apple, and Peter too was listening for the echoes of a distant rustle in the depths of the house and wondering why that rustle should make her uneasy, and also what it was she was hiding from him, because she must be hiding something if Gavryluk had attacked Chupryn not for Madame Irène (there had been too much obscurity in all this for him not to notice); he observed that she was a head shorter than he and had become indescribably tiny, fragile, all delicate little bones enveloped in crumpled tissue, and when he saw her thus—aware of her preoccupation with what she was telling him—his eye was caught by his grandmother's hand, nervous and limp, opening and closing in time to the rhythm of her phrases, and there was something indescribable, unutterable, in that hand and its movements, just as there was in his grandmother's words, and it was no longer that small but determined hand which had once ruled the house, but something crippled, withered, not repulsive though, on the contrary it was familiar, good, dear, yet sad and as blind as a newborn mouse, helpless, beloved but at the same time corpse-like, phosphorescent, and he looked away. This hand used to stroke his hair as he crouched over a book, had gone through his notebooks, corrected his homework, but now, just opening and closing, it accompanied the narrative of Madame Irène's death, and not until now did he envisage Madame Irène as though she were still alive, as his grandmother wanted him to, recalling those brief but diverting stories in the French grammar-book, whose heroes were always the same Charles and Pierre, or more precisely he recalled one of the first stories which was so firmly embedded in his memory that even if he'd been wakened in the middle of the night he could have recited: '*Charles et Pierre vont à l'école.*' Madame Irène had made friends with Catherine, they'd go to bathe in the stream together or play duets on the piano;—her husband, a fat, good-natured music teacher (he had a beautiful, strong baritone voice, and used to show it off in Schubert's songs when company came), sang solos in church and Catherine helped him with the children's choir. Also he recalled some dance or other, and couples waltzing, himself in a navy-blue, fashionably cut jacket (yes, Catherine had been whirling round and round with her fiancé in the very centre of the floor, for her engagement to Alexei Woynovich had been announced just the day before); that cold, slippery twist of pain in his chest, he recalled that too, and also the dark stairway to the 'blue room,' an arm in a long white glove moving up the banister, a strong masculine hand an inch behind it, and how each soundless step he heard as he hid behind the drawn folds of a curtain had been evidence of the lightness of that step going first, of that woman he loved in his childish dreams; and the thought of what they were going to do there; then suddenly his father coming up, his surprise: 'What are you doing here? Go away and play.' (Why had he ever pretended he didn't understand, when in fact he knew perfectly well!) Then the cracked mirror in the hall, in which his own face, Peter's face, looked shapelessly diffused, forming crooked zigzag lines like the ruins of a real face down which tears were streaming, but that was already much later, when Madame Irène calmed him: 'Peter, you surprise me. Control yourself, Peter,' then her oval room under the tower which linked the right wing with the main building, that room in which the tapestries had no doubt once been bright but had faded with time and looked heathery, and many discolouring patches of damp glistened like dew in the early sun; and how he used to come to her pretending he was having trouble with grammar so as to have moments of private confidences and to listen, as he drank raspberry juice through a straw, to the shrill squeaks of bats circling the park; that she alone had known all this, how he'd survived Catherine's departure with Alexei, well, perhaps her husband too, they'd been so understanding and tactful, and that had a soothing effect on him: but now all these people were dead; his own father, Alexei himself, whom he'd hated so much then, he'd left for the front just after his marriage and been caught by the Bolsheviks in the Pinsk marshes, he never came back, Madame Irène and her husband—only time had arrested these figures on the film of memory, they were already cold, caught in motion, hence their hieratic and unnatural gestures, and soon they'd be forgotten entirely, he thought, just as the time in which they'd lived was becoming more and more impenetrable, silent, enigmatic; and yet there emerged from that tangle of momentary, interrupted reflections passing like lightning through his brain, some dim masculine face, dark, embittered, with black hair and teeth white as ivory, which he couldn't at first associate with anyone familiar, although it was like the face of someone he knew, but another memory—bringing with it a wave of something dirty, clammy, the echo of a primitive, half-conscious fear which he'd experienced still earlier, much earlier, even before he began to understand the meaning of the painful differences between his mother and father—this memory set the face in juxtaposition with the sombre setting of the old water mill in the forest where he'd once gone with his friend Nick Fiodorchuk and Julia the Second to look for buried treasure, and he'd accidentally dropped a ball he was carrying. Its diagonal coloured stripes rotated in the air now as they had done then, and the rest of the picture emerged from them: the three of them standing on the path as the ball rolled away downhill, mesmerizing it by their gaze, still childishly confident that they could bring it to a stop, then it had bounced a moment on the surface of the water, ever widening circles moved away from it, until it finally stopped, motionless, and a lazy current or perhaps a breath of wind moved it towards the far bank, and again now, just as then, he caught sight of a young man attracted by their cries, from the mill perhaps or maybe he had been standing at the sluice, in any case unnoticed by them, but who'd been watching them for some time with suspicious attention; he had emerged from the shadow of the mill to the water and the path, had rolled up his trouser legs and gone into the pond, tried to reach the ball but couldn't, so had plunged in waist-deep, fished out the ball and then, as he handed it back, had asked him, Peter: 'Who're you?' addressing him, Peter, not Nicholas or Julia the Second, thus betraying that he knew them, and when he, Peter, after thanking him, had carelessly replied that he was Cherestvienski, the man had stood over him, rubbing his chin, unable to take in what he'd heard, so that in the end he'd had to repeat to himself in an undertone: 'What? Cherestvienski?' gazing at him with burning eyes, as though on the point of striking him, so that Peter had taken a step back, whereupon he'd at once turned violently away and gone springily over the bridge, rockingly, like a wildcat on a branch, and had disappeared into the grey building of the mill, though he didn't live there (he couldn't have, for the mill belonged to the manor, had long been deserted and was avoided by all right-minded people in the neighbourhood, for they said it was haunted), and they'd never met him again, either then or later, for after waiting a little and after some discussion, they'd peeped into the interior, and later on had come here several times, but neither Nicholas nor Julia the Second had ever said who the man they'd accidentally met was, though he couldn't have been a stranger to them, so he didn't learn until much later and from other sources; and just as that man had muttered Cherestvienski, so now Peter incredulously muttered to himself in an undertone: 'Gavryluk?' feeling the renewed shiver of that long-forgotten primitive terror which he'd known then, but his grandmother asked: 'Did you say something?' and he, eagerly shaking off the unpleasant mood, said: 'No, you're imagining things,' but his grandmother said, 'And don't speak of this matter to your grandfather either, please,' so he: 'What matter?' and his grandmother: 'I thought you understood . . . Gavryluk,' and he: 'Oh yes, Gavryluk. But I thought we were talking about Madame Irène, not about him,' and his grandmother: 'Yes, but it was he who did it. And not only that. Avoid the topic with Julia the Second too,' and he: 'I don't care for unexplained mysteries,' to which his grandmother said firmly: 'I'll explain it to you in good time, and he: 'I didn't realize that so many things could become taboo in the course of a few years,' and his grandmother: 'You're old enough to take care of yourself if you're threatened physically, but you're not old enough to endure disappointment and the loss of illusions,' and he: 'What do you mean?' and his grandmother implored feebly: 'My dear, don't talk about it, it's not at all pleasant for us or for you. At least not today. The time will come for everything,' so he: 'Very well, Grandmother. I'll go for a look around the park. But I didn't think things had gone so far.' 'What things? What things?' she fluttered her hand, 'Well, the things we've been talking about,' said he, to which his grandmother said: 'Don't be late for lunch,' as if she hadn't caught that last phrase of his.

He didn't move from that spot, merely waited for his grandmother to go away first, and in fact she did. He followed her quiet footsteps into the depths of the room, trying once more to recall how they sounded, for she used to walk differently, more firmly, more assuredly, and he didn't turn back until the oak door with its heavy brass latch had closed after her. Then he set off across the terrace into the depths of the park, thinking that the future she'd spoken of, when she would explain everything, was still far away, while the present was beginning to grow complicated, and thinking also of what she'd said about Gavryluk, but not too attentively now; it was stiflingly hot.

It occurred to him that he hadn't anything specific to think about, but was wandering at random amidst things far and near, unable to concentrate for long on anything. His entire body felt exhausted, there was a spongy dullness inside his head, maybe I got up too late, he thought, but it was also as though, now that he was back in the world he'd yearned for and which had always seemed to him to be rationally ordered (like a chessboard, where the players set out the men then interrupt their game for a moment to go away, confident that nothing will be touched, and are amazed when they return to see the chessmen rearranged), now that he was finally there in a physical way, the specific elements constituting the image of this world whenever he was absent from it, had—he now saw—undergone too much of a change, or were simply absent altogether; he couldn't get rid of this impression.

He walked along a gravel path, brushing the drooping clumps of grass at the edge of the path with the tips of his shoes. The gravel was white, baking. He couldn't look up for long because a black light at once flared in his eyes; the sky was completely naked, and the ball of the sun was drifting across it in solitude, drawing away all the strength out of the earth and nature. The fermenting smell of rich earth drenched by yesterday's rain and nourished by the leaves of the past went to his head like wine. The silence persisted, roasting, stagnant, nothing was happening in it, there wasn't even the solitary buzz of a bee or wasp, or of the cicadas, not even the dry rustle of lizards scuttling through the grass, and not until after a time, where the park descended into a valley and the horizon stretched across like the white shore of some glacial ocean, did he notice a bird slowly gliding from its surface. It was the hawk he'd seen that morning, but soon it too disappeared, plunging into the smouldering foam of the sun's glare. He walked aimlessly along, not thinking about anything. He couldn't force any rational decisions out of the spongy, rather dry and unpleasant stupefaction that filled his mind, and he felt clammy and damp, he'd have to dry off the sweat again, he'd always be in the light no matter which way he turned. Everything around, every tree, every bush, the steep stony mass of the house and the lamps in the main drive—all were blurred, quivering, as if not supported by the earth but suspended in the air so that they had to yield to its vibrations, looking as if they'd been sketched by a child or half-wit with thick, irregular and blurred lines which only marked the black outlines of everything. He grew increasingly irritated as he walked on, unable to come to any decision, not really knowing what it was all about, and he even paused a few times, for he seemed to catch a far-off cry somewhere: 'Pete! Pete! Peter!' but the sound was thin, shredded by the expanse, so that it came to him rather like a whisper which nevertheless shook the foundations of the burning silence. Looking back towards the house, he tried to stare through the wall of bright light and to see a figure, man or woman, calling from one of the windows, but all were closed, mostly screened by green blinds, and although it seemed to him that his gaze, as it wandered in search, was meeting the gaze of another person, nevertheless that voice might have been only an illusion. Not until he approached the spot where the *allée* passed by a thicket that was overgrowing the ruins of the orangery and turned to the right, did he observe his uncle Theodore seated on a bench.

Uncle Theodore nodded and smiled to him from the distance, either to greet or to summon him, but his face made Peter doubt, for it was dissolved in an ephemeral glow, like that in Renoir's paintings, and even before Peter came up to him he wondered whether this was real, or only another of the illusions he'd been having that day. The misty unstable mass was as mutable as the light which impregnated it and everything all around, it was given up to the destructive action of this light, but in the end he approached and without asking, or wanting to be asked, he suddenly, violently, quite instinctively yet violently, on the very edge of an outburst, without even thinking, said: 'I'm going to Gleb, Uncle.' His uncle Theodore looked him in the eye and, as if he knew or had perhaps been awaiting this decision, said: 'Very well, of course—except that Catherine was here just now, after all . . .' still smiling, however, as he gasped: 'When?' His uncle said: 'Yesterday, when you all arrived, and today too,' 'How could she have been?' he exclaimed, losing control, and his uncle said calmly: 'Didn't you see her, or say good-bye to her? She left after breakfast,' but not without some surprise, and it was as if something were about to happen, or already had. The day went out like a light, though only half the day had elapsed, the world rocked though it was motionless, a butterfly swooned in the air, a flower faded on its stem, but no, nothing happened.

Striding behind Cherkvas along the edge of the ravine, he watched the hawk he'd seen from the windows of his room when he woke up and then for the second time after he had left his grandmother. He was carrying his pre-war shotgun, the old man on the other hand had an incredibly archaic weapon, which only he could manipulate and with which he could hit even the swiftest creature in motion. They were talking a little about all sorts of things, cautiously, as though the fact they hadn't met since that memorable September had created a certain distance between them and meant they weren't altogether sure to what extent they could trust each other, though this applied to Cherkvas rather than to Peter, for Peter was prepared at once to return to their former intimacy, only the old man betrayed some doubts, as if he weren't yet quite sure whether he might trust Peter as he had done in the past. He told him Nicholas, the son of Fiodorchuk, had grown up, also that he'd become the right-hand man of Mikolai Fiodorovich (the Cherkvases and Fiodorchuks were Russians, like Peter's grandfather, they'd emigrated with him, had settled in Poland and always referred to him as 'Mikolai Fiodorovich'), he said Nicholas was his contact with the Polish partisans in the district, but didn't go any further, as if he couldn't have explained their existence, though Peter had heard a good deal about them even in K., and nothing Cherkvas could say would startle or surprise him, and in the same way he said, suddenly changing the subject, that Julia the Second now lived in the manor following the death of her father who'd led the local peasants against collectivization in 1940. She was entirely separated from her mother in the village, but when Peter asked whether she was going to get married he suddenly fell silent. The conversation halted, there were more and more of these silences, and Peter felt that Cherkvas didn't want to arouse his curiosity and that something inside him prevented him from speaking out as he wiped the sweat from his bald skull, groaning, then put on his cap and said: 'Nicholas has become a sly one, he has! Mikolai Fiodorovich keeps him away from Chupryn mostly, to look after his affairs for him, you won't be seeing him for some time, sir. These are hard times. They're terrible ruffians, and Gavryluk is the worst of them. But Nicholas has got the better of him more than once,' or, concealing something cunning and sly in his face, he said: 'Yes indeed, Julia the Second lives here. It's too bad she hasn't always lived here. That Gavryluk will visit us, sir, that he will, there's not enough to keep him where he should be,' and if Peter hadn't just discovered that he'd missed meeting Catherine and therefore wasn't inclined to talk Cherkvas would not have got off so easily with his vague remarks. The dust rose in clouds around their feet as they came to the road that led into the village. 'I suppose we'll turn back here?' the old man said at this point; it was too hot even for the hawk, which had alighted no doubt on the branches in some grey ravine, he couldn't see it, so Peter willingly agreed: 'Yes, it's hot.'

The air was vibrant, weighing down the thin grass along the edge of the ravine. Ragged weeds, sprouting out of the earth where the ditches crossed, looked withered. On the right side of the road the yellow steppe extended, dotted here and there with burial mounds covered with mint, lady's-fingers, and wild oats, above which sharp points of burrs towered, looking from the distance like upturned broomsticks, and though the wind couldn't be felt, a whitish cloud of dust rose above the ravine, and the distant horizon also had that same dusty, smoky tint, as if a herd of startled horses were galloping along it, raising the dust. 'And the village? How are things at the village?' Peter finally asked, glancing down the road which, as a child, he had often walked along on his way to Chupryn village, where he knew almost everyone, and, even before Cherkvas replied, he felt a painful stab under his heart, then finally heard his own question repeated: 'The village?' followed by a meaningless yet at the same time significant reply: 'Nobody goes to the village much now, you must understand that, sir . . .' and suddenly, for one brief moment, in that stifling expanse where the Ukrainian houses were almost lost in the distance, Peter saw as though it were a film close-up the interminable pastures, the winter corn drying before harvest, and the still green fields of summer wheat with white clouds passing endlessly over them. He saw barns and fenced-in lots. He saw the red-faced buxom wife of the Orthodox priest putting a dish of chilled, sour milk on the earthen bench in front of her cottage. Her invariably sleepy son Oshka was just taking hay to the cows and horses. The creaking door of the shed. The warm comfort under the gabled roof, surrounded by pigsties. Manure to the ankles. Piss and rain water flowing thick and brown into a puddle between the buildings. Horses with matted coats trotting across the pasture. Sheep and goats crowded in a dirty, grey mass into the corner of a yard. The schoolmaster's old dun gelding dozing alone behind the school, over an empty trough stained with bran and saliva. The painful grunting of pigs. And 'How boring,' said the schoolmaster. He got up from the goatskin jacket he'd been lounging on in the garden, cautiously circled the barrel of slops, swearing: 'Damnable country. For six months of the year it's like a stove, for the other six the snow drives you insane. And a man has to go behind the stable or into the orchard to relieve himself,' he stalked away, unbuttoning his pants. The mayor's wife was asleep on a bench in the shade of a pear tree, her face covered with her apron, her rump sticking out, her legs—caked with loam and earth—tucked up under her. But when dusk fell, the kerosene lamps were lit and everything seemed tranquil and right in the huts. The wind blew down the ravine and into the brushwood scattered on the rafters of the pigsties, a greying dusk covered the straw roofs, with odorous smoke rising above them. Girls were singing songs about summer evenings and unfaithful lovers in the meadows behind the village. He longed to go back once more.

They set off again in the direction of the manor. Cherkvas, who evidently attributed Peter's sudden silence to his own words, hastily explained: 'I don't mean to say that anything threatens us from them now, no. We're well protected. Besides, Mikolai Fiodorovich was always just, though stern. Those who were on close terms with the scoundrels before the war were the ones who came off worst. They were lucky to be left with a shirt to stand up in. They have fighting in the blood. Now they're slaughtering the local Jews and Poles wherever they can find them, by the thousands—but the time will come when they'll turn against their German protectors. There's nothing to go to the village for. It's not done any more,' and he paused, leaning on his obsolete rifle, then introduced Peter briefly into the complex relationships between Chupryn estate and that green island beyond the ravine which surrounded the late-Renaissance manor bought by Peter's grandfather after the First World War from the Polish Firlejs.

When the area had been occupied by the Soviets, they deported most Poles to the East. They established collective farms for the local Ukrainians in the villages. The Soviet rule was worse than the German. For no matter what, for a single word, without even doing anything, an NKVD official would appear and stand a man up against a wall or exile him to Siberia. Then the

Germans chased away the Reds and they bought for their own dirty work the special proclivities of the local hooligans. Chupryn, fortunately, wasn't a manor village. Peter's grandfather owned little arable land, but mostly forest and wasteland which he used for hunting. Apart from his own Russians he employed no one but Poles, so there was no reason for close contact with the Ukrainians. But if that were peace, it was also armed. For who knows how many of the local villagers were merely afraid, and how many supported Gavryluk? Perhaps only a few, or perhaps all of them? The manor carriage as it drove past the Ukrainian shacks was no longer greeted with bows, smiles, or the plea for a decision in some family quarrel over land, or advice because someone in a family was sick. A silence had fallen. The black sources of poison, which had been throbbing under the skin since the days of the legendary Gonta, were again coursing fast. The earth round about was turning a baleful red. The Polish and Polonized villages in the area were like outposts resisting engulfing waves. The little towns, inhabited for the most part by Jews, were dying. Weeds grew over the scenes of conflagrations. The crooked streets had emptied. Black chimney stacks loomed amidst burned-out ruins. Men from the German police ransacked ruins, searching for hidden gold and dollars. Although Shames Agatstein himself never sang, yet he'd chanted the Kol Nidre over a lime pit for his dying brothers, then was himself pushed into its depths with rifle butts. The synagogues were despoiled, sacred tablets from the Jewish school were trampled under nailed boots. Churches were looted. The wonderful old chasubles, embroidered by earlier generations of women, were cut into carpets and canopies for beds in peasant huts. The front-line infantry kept stores in convents. Even the Ruthenian intelligentsia in the little towns were dying out, vanquished by a dark, primitive, revengeful element in themselves, driving from their own grass roots. Secret agents, auxiliaries, Bandera's supporters and those of Mazeppa in the SS-Galicien, and lesser, armed bandits protected by their Church killed anyone who made the sign of the cross in a manner different from themselves. A mob. It was a rotting world which bred vipers in its own putrefying carcass. They wriggled from the underground sources of hate. Rifles barked out eerie nocturnal music.

Cherkvas's narrative thus revealed to Peter what his grandmother hadn't told him. That world of values he'd loved and had come back to, thinking to find it unchanged, was whirling away into oblivion. Hordes of drunkards thirsty for blood, for violence, until recently had been peaceable rustic squires—as if this war had some accursed power to transform anyone it touched. The image of smashed windowpanes and shattered mirrors, the crash of rifle butts on the door at dusk, grenades thrown into human shrieks, the feverish breathing of children hidden in cemeteries. And all this encircled the green island of Chupryn, hardly touched by the fire as yet.

They were walking back along the narrow path that wound along the edge of the ravine, one behind the other, in silence. Stones dislodged by their feet rolled and plunged with a hollow rumble into the depths. Swallows were flitting out from under the projecting roots and overhanging sod, squeaking. When they finally stopped in the shadow of the park's cool wall, Peter turned back once again in the direction of the road to the village and sighed inwardly: That wonderful yesterday of mine—will I ever think as badly of you as I do of today?

His uncle Theodore stood brooding by the window-sill. He was staring not very attentively at an unfastened silk cord hanging from a loop in the wall, then he fastened the curtain back with it, so that the cord formed an elaborate knot at one side. Immediately a sunbeam, which had been making a blurred square on the floorboards, became vivid, and the brass rod of a gnomon on a table facing the window distinctly showed the hour on its flat face. A shadow edged by the bright light lay across the Roman V engraved in the marble though almost obliterated by age. His uncle brought out a watch from his waistcoat pocket, glanced at it and muttered: 'A quarter to five. We still have plenty of time,' then went back to the table and carefully stroked the yellowish pages of a book from which he had just been reading to Peter a long passage relating to the early history of Cilicia, a kingdom founded—so the passage said—by an Armenian prince of the Bagratid family, named Reuben.

Peter sighed. Did this still mean anything? His uncle's tales, his mysterious and thrilling discoveries, his archaeological excursions, both the ones he'd actually undertaken at some time, and these later ones, based only on old maps, chronicles, and notes. Filled with the risk and exciting poetry of exploration. The treasures of Byzantine Emperors, of Teutonic Knights, of Spanish conquistadores or corsairs, discovered or if not exactly 'discovered' yet at least shown on maps, with his uncle's solemn assurance that they were definitely there, that error was entirely out of the question, so that it was as though they'd really been found, for Peter had believed his uncle: treasures were to be found everywhere, other searchers lacked the imagination, the inspiration, and the ageless, almost boyish heart his uncle possessed. He'd always participated in these excursions with glowing eyes and fevered brow, he even went further than his uncle in his dreams, for it had seemed to him that with the treasures he found, his uncle would buy a boat in which they'd undertake a long voyage to discover some new land or other, for after all there must still be something left in the world to be discovered, or else his uncle would form an army and march into his homeland in the East to dislodge that bloodstained Georgian with his moustaches, or perhaps he'd drain off some huge coral reef in the Pacific, and populate it with runaways and *émigrés* from all the countries where evil prevailed, and would establish a just kingdom for them there, in which everyone would be kind to everyone else, all would be equal, money would be unknown and unnecessary, and they'd pass their lives far away from cruel, destructive civilization, in peace, fishing and talking about fine and useful things, such as Peter had once read of in a book called *Jim the Sailor*. There were many alternatives, as many as there were forgotten treasures which his uncle wrested from the earth and sea, and all were equally thrilling. Oh, those carefree dreams of a child, for which he was grateful to his uncle to this day! But now, his thoughts were elsewhere. This day had held too many completely different surprises in store for him, more than he'd ever expected, and although he subconsciously felt his uncle wasn't taking his own narrative as seriously as he'd used to, that he was only making an effort—as if nothing at all had happened in between, time hadn't moved on, and they both had the same enthusiastic, unsullied hearts—to play the part he used to play to him, Peter, he found it increasingly difficult to surrender himself to the delicately murmuring stream of his uncle's words, which were intended to evoke in him old, very old images of events, and it was increasingly difficult to concentrate. He repeated unthinkingly in his mind: The Bagratids . . . Reuben, son of Gagig II, the last Ani king . . . and he thought: I've heard of him somewhere before, could it be that his uncle was rehashing one of his pre-war tales because he couldn't think of a new one? All this was jumbled together in his head.

'Tired? No? That's good, excellent . . .' his uncle said, catching the fleeting negative movement of Peter's head and interpreting it to his own advantage, 'because before we get down to our, well . . . search, I'd like to tell you a few general facts. But it will sound rather like an academic lecture. You won't be bored?' to which he answered, with an apologetic smile, for he was truly sorry he couldn't regain his former degree of interest: 'Of course not, please go on, Uncle,' and his uncle: 'Well then, look at the map. Just here. There's a narrow strip of land between the Black Sea and the Mediterranean—Asia Minor: the Pontus mountains rise in the north, along the Black Sea coast, and in the south there's the steep, rocky wall of the Upper Taurus along the Mediterranean coast. All these coasts of Asia Minor, with their devious routes leading towards the green valley of the Euphrates and the yellow sands of Arabia, were at one time a stage on which important historical events were enacted. It was here that the ship of the Egyptian Ptolemy, bearing Cleopatra, sailed majestically from the Mediterranean Sea to the mouth of the river Cydnus, as the Romans used to call it. Its poop was said to be of pure gold, its sails purple, and its oars adorned with burnished silver. Accompanied by flutes and harps (so a chronicler wrote), that ship sailed up the river to the city of Tarsus, where Antony was awaiting Cleopatra. It was here that Alexander of Macedonia's army fought the Persians. Here, in the city of Tarsus, a Roman citizen named Shavel, of Jewish descent, later an Apostle, spent his childhood. And in the Middle Ages the Crusaders came this way to the East. In brief, this is the region of Asia Minor where Reuben fled into the inaccessible mountains and hid after the Byzantines killed his father in the year 1079. His kingdom apparently originated when he succeeded in seizing and holding first one fortress, then his son added another, but it wasn't until later that his grandsons Prince Toros II and King Leon II extended the frontiers of the kingdom throughout Cilicia. I'd gladly show you drawings of the ruins of these towns. I had them here somewhere,' and he began searching amidst the books, piles of yellowed papers, manuscripts and maps spread from one end to the other of a massive Danzig table which occupied almost a quarter of the room.

Peter made himself more comfortable in an armchair and pulled up a footstool. There were two worn, rusty places in its velvet covering left by his uncle's feet, for as he sat reading he usually did so with his knees up almost under his chin. Putting his feet in these same places, half sitting, half recumbent, Peter felt as if he were weighed down with the dust and stifling smell that had been fed over a long period of time with the paper which filled the room to overflowing, a heat untouched by a draught of any kind, although sparkling particles of dust continually spiralled in the still air; this heat was crushing his resistance, was slowly defeating him, was pressing the strength out of him, and although his eyes were open as he watched his uncle impatiently rooting among piles of ancient rubbish heaped on the table, he wasn't sure that he wasn't dreaming. His uncle's voice sounded like a series of monotonous meaningless sounds, first approaching him then ebbing away, and although he tried he couldn't get very much sense out of them.

For the first time in years here he was, sitting in this room, and although it was the same room as before (well, perhaps not entirely, not completely, for earlier it had seemed immense to him, sufficient for the whole world, and—like all these journeys and excursions undertaken with the help of nothing but books, maps, globes, and his uncle's tales—girdling a huge and mysterious expanse: mysterious and full of surprises too), now the room seemed much smaller and even rather absurd, not unlike an attic or a mad collector's pile of junk, who thought that a woman's hand seeking to introduce order of some kind would profane his collection. But despite this sudden diminishing, which the room had undergone in Peter's imagination, it was still the biggest room in that part of the house. It was really a hall rather than a room, shaped like a halved octagon, strikingly odd. Apart from the longest wall with the windows, the other walls were covered with shallow, high bookshelves put up in such a way that mirrors could be placed between them: two shelves and one mirror to each wall. The gilt frames of the mirrors contrasted strikingly with the black wood of the shelves. Behind one of them was the single window overlooking the far side of the park, with a view of the orangery, but perhaps he wouldn't even have guessed it if his grandmother hadn't told him before. And in each square yard of the space between the shelves, the huge cruciform table, the desk which was almost as big, and little tables were crowded, with globes, wind roses on iron stands, clocks, heaps of excavated shards, urns, tear flasks, piles of foreign atlases dumped on the floor, a cheap music box, tall chairs like bishops' thrones, two mahogany cupboards each with twenty-five flat shelves in which, he recalled, his uncle kept old coins and medals commemorating various occasions, also a set of eighteenth-century English medals, on velvet, under glass, while little candlesticks, some without candles, stood wherever they could be fitted in.

Under the mirror covering that window which overlooked the unhappy orangery, amidst oddments of silver and lacquer, he caught sight on the sideboard of an oblong photograph in a cheap frame made of shells, such as small-town Jews used to sell in market places before the war; it had probably been taken somewhere in Nikorycha, most likely in the market, for in the background he could see a countrywoman passing by, a water carrier with his yokes, and some booths under canvas. In the foreground of the photograph Madame Irène was walking briskly along against the wind, her legs and hips outlined under the light dress. The little jacket she was wearing around her shoulders was unfastened and had been blown up like a balloon by a gust of wind, and she was smiling and turning her head as though speaking to someone on her right. The photograph must once have been much larger, because Peter could see part of a man's hand holding her by the arm at the curve of her left elbow, but that someone to whom she was smiling and speaking at the moment when the picture was taken had been cut off. Thus deprived of her surroundings she looked rather unnatural, as if turning back to some object outside space, speaking as it were to the Buddha statuette on the sideboard next to the photograph. Peter glanced at his uncle then suddenly asked: 'Uncle, who's Gavryluk? Truly. I'd like to know,' but his uncle, who was at this moment considering some engraving or other he'd extricated from a pile of other engravings, shivered and turned his head away as if he hadn't heard, then went to the window. He stood there for a while, raising the engraving to his eyes as though there weren't enough light at the table.

'Just look . . .' he said presently, coming back to his previous position, 'here's a picture of Tarsus, done for John Garne's album *The Holy Land—Asia Minor,* published early last century. I had more of them, but I don't know where they've got to. I keep losing things nowadays, one day I have a thing, the next it's gone. A few days ago they were all on the top, but now that I want them I can't find them. One day you ought to glance through this Englishman's account, it's still relevant. I remember in 1910, I was travelling through the same part of the Ottoman Empire and the country was still as wild and inaccessible as it had been when he saw it a hundred years before,' and after meditating as though he were again crossing those regions in his mind's eye, he went on: 'Steep cliffs, deep abysses, dark-blue seas washing the deserted coasts around the port of Ayash, the devastated towns, the ruined castles on mountain terraces, the vestiges of an old canal that once linked the town of Tarsus and the sea, and Tarsus itself, an ancient Eastern settlement with minarets and gardens, with genuine Roman gates in the north-east section and the ruins of an old theatre by the river. I met several Armenian familes who'd kept their religion and language.'

'Uncle, what was his purpose?' Peter interrupted, 'his purpose? That's what I want to know. He must have had some purpose since he made that attack on Chupryn. I gather it wasn't a question of robbery. There was no looting, was there? So what was his purpose? Was what happened in the orangery what he came for? Or was that only incidental? How was it? I want to know what his purpose was,' but his uncle Theodore, without altering his expression, only getting paler and more hunched, went on in the very same voice, which seemed hollow and meaningless, to say that in Tarsus, Sis, the ports of Ayash and Mersin, Silifke, in the mountainous nest of Zeytoon, a life typical of the Middle Ages had run its course under the Reubenites: 'Here ships anchored from Genoa, Nîmes, Montpellier, Seville, London, Messina, Majorca, Crete, and Turkey. Yet although the Armenians adopted European customs, dress, and names, they retained their ancient social order and behind their adopted titles of nobility, for instance, were hidden their national Armenian inherited titles of "sparapet" and "sharapet," handed down from one generation to the next. Arts and crafts were highly regarded in Cilicia too: painting, poetry, music, sculpture, the illumination of manuscripts. Many manuscripts they'd brought away with them from their ancient homeland beyond the Ararat were preserved from destruction in Asia Minor. You should know that music was so highly thought of in Cilicia that an "expert in song" would acquire the title of philosopher, or wise man. Even today, traces of the architecture of those times have survived in the remaining monasteries, in the superb arches of bridges, especially the aqueducts in the Bajlan pass, in the ruins of the medieval castles, in the once inhabited caves of Silifke which are surprisingly reminiscent of Goris in their ancient homeland. Valerii Biurov has written that in the twelfth, thirteenth, and fourteenth centuries Cilicia was one of the most animated centres of the intellectual life of that world. And it was so. In the second half of the Middle Ages, Armenia succeeded in creating a centre of genuine culture in the East, and was herself in the forefront of all Asia,' but Peter: 'Uncle, please tell me whether Catherine was living with the Woynoviches at Gleb at the time, or here? I remember Grandfather writing to say that once she had some disagreement with her mother-in-law. So was she living at Chupryn then, or did she merely come visiting more often? When Gavryluk made that wretched attack . . .' However, his uncle Theodore had just found the case containing the other engravings and, with unnatural animation, he made room on the table among the books, and began laying them out, dusting them, straightening them, and commenting on the views they depicted. All this as though the definite questions Peter had insistently asked hadn't reached him at all.

His uncle's thin face was white, as though powdered, his oval chin disfigured with a twitch that also affected his cheeks, and there was a blind amber light glowing relentlessly in his wide-set, rather feminine eyes. And then suddenly something in Peter went into reverse, he no longer wanted to hear his uncle's answer and, smiling palely, forcing the words out with an effort, 'It's tremendously interesting, Uncle . . .' he said very feebly, '. . . how this small group of immigrants managed to create a national state organism under such different and difficult conditions,' but his uncle (evidently not expecting this) looked at him with unconcealed amazement (though only for a moment, for he instantly reverted to his previous role) and quickly shifting a footstool over to the chair in which Peter was sitting, he unfolded the case of views he'd found on his knees.

'This is Ayash,' he said, pulling one of them out. He spoke fast and too loudly: 'Ayash the harbour, Ayash the town, and finally Ayash the watchtower, the oldest part, which I'd like you to consider particularly,' and in the deeply folded plan of the desert, over the walls and buildings of a town hardly visible on the engraving, Peter, trying to submit to his uncle's words, saw the ruins of what might have been a watchtower or temple or perhaps a royal castle, but at any rate a building of lofty and impressive dimensions, though damaged in the middle as though by someone's angry fist, and then he made one last effort and imagined it as his uncle wanted him to as he showed him particular elements with a finger that was trembling nervously and tapping the paper, perhaps afraid he might interrupt again with a question about Gavryluk. For a moment Peter even succeeded in following one thread of the narrative. His uncle was explaining that what he was looking at was the basilica of the local kings, built in the second half of the thirteenth century on the model of a temple of St. Gregory, erected earlier by Gagig II in Anah. However, it was a boring and dry narrative; it reminded him hardly at all of the earlier, almost poetical tales full of imagination his uncle had evoked in this very room. A single brief reference to royal jewels and gold caught his attention, revealing that he hadn't yet lost his former passion for finding supposed treasures or ancient works of art. 'Yes, I think that the graves of some of the kings of Cilicia and probably the royal treasury too are to be found in this basilica. I've come across several references in Arab writers. I reported on them at one of the archaeological congresses, everyone agreed I was right but no one would believe that any of it has survived to our time. I differ from that view,' he said, and then Peter understood that his uncle only wanted to expand his monologue so as to prevent him from speaking, the narrative itself wasn't important at all, and he spoke without even thinking what he was saying, for his voice sounded hollow and somehow absolutely empty. Moreover, everything in the room in which they were sitting sounded hollow and empty, all the superfluous objects collected there absorbed the sound, but as he listened now to nothing but that voice, letting its entire content flow past him, Peter suddenly caught, as he'd often done before the war, a certain characteristic, a characteristic which had always impressed him, and by which he'd have recognized his uncle even in a crowd, if he'd heard him. The monotonous voice of his uncle, tired now, was free from any of the faults to be expected from foreigners. He spoke a Polish that was too refined for a Pole, an academic language really, somehow rigid, and had it not been for that imperceptible emotional undercurrent which usually vibrated in his voice, coming to the surface of phrases at the most unexpected places and colouring them with warmth, it might even have seemed dead. At this moment, however, that warmer colouring which usually gave it sharpness and clarity was absent, his uncle was speaking as if he had no strength left in him, and in fact he soon stopped. Silence stalked through the room which wasn't really silent at all: all the sounds from outside, and the insects banging against the screens went on sounding in it.

His uncle sat staring indifferently at the engraving he held, then put it away in the case. He took out a blue lace handkerchief and waved it in front of his face like a fan. Then the case slipped off his knees and scattered the engravings on the floor. But he didn't lean over to retrieve them. He rose from the stool and looked out of the window. Peter collected the drawings, then did the same as his uncle. 'Dusk is falling,' he said. The sun was now pale in the milky sky as it set. He noticed that it was reflected flatly in his uncle's eyes which still held that amber-coloured unseeing gleam, as before. His uncle said, 'I thought it would amuse you,' to which he: 'It's very interesting. I often used to think during those years that when we met again we'd surely make some great new discovery. And so we shall. For you, Uncle, certainly know where to find this treasure in the basilica vaults. I'm right, am I not?' and his uncle began in reply, as if to himself: 'Dusk was falling the first time I was there. An Arab guide had driven me up the mountain on a donkey and was waiting at the bottom of some steps, lighting a fire. Shepherds were coming down into the valley and veiled women in black, faceless, carrying baskets of fruit, were resting as they leaned on gaps in the walls before they started going down slowly. The guide had already lit the fire and called to me. I went down to him and behind me, beyond the horizon, almost enveloping me with the desert's heated air, rose the circle of an unusually large moon. People passing on the road stood out against the ruins with the sharp outlines of Rembrandt's figures, in a shifting, double light. That was a very long time ago, Peter.' So he quickly said, 'Let's spread out the map on the floor tomorrow, Uncle, and retrace that journey. It's exciting. And we'll guess where the royal treasure is,' and his uncle: 'Yes, of course . . . But I don't know whether we'll succeed. Even here in this house, where so many things are not mentioned, it's hard to forget the real world,' and he: 'Oh come, Uncle!' and his uncle: 'We're plunging into the darkness, my dear boy, and though everyone is doing his best, we're only plunging still deeper and deeper. I don't know whether we'll even find the power to resurrect that world,' and he fell silent, and although the sudden gleam of a window pushed by Peter illuminated his face (his parchment-like skin seemed to absorb all the rest of the light remaining in the air) so that it seemed faultlessly pure and noble, his mouth twisted into a grimace of dismay and guilt. As if guessing Peter's thought, he said, 'Forgive me, my dear boy, I've been a bore and tiresome today. Besides, I didn't answer your questions. Of course we'll talk of what you want to know later on. Although it's also wise to know nothing. But now it's supper time,' and Peter then noticed that the first dusk had already fallen outside, and would soon scatter the whole room with deep blue. As always before evening the sparrows were flying about in the park, and swallows cut through the air just above the tree-tops. Below, everything was changing and shifting in the fading light, and only a laburnum bush in the flower bed burned with the yellow glow of its bright flowers. When he turned his gaze to the room, his uncle stood expectantly in the depths, and the gnomon, drowned in the twilight, no longer indicated anything.

The rain had been drumming, monotonous and hollow, on the gutters for an hour. But that was outside the house, in the fading day; the rain was cleansing it of the remaining dust and heat while the lamps in the little drawing-room cast delicate nets of light from corner to corner, catching in them the moths and butterflies that flitted through the open windows. It smelled of comfortable warmth and the smoke from those long-tubed cigarettes which all the Russians Peter knew smoked wherever he met them; a pale-blue spider web enveloped his grandfather's chair, emitting an acrid and mildly soporific aroma: 'You don't express yourself clearly, my boy,' said his grandfather (brushing some invisible dust off his sleeve), 'at least not clearly enough for me to understand what you mean. Surely you don't think I want to hide anything from you?' he asked in a voice that, as always, had no particular accent and contained a touch of that scepticism of his, although it wasn't flawed at this moment by irony: pondering, he stroked his pointed beard, gazed at the ceiling as if he wanted to make it clear he was weighing with the utmost solemnity all the various alternatives. The door opened and Fiodorchuk, wearing a white linen jacket which he put over the bright green shirt of military cut when there were no guests in the house, came soundlessly into the drawing-room with the tea things. A short silence ensued, broken only after a moment by Uncle Theodore's irrelevant comment that it had been merely the heat wave that had recently affected everyone: 'People have gone mad! The sun hasn't stopped blazing down for ten days. It's all very well when it rains a little at night. But when it scorches so by day, then everyone says the oddest things! Who knows what they really mean? What do you think, Father?' and he turned to the grandfather but stopped when he received no reply, perhaps he hadn't even expected one. Peter, who had recovered a little from the surprise sprung on him unexpectedly by this conversation, thought that in fact the hot weather had transformed everything he'd come into contact with so far into something very distant from reality, not at all what he'd expected to find on coming to Chupryn, it was depressing.

This is what had happened: during supper he'd given an account of things that might interest his grandparents: that he had finished revising the material for his third-grade examination and next year would be preparing for the Minor Matriculation, also Constance's progress in her studies and what his mother had been doing. Then he talked about Rommel's defeats in Africa, amidst the silence of those present, not realizing yet that they'd decided not to talk about the war, and later on, recalling Julia the Second, but without knowing what persuaded him, for after all he didn't expect any explanation since he himself wasn't at all sure whether he'd really heard anything of the sort or not, or whether it had only seemed to him that he had—he asked: 'Why would it be a bad thing for me to resemble someone else?' then, feeling at once he'd committed an indiscretion, for the question didn't mean anything, he tried to explain, forming the phrases awkwardly, that it had been due to the uneasiness which her words had evoked in him, then the question: 'What words?' was asked, so he briefly quoted that strange morning dialogue of theirs. When he ended he got from his grandfather this brief explanation, preceded by a loud sigh: 'Even when she knows what she's talking about, she rambles,' and 'You needn't be afraid, you're not in the least like Semeon Gavryluk in looks, everything she chattered about was disgusting. Besides . . .' but he rebelled: 'What does it mean? What does it all mean? Why should I, or could I, be like him? I don't understand,' for again that penetrating, incomprehensible fear which he'd already experienced that day when the name 'Gavryluk' had been uttered for the first time by his grandmother, or rather not when it was first uttered but later, when it aroused in him the recollection of that long-ago encounter at the mill, that all-pervading, incomprehensible, hideous, and somehow panic fear which surged into his throat with a hot wave, mingling with yet another feeling which bordered perhaps on shame, if he'd anything to be ashamed of; and realizing at the same time that they knew something they didn't want to tell him, for after all it wasn't Julia the Second who had mentioned it, it was they who were putting the name 'Gavryluk' into her mouth now, as if taking it for granted that she'd been thinking, as she spoke, that he, Peter, wasn't like him in looks; and also understanding that they wanted to keep what they knew a secret from him and even (having noticed a touch of impatience in his grandfather's gesture as he lifted a cigarette to his lips, and the embarrassment on his grandmother's face, and that only Uncle Theodore's face was still friendly as before, though flavoured, as it were, with a pinch of sympathy) seeing that they regretted the conversation taking such an unexpected turn and that despite themselves they'd betrayed their knowledge of what Julia the Second might have been thinking when she told him, Peter, that he wasn't like anyone in looks; still feeling this incomprehensible fear, the more incomprehensible in that it couldn't be logically justified, and which gripped his whole body with a shiver as it overwhelmed him; in order to shake it off, and knowing that in a moment he'd weaken and agree to any lie with which they might seek to veil the truth from him, was already weakening indeed, and protecting himself from it, seeking with his eyes his uncle's sympathetic glance—he once more insisted impetuously, almost furiously: 'So what does it mean? What's the meaning of all this talk about likenesses?' and then his grandfather, brushing invisible dust from his sleeve as if he wanted to gain time, had just said that he, Peter, wasn't expressing himself clearly, at least not clearly enough for him, his grandfather, to be able to understand him, and Uncle Theodore had begun right away talking about the effect of the heat on people's thoughts and saying how some of them had lately suffered as it were heat stroke and had said the oddest things; Peter didn't understand at once whether this referred to him or to Julia the Second in connection with what she'd said to him that morning when she'd brought the water to his room, but in any case he didn't care.

Fiodorchuk went out and for a time no one tried to break the tense silence. The melodious bubbling of the samovar could be heard, his grandmother presently began filling cups with tea, passing the sugar bowl to each person in turn, and when Peter whispered as she passed it to him: 'You always serve such delicious tea, Grandmother,' her frozen, severely drawn face seemed to melt and become gentle with pleasure.

It had already happened. Inwardly he had weakened, the desire to argue had died, the desire to rend from them this truth of some sort which they were concealing; now he was ready to accept any false coin, without even admitting to himself that he'd discovered its falsity, for the fear which a moment ago had dominated him very strongly also went out as suddenly as it had appeared and—watching the spaniels Hook and Pook stretched at the empty hearth, dreaming of hunts past or to come, sighing in their sleep, twitching their legs and trying from time to time to bark without opening their jaws, until their imagined pursuits irritated his grandfather who shouted at them so that they lifted their heads to look at the seated people, only to confirm that nothing of any interest was happening and replace their heads between their outstretched paws—watching them with a sort of almost thoughtless indifference, he said dully: 'Of course Uncle is right, this heat is enough to turn anyone's head.'

His uncle, pleased that his explanation of the entire matter had been accepted, smiled apologetically and hastened to add, as though he didn't want too many unspoken things to remain between them: 'You ought to know that this girl has been through too much lately. If it had happened at some other time . . . Well, even now . . . But if everything that has happened hadn't happened, if Gavryluk hadn't become such a rabid Nationalist scoundrel, for apart from a number of open attacks, still worse things are being attributed to him in the neighbourhood, if it hadn't been for that, my God, perhaps one should be glad she fell in love that way. Yet was it love? In any case, we'd certainly have arranged a wedding for them soon, and your grandmother would have been a godmother once more after a certain time. For that's what it was . . . For she and

Gavryluk to . . . That's her misfortune,' and he stopped, evidently expecting Peter to ask a question, but Peter didn't. His uncle then smiled palely in the direction of Grandmother who replied with a similar though less expressive smile, and he went on that he, Peter, probably hadn't met Gavryluk before because . . . 'before the war we sent him to the high school at Tarnopol. He was our foster son, after all. But sometimes people spoke of him, you remember?' as if he didn't remember whether Peter remembered that sometimes during his school vacation a sombre youth, with an intelligent though impenetrable face in which only his black eyes burned with an animated glow like coals, would come to their house with evident reluctance and unconcealed constraint in order to give his protector an account of the progress he was making in his studies. And: 'You must understand that it came upon her like a thunderbolt, that love of hers,' he said, 'the girl thought the world of him (a handsome young man in any case, I don't deny that, if one can refer to such a man as handsome. A good-looking Mediterranean type, though taller and with a somewhat longer skull, a mixed type you know), but meanwhile all sorts of reports about him used to reach us here, about his—vile isn't the word for it—but unethical acts,' and turning to the grandmother: 'May I have another cup of tea, Mama?' he snorted somewhat contemptuously but at the same time with self-irony: 'Ethics! Obviously the heat has got me too. I'm beginning to talk utter nonsense. In a word, my boy, her mother came to the conclusion that he wasn't a match for your Julia the Second. But they couldn't drive her lover out of the girl's head. Even after the attack on Chupryn, after . . . the murder of Madame Irène . . .' (he uttered the name of Madame Irène quietly, colourlessly) 'nothing changed either. It was a sort of subjection, if you know what I mean. A passion which perhaps the crimes and sinister reports surrounding this man merely inflamed still more,' he pondered a few seconds, then: 'So there's no cause for you to be surprised,' he concluded, and having added sugar he sipped his tea, replacing the cup in the saucer: he looked somewhat melancholy but also gratified that he'd said what he had to say.

Grandfather in the armchair seemed to be dozing to the monotonous sound of raindrops outside the window and only the slight trembling of his closed eyelids revealed he wasn't, but was listening, perhaps even attentively, not only to the echoes of the rain drumming in puddles blended with the soporific melody of the trickle of water in the gutters, but also to what Uncle Theodore had been saying. Grandmother's face again took on a troubled expression, characterized by the helpless dissolution which Peter had already noticed about her when she was telling him of Madame Irène's death; he felt sorry for her. He then said something hastily about his other grandmother, the one at K., and the atmosphere seemed to relax a little, and his grandfather was able after a moment to reach for another cigarette without irritation. His grandmother, stirred from her meditations, recalled several incidents of past years, when Julia the Second had led a gang of young scamps and he, Peter, had blindly carried out her wildest notions; they were comical, everyone burst out laughing. For a moment, those other disturbing matters, those questions struggling to be answered, and the trivial unsatisfactory replies ebbed away from Peter and were absorbed by the darkness outside the windows. His uncle interposed something about excursions in the swamp by the mill, yes, Peter remembered them very well; they'd made their way across the marsh by hummocks of turf, it had been down in the valley where the swampy meadows came right up to the forest, though in summer they dried out and there was water only in the gullies and when they crossed fat red leeches had at once clung to their legs (when he thought of them, he felt the sickening pain where they sucked at his flesh); and 'other night wanderings too', he gazed at him significantly and indulgently, so that Peter flushed because he couldn't remember; meanwhile Grandfather contributed a few words about Philip the pony which Peter had drowned in the swamp adjacent to the Motren Forest during one such excursion (I've still got a white twist of its mane from the spring clipping somewhere, he thought—and in fact he recalled how he'd added that clipping to the other treasures kept in his little desk, and he at once remembered those few issues of the *Prehistorical Archaeological Quarterly* containing an exciting article in several instalments on Scythian burials, Karol Plage's book *Brass Coins*, an engraving of a Lithuanian half-kopek piece from Prince Uvarov's collection, also a diverting 'Two Thalers—State Currency of the Duchy of Warsaw,' which in turn brought back his earlier numismatic interests, due in great part to his uncle Theodore, and the description of a steppe burial mound torn out of some book, also a fragment of an old gravestone from a Jewish cemetery which the Germans had certainly destroyed by this time, with an incomprehensible Hebrew inscription cut in blue letters, and there had been other things in that little desk as well, for example an excellent recipe for pistachio ice and photographs of film stars from chocolate box lids, and he'd kept the clipping of Philip's mane in a small box made of Chinese lacquer—he remembered—there he'd put bits of amber and shells found on the seashore, and he also recalled unhappily: I haven't looked into the cupboard yet, I didn't check what's left), and he said to his grandfather: 'But if Julia the Second had arrived in time, she'd have pulled the pony out of the swamp. I remember Nick Fiodorchuk and I couldn't. Yet all we needed to do was to cut some reeds and slip them under its belly. She was the only one to think of that,' and he suddenly asked whether Julia the Second still went on meeting that man. 'Why?' his uncle asked, looking up and betraying his surprise. 'What do you mean "Why"?' he countered. 'Why are you asking questions about this again?' said his uncle, and he in amazement said: 'You were telling me, Uncle, that she fell in love, she thought the world of him, so that's how I took it, but it was all in the past tense, as though . . .' 'Ah yes, of course, so I did. No, my dear boy, I don't know. But you certainly won't be meeting him again, it's all over . . . In any case, she must think of herself, I suppose,' he added, with barely masked embarrassment, and his grandmother called at once: 'Mikolai' to his grandfather, 'Mikolai, you ought to go over to Gleb tomorrow with the boy,' she said, beginning to fuss awkwardly between the little table with the samovar and the little table with the lamp, and his grandfather: 'He can go by himself if he feels like it, don't worry,' then Peter, moving aside his grandmother's hand as she reached for his cup with the intention of pouring him more tea, and looking at his uncle, understood. Yes, at this precise moment, as he was insistently gazing at his uncle, though the latter's face with that somehow helpless and embarrassed expression looked very blurred to him, yet nevertheless he went on gazing, not wanting to lose sight of his face, though already he could hardly see it, seeing at the same time, clearly, that morning scene in his room (Julia the Second sitting heavily in the chair, hands on her slightly parted thighs as if to keep her balance better, and how they'd bulged at the sides, full and womanly), finally he understood what he hadn't been able to understand before, and he exclaimed: 'She's pregnant! By Gavryluk!' still more loudly, visualizing that morning scene far too clearly to have any doubts, although now not only his uncle's face but everything else too looked blurred, and his grandfather: 'I didn't realize you were so involved in these matters, my boy,' said with remote irony, frowning, as if that exclamation of his had been unbearable and over-insistent, and his grandmother: 'Since you know (I don't suppose she told you anything of the sort, but you guessed it, didn't you?) you needn't be particularly surprised to hear that sometimes she wanders in her talk,' and hastily: 'Well now, Mikolai, won't you go with him to Gleb? A little trip would do you good,' and Peter: 'She didn't want it to happen, did she?' already more quietly, stifling that cry within himself, and Uncle Theodore reluctantly: 'Who knows what she wanted? She was away two months, she disappeared and she certainly went to him. You're asking too much of me, Peter,' and his grandmother: 'It's such a sad story, I wish you'd stop it,' and finally his grandfather sententiously: 'Everything in this world is sad, my dears,' and he sighed.

Slowly the drawing-room and the objects in it regained their own colours and ordinary features. On the walls the vertical gold and red stripes undulated, the windows were deep and black. Pink light flowed radiantly from the lamp, smudged a little here and there by the shadow of a moth as it flitted over the window sill and brushed against the beads suspended from the lamp shade as it passed. The tulips in a vase on the marble mantelpiece had opened their white petals to reveal waxen interiors. The mechanism of the clock creaked loudly. Peter awoke as if from sleep; he looked up, glanced at each of the seated people, and it seemed to him they were watching him discreetly. He could still hear his own voice unpleasantly loud in his ears, could still feel the anger which had suddenly boiled up within him a moment ago, but was already aware of the futility of his outburst and only now found the somehow warning thought that he'd never reach those distant parts he'd formerly visited with Julia the Second, he didn't even remember where they were or whether they'd been dreams or reality, well never mind, for they'd gone now, and it was as though they'd never been, and this was the only thought he found in his head, together with something not unlike disgust which penetrated him through and through, so foreign was it to him; this must have been evident, for immediately afterwards he caught the troubled gaze of his uncle seeking his own, and in the tiny points of yellow light in his pupils, he perceived his own face focused: it looked indifferent to him, and then all this passed him by.

A moth, beating against the wall, banged dully on the tapestry, fell to the ground, fluttered a moment, then could no longer be heard. Not until this moment did he realize that the sounds of the downpour outside the window had stopped. Even the metallic drumming in the gutters had gone. Either the rain had stopped or it had changed into a fine, silent drizzle. The cold air was seeping in from outside. A breeze made the reddish-brown curtains swell and brought the scent of laburnums into the drawing-room from out there. Somewhere very far off a dog barked, but the spaniels didn't react.

Even before supper they'd talked about Gleb, but Peter, his pride wounded by Catherine's unexpected departure, didn't take the matter up (no, he didn't regret it, except that he'd promised himself too much from meeting her. A few hours ago he'd have rushed head over heels to Gleb, but when he found out she'd really been at Chupryn yesterday and had left without exchanging a word with him, he felt humiliated. Then, for the entire afternoon he'd tried with varying degrees of success to rid himself of all those intrusive thoughts about her); now, however, he controlled himself and, so as to change the conversation, he took advantage of his grandmother's so earnest encouragement to visit the Woynoviches and asked whether Mrs. Woynovich had been able to resign herself to the loss of her elder son (he called her 'aunt' but privately regarded her as his mother's sister-in-law and as Mrs. Woynovich, and Paul's brother Alexei—because of what had happened between them long ago—as her elder son and nothing more), his grandmother at once reacted sharply, saying that it wasn't so, Alexei was still alive after all, and then: 'If you don't have any particular desire to go to Gleb within the next few days, then you might see Paul on Sunday. He'll be at Mass in Nikorycha. I expect he'll be very pleased indeed,' 'I daresay . . .' he said, but he doubted whether he'd go to Mass, he hardly ever did. And something of anger and loathing must have been wandering in his mind and seized hold of a desire to vex his grandmother somehow, or even to provoke her, but his grandfather meanwhile, evidently sensing his mood, interrupted with a smile: 'Caroline, for goodness' sake! Can you have decided to convert him? Let's let him do as he chooses with his own time,' and then his grandmother mildly and in a tone attesting that her head had been full of far more remote matters said: 'Goodness, Mikolai, I was only thinking of how to make it easier for him to see Paul. He'll bore himself to death here.' 'You keep on treating him as if he were a child . . .' said his grandfather, 'after all, he's nearly grown-up now. If he starts feeling bored he'll find himself suitable things to do, and company too. In any case, please don't force him to go to church,' and he glanced with an amused, somewhat inquisitive expression at Peter, who at one time had been the object of a quiet but insistent conflict in the family with its religious divergences, and he'd changed his views on religion or succumbed to a different species of mysticism according to whose influence he happened to be under at a given time, although they'd been quite mild species of mysticism and not harmful (his grandfather had found them merely entertaining), quickly dislodged, however, by the mysterious notions his uncle implanted in him, but just now he wanted of course to spare him such things.

Catching his grandfather's intention as it passed, Peter reflected that what his grandfather had been thinking about was now long past, so long past, indeed, that it wasn't a threat to anything. Oh, much later, after that first period, he'd lived through similar states of mind, true enough, there had been those various kinds of uneasiness just before his first Communion, evoked within him by Father Ignatius, the instructor at K., with all his strict lessons, his visions of temptation, of impurities, of sin (those two girls he'd watched as they bathed naked in the lake one hot afternoon in the wilderness, who later had lain on the warm grass in the sun, and there had been a glow which ran through him like an electric current, pleasant, mysterious, exciting, delicious, incomprehensible, when he hadn't been able to take his eyes off them, and what he'd done afterwards, yes that was certainly what the instructor had been thinking about), when his sermons evoked images of damnation, in which the abstract tortures of Hell had mingled with specific earthly ones, and he was never quite sure which to fear most, and although in the end he decided it wasn't true and that the Catholicism in which his mother had brought him up was benevolent and quite tolerant (typified essentially by bright colourings, as in the windows of the K. parish church, colours which even the centuries hadn't been able to dull or to veil with a patina, and the plump cupids with wings sprouting from their pink shoulders had wandered prettily in the clouds amidst a crowd of angels dressed in transparent garments blowing their trumpets over the heads of smiling saints, with a Virgin Mary openly and simply feeding her heavenly infant in a pose reminiscent of the worldly women in pictures by Dutch masters—yes, it was benevolent and prepared to tolerate all earthly pleasures, so different from the Orthodox faith which he came into contact with through his father, a gloomy medieval religion, dazzling with tinsel, its abstruse ceremonies essentially unquestioned, which jealously guarded its deeper significance from the eyes of the profane beneath a complex ritual), yet the impression the sermons and lessons of Father Ignatius had made hadn't been without effect on his state of mind at the time, a state of mind in which faith and scepticism struggled for primacy, especially because he was subjected at the same time to a wave of scepticism from reading Renan's *Life of Jesus* stolen one day from his mother's personal library (it caused him a terrible confusion of ideas, it was as though someone had lifted him high into the heavens then brutally thrust him down into the depths of the earth). But with time he became indifferent to such matters, once he began reading *Gargantua* and *Pantagruel,* then *The Death of Ivan Ilyich* and *Anna Karenina,* though he always put the philosophical tales of Voltaire and Diderot ahead of all these (not only because they were Grandfather's favourite writers), for their witty irony corresponded most to the state of mind which the various faiths of the members of the family in their mutual friction had brought about in him as they tried to attract him to their respective sides: a total lack of feeling for that specific kind of spiritual longing with which their churches wanted to calm him. He thought of all this, well perhaps not exactly this way, but more or less, as he caught that gleam of amusement in his grandfather's eyes and guessed he didn't want to let his grandmother try, when Peter refused to accompany her to Mass on Sunday, to concern herself any more closely with his present religious beliefs. At once, however, he understood that both his grandfather and he himself were wrong.

Grandmother sat deep in thought, gazing in the direction of the windows, over which the heavy curtains were billowing in a cooler breeze (it looked as though shadows were going in and out of the circle of light); she was remote not only from the matters which his grandfather feared any mention of, but did not even react to Peter's disappointing refusal, and when she noticed they were silent and that enough time had passed so that she needn't react at all, she said in the same tone as before, although previously that tone hadn't made Peter think, as it attested, that her thoughts were preoccupied by very much more distant matters (only now did the tone of her voice make him wonder, and he felt a recurrence of that uneasiness), that she didn't want him to rely 'on the domestic servants for company', she enumerated each one in turn, pondering, as if she had difficulty in recalling them. When he still said nothing, she added after a moment, in explanation: 'On the domestic servants and on Julia the Second,' and then that which had died out within him, had become a matter of indifference to him, that which had passed him by and which he no longer wanted to have anything to do with, that mysterious something which had emerged from his morning conversation with Julia the Second, and what he'd later learned from them, or rather from what they hadn't told him (well, after all, perhaps they couldn't, but in any case they hadn't), then it all came back to him and he thought: So that's what she was thinking of all the time we were talking about various other things, yet she was thinking of nothing but that, of God, and he felt his throat contract again with horror, for he couldn't correlate those facts: the inquiring look of Julia the Second that morning there in his room, as she studied his face feature by feature, seeking resemblances known only to her, as moreover she herself had carelessly let slip out, and her appearance, in which there had been a sort of (he realized this later) springy, catlike, lurking indifference, and that swelling of her breasts over the bodice, and the coarse curve of her belly, and the splaying of her full thighs, and, in a word, sensuality blended with hauteur (he realized this, too, much later), which had deprived him of all his previous calm and, finally, what he'd learned about Gavryluk and about her, but more especially about Gavryluk; no, he couldn't link these few facts together, nor draw any conclusion from them, it was like deciphering a complicated code to which he hadn't been given a key, and even if he'd succeeded in doing so, he'd have discovered that what he'd deciphered was a narrative written in some foreign language, in fact it was (feeling this all too terribly clearly) purposeless, which only increased his horror which had previously been merely uneasiness or a strange fear, but had now become horror, so much so that it definitely paralysed his mind, and it contracted his throat as he realized that he knew; he asked no more questions, for he'd have betrayed himself by his own weakness, and suddenly still feeling that the thought which had already been vibrating in his head earlier, the vague suspicion which had cast a new light on these facts, on each one individually and on all of them put together (he saw them naked, as if in a brief flash of magnesium), this thought again dominated him and, in an attempt to protect himself against it at any price, he said: 'It's late, I'll go to my room,' and he rose, knocking aside a chair, and when he'd crossed the few yards dividing him from the door, counting his own heavy, stiff steps, without turning his head he added quietly: 'Good night,' and heard the replies: 'Good night,' and at once the door closed behind him of its own accord.

He leaned against the doorpost and gazed into the darkness unable to penetrate it, trembling a little, as if the cold had entered his marrow and was coagulating his blood, and he sighed loudly. Behind him, beyond the drawing-room wall, it was silent. After his exit, apparently no one had taken up the conversation, and it seemed there was still time for him to go back, but no, he couldn't bring himself to. The darkness was simmering with a sort of close, monotonous whisper, and his own uneven, loud breathing mingled with that same whisper. Finally his eyes grew accustomed to the dark, and he discerned the windows. They reflected a distant gleam of the sky that was now clear after the rain, and a creeping vine against the wall outside tapped a damp and mysterious narrative. Crossed by still undried little rivulets, the panes glistened strangely when he looked at them; perhaps stars had appeared in the sky. After a moment a dog's paw scratched at the drawing-room door, there was a sniffing and low whine to be heard in the crack between floorboards and door. When the door opened, his uncle was standing there, he noticed him and, with his face frozen into a motionless smile, without speaking, he came into the room, closed the door behind him quickly, as if he didn't want the others to learn that he, Peter, was still there. He said quietly to Peter: 'Come, I'll go upstairs with you,' took him by the arm and led him in silence through the rooms. Everywhere was deserted. Not until they reached the stairs did Peter catch hold of the banisters, which creaked under his dry hand, and his uncle, as though touched by a premonition, paused: 'Surely you're not going to make a fuss because of this?' he asked dully. 'It was only an unfortunate incident,' and already in his voice he had the limitless sorrow of the facts previously concealed from Peter but of which he had known, the cause and the final consequences, and Peter replied: 'No,' also thinking about them, about those facts which up to quite recently he hadn't been able to interpret but now he could, and his uncle: 'Well, then?' to which he answered: 'Nothing, nothing, Uncle,' and although the chandelier connected to the switch downstairs cast a ray of dull light at their feet, they were standing in darkness from the waist up, and couldn't see each other's faces clearly, so 'I understand it all . . .' said Peter, 'I understand it all, but it's hard for me to accept,' and his uncle: 'All?' and he: 'I've guessed,' he replied, and his uncle: 'All of it?' and he: 'That . . . either Grandfather, or . . . you, Uncle, or . . . my father is . . .' 'Yes, your father,' said his uncle. 'My father, good God . . .' he said, and his uncle: 'Your father is Gavryluk's father, yes,' and he: 'Well, yes, I felt it,' he said briefly and soundlessly.

A draught shut one of the doors down below: it creaked and slammed with a crash against the frame. Demoiselle emerged from the end of a corridor, wearing a long robe that swept the floor, her head wrapped in a compress, carrying an empty glass in a saucer; evidently her head ached, she couldn't sleep and was on her way to the kitchen for tea. She passed soundlessly through the hall like a ghost, without noticing the banging door. Peter wanted to go down and shut it, hesitated, then at once began to go on upstairs. His uncle followed. Now they couldn't see each other's faces at all.

II

NOW THAT HE KNEW HE FELT A STRANGE tranquillity which didn't, perhaps, have much in common with calm.

He didn't sleep for a long time that night, through the wall he could hear his grandfather's steps as he walked in his study from windows to fireplace and back again, regularly, slowly, indifferently—really there was nothing in his step, nothing whatsoever from which anyone might have learned what was happening within him, no feeling—they sounded dull, like the knock of wood on wood, as if they weren't the steps of a flesh-and-blood man at all, and then, when Peter fell asleep, or perhaps it merely seemed to him he fell asleep, for he could still feel the chill of the bedclothes penetrating his skin, although he was feeling overheated, but it was a fever that merely flowed from within, from the depths of his body, for the sheets were chilly and the wind coming through the window was too, and sharp even after the recent rain, as he clearly felt without for a moment losing contact with surrounding reality, so perhaps he didn't fall asleep at all, it only seemed to him he did, in the end though it didn't matter, for his dreams blended with reality and reality with his dreams, without altering the state he was in either for better or for worse, then too he could hear his grandfather's steps behind the wall; to and fro, to and fro, as if he had too much to think about and so couldn't remain in one place, or else he wasn't thinking at all and was going through motions he'd decided upon earlier, at some moment of great tension which he'd long since forgotten, it was one or the other, so Peter judged, and later he heard the house full of those steps, surrounding him on all sides, penetrating into his brain with their wooden thumping, behind other walls and in the corridor and in the old gallery under the floor of his room and even under the windows, actually in the park, all was full of those regular, indifferent, slow steps, and he thought of nothing, at least not consciously, experiencing that very strange tranquillity (stupefaction, perhaps) which certainly derived from the state he was in, it somehow freed him from any necessity of thinking, and next day nothing, absolutely nothing happened, not until noon did his cousin Paul arrive, summoned perhaps by his grandmother; he left his horse in the drive after tying it to a tree, and walked to meet his grandfather who was taking a daily before-lunch constitutional just then around the flower bed by the waterfall, and when he'd greeted him they didn't talk long, so that after a moment Paul reached the stairs where he was standing, leaning against a pillar, he'd been standing there ever since he first heard the galloping of a horse near the driveway and also all the time Paul had been talking to his grandfather, watching them in that powerless stupefaction, knowing in advance that this was exactly how it would be: they'd talk briefly, then Paul would come up to him, shake him by the hand and, in order to appear natural, would ask how he was, and then without waiting for a reply he'd say why didn't they go to the meadow behind the Motren Forest where he had a fine stallion tethered, he'd just broken it in, so he'd show it to him, and this was what happened. Paul said all this more or less as he'd expected he would, with that superficial smile masking entirely different preoccupations, perhaps inward uneasiness or something of the sort, and they stood facing, eyeing each other and inspecting the quantity and quality of the changes which time had brought about in them, and which they could neither evaluate nor enumerate, for they were almost imperceptible, as each had changed in the same way during the years in which they hadn't met, and Peter said nothing, but Paul, startled, asked: 'What's happened?' to which he said: 'Nothing. Nothing that could matter to you,' a statement he'd prepared in advance for this occasion, and then: 'I daresay you'll stay for lunch, we can talk,' in a somehow courtly manner, so that it was almost clumsy, thus giving him in advance the status of guest and himself that of host, and not taking into account at all that idea of his which might have brought them together again, to recall how they'd chased about the district, broken in horses, and been the best of friends, so that Paul must feel hurt; he was gazing at him steadily and already had a question of some sort on his lips, while he himself went on standing there, leaning against the pillar, his back pressed hard against it, stubbornly silent, full of that fever which was disintegrating his body, and it was surely then that he gave himself away, something of the sort must have gleamed in his eyes, he didn't yet know how to control himself, for he'd known about these local matters and about Gavryluk since only the day before, whereas all of them, even Paul, had known about them a long time, perhaps these were quite commonplace facts to them, while he'd learned them only yesterday, and he also knew he would never come to terms with those facts, even if the other had done so and were not simply waiting, appearances might be misleading, of course, but matters had gone too far, and that gleam in his eyes was certainly either rage or hatred because Paul had betrayed him; for, if they'd ever been two of the best and most loyal friends, and were to become so again, friends through life and death, then they ought to tell one another everything without holding back, but Paul hadn't told him anything, and although he soon realized he couldn't, after all they hadn't met for three long years, yet that gleam which he felt in his eyes he couldn't extinguish at once, only later he succeeded in doing so, with a certain amount of effort, of course, and in order to erase the disagreeable impression, he said in a tone that held many implications and was understandable to Paul: 'We'll talk after lunch. We'll talk about everything,' he added once again, hastily, but they didn't talk either after lunch or later, as they were sitting in his uncle's room and were entertaining him with some trivial conversation, avoiding each other's gaze, and only on parting, in the drive at dusk as a stableboy brought the horse around, and feeling that this was the last moment, they looked one another in the eye and then Paul said significantly: 'You can always count on me, you know,' to which he, Peter, replied with gloomy understanding: 'I see,' responding to that strong pressure of the hand, and then that night again he didn't fall asleep for a long time, he could hear his grandfather's regular footsteps through the wall as he paced to and fro in his study, steps that had an empty soundless noise, in which he guessed there was nothing and which meant nothing, they couldn't mean anything except that he was suffering from insomnia, for otherwise he wouldn't have waited so long, he wouldn't torture him and would have talked to him frankly today at least, even if he hadn't been able to yesterday, but no, he hadn't spoken and it seemed to him he hadn't the slightest intention of doing so, but when he finally fell asleep the steps continued to resound in the vaulting of his skull, as if someone were tapping wood on wood without a moment of respite, and he finally understood what it might signify, or at least he supposed he was beginning to understand, this was more or less the meaning of the thought: that his grandfather didn't in the least regard him as a partner equal in all things, for he certainly thought he wasn't yet sufficiently mature, and then he also understood the origin of that startling tranquillity which he'd experienced immediately after finding out who Gavryluk was, a strange tranquillity bordering on helplessness, though he at once suspected it of having little to do with tranquillity, and that it was only the appearance of tranquillity, and now he guessed it originated from the same premonition his grandfather had had, a premonition deeply hidden hitherto in his unconscious perhaps, yet existing there, and only now revealed to him.

He suspected that he felt himself already a man, although he hadn't yet matured to the point of being able to face those cruel facts, of bringing himself to make one unequivocal decision and confirming his maturity by some decisive act, to undertake that test which would prove he could represent the Cherestvienskis in cutting the bonds in which cruel circumstances had entangled them, and now it wasn't either tranquillity or calmness, if these words meant one and the same thing in the end, but a deeply felt helplessness, since it wasn't so much that he couldn't say how he ought to behave as that—vaguely feeling what sort of attitude he ought to adopt and what to do—he knew he wouldn't be able to steel himself to it soon, not because of his youth and inexperience but because once he'd made up his mind, his courage would instantly fail to tackle the sombre flow of acts which would irresistibly propel him towards new facts, taking on who knows what disguises and he realized too that no one expected him to make these decisions or perform these acts, at most they were afraid that he might commit some folly in his youthful rage, or perhaps break down psychologically upon learning things they hadn't in the least prepared him for, and he noticed he was being watched with a fear impregnated with concern, the fear he'd already seen in his grandmother's eye on that first day, when he'd started asking what was happening here, and later, when she tried to persuade his grandfather to take him to Gleb, in the hope that by letting him meet Paul and Catherine they'd provide him with some normal social pastimes which might detach him from the confusion of the war, and by doing so give him one more tranquil, delightful summer at least, and then he'd seen that concerned fear in the eyes of his grandfather and his uncle Theodore when he refused to take part in the latter's imaginary archaeological excursion just as he'd refused his grandfather's invitation to go shooting quail; and he also realized that even Paul didn't expect this of him (the taking of decisions and performing of acts), Paul who for the last three years—while he himself had prolonged his childhood under the close and tender care of his mother at K., protected carefully from anything that might by a sudden shock have made a man of him, and which after all was the lot of almost every fifteen or sixteen-year-old boy in this region, forced to take part in the cruel struggle which had become this country's fate—Paul already was this man, he'd preceded him, Peter, by precisely these three years, he'd grown up, even though in September 1939 he'd been still a boy like himself, but he hadn't been kept in cotton wool for those three years, hadn't basked as he had in a greenhouse or under his mother's protective wings, shielded from everything which constituted the daily bread of adults, but he'd come in contact day after day with what was happening here, with the murders, arson, rapes and he'd perhaps stained his own hands with blood; he realized that even Paul, his best and truest friend, wasn't expecting any decisions from him, or actions, but that he feared for him, rather, as they all did, lest he commit some folly which he'd have to regret later, and he wanted to shield him from this whatever it was that might be awaiting him if he made a decision, and that Paul even wanted to prolong for him that childishness or boyhood which he himself had prematurely lost, with this difference, however, that Paul certainly had a premonition that he wouldn't be able to shield him, nor would any of the family, for he would make this decision sooner or later, and indeed he'd have to, since he belonged to these people and had their blood in his veins, hence no doubt those words of his: 'You can count on me,' as he offered him help or at least sympathy in that which perhaps ought to be done though he, Peter, didn't yet know what it was, and had merely a vague inkling of it.

Between Friday and Saturday, Nicholas, the son of Fiodorchuk, came back from Krzysztopol. He'd spent the week with the local lawyer, a friend of Peter's grandfather, seeing to some of Grandfather's business in the German office for harvest consignments, and when he got back they didn't meet, as Peter had expected earlier, to greet one another and enjoy their former friendship, but he remained in the background all the next day until the evening, that evening between Saturday and Sunday. That evening—after a long talk with his uncle and a somewhat shorter one with his grandfather, although not much emerged from either the first or the second—Peter himself went to Nick, filled, as a result of both conversations, with an indignation that was natural in the situation he'd involuntarily become mixed up in, although perhaps the truth was that he hadn't matured to it yet, and just then, late that evening, sitting in Nicholas's dark room in the attic of the north wing, in that room with its beams and gable from which a window overlooked the overgrown ruins of the orangery; behind the fire-place was Nick's father's room, from which no sounds came, perhaps old Fiodorchuk hadn't finished his daily chores yet and was in no hurry to get back to his room, besides he never hurried anywhere since his wife's death, happy to sit about downstairs so as to be near Grandfather; Nick and Peter were sitting quite close to one another, they could see the outlines of their bodies in the darkness illuminated only by a pale ray from the new moon rising beyond the park, which cut the room in half and separated them, but it hadn't been there when Peter came in, or more precisely ran in, of course he ran in, he'd run up the stairs three at a time and he ran along the corridor to the Fiodorchuks' quarters, and ran into Nicholas's room without knocking, and it might even be said that he forced his way in uninvited, although he was perhaps expected, and this emerged from Nick's first words when he exclaimed: 'Nick, I have to talk to you,' and Nick had replied: 'I was thinking the same thing,' calmly, and had told him to sit down, and he did, still out of breath, suppressing with an effort the indignation caused by those two conversations and already feeling from the tone of Nick's reply that he had been wrong in assuming that their friendship hadn't outlasted the years of his absence; just as he sat down, thinking: What a good thing it's dark in here, and Nick hasn't lit the lamp, it's better we shouldn't see one another, although he didn't understand why he was reluctant to see his friend's face and eyes, but he was, that was certain. In this darkness they exchanged their first words and there was no need to break the ice, and when a moonbeam fell between them they already felt as if the three years hadn't existed, but they were still unable to see much, only the outlines of their bodies, or to be exact it was Peter himself who didn't see much, except that Nick was sitting on an old carved chest used in his room as a wardrobe, a little to the side, one hand on his knee, the other behind his head which he'd leaned against the wall, gazing perhaps at the ceiling, talking fast but at the same time calmly, at most with some emphasis now and then, but really as though he were telling him of long outdated matters which, judging from the tone in which he was speaking, were at least outdated as far as he was concerned, and he certainly wanted Peter to consider them as such too, and without pausing—as if he didn't want them ever to have to revert to them—he told him and went on telling him for the rest of the evening how things had been between Julia the Second and Gavryluk, what he himself had seen and what she'd confided in him, and how he himself hadn't seen much and she too had confided little in him; he told him what he'd guessed and how he pictured the affair, in rough outline of course, and precisely at this moment, though it was already quite late in the evening, Catherine arrived for the second time that day; first of all he heard the horse-drawn carriage coming along the drive from the gate, and he leaped to the window but saw only the black ruins of the orangery, overgrown with weeds, for the drive on this side was hidden by the trees, but then he heard her voice in the porch as she said something to Fiodorchuk, who'd hurried out to help her down, but he, Peter, after his conversation with Nick, and after what Nick had told him, didn't feel up to facing her right away, for he guessed as soon as Nick had started talking that it hadn't been a question of Julia the Second when Gavryluk had attacked the manor, or of Madame Irène either, but that it was she who was to have been his victim, and only by some miracle had she escaped what wasn't difficult to guess, despite Nick's moderation, but he'd found out enough to have a definite opinion of the entire matter, precisely at that moment, despite the lateness of the evening, as they were sitting close to one another in Nick's dark room, divided by the pale ray of the moonlight which barely enabled them to make out the blurred outlines of their own bodies (throughout that long Saturday, until evening, it had been evident that Nick was keeping in the background, and even, as Peter had started to think, avoiding him deliberately as if he'd learned something of what had happened here), well and in the end nothing of the sort had happened, for if everything he, Peter, had imagined were jettisoned, then, from the point of view of the others, the matters he'd stumbled on hadn't much significance, then certainly nothing particular had happened, and life in this house could go on as before; or Nick sensed what was happening in Peter, and didn't wish to intrude into matters that didn't concern him; so that for the first moment Peter didn't quite know what to make of Nick's behaviour, after three years he'd stopped realizing where the lines dividing his own people from others ran, and in the end—this thought was so intolerable to him—he'd asked his uncle (they were sitting by the stream on dry rocks, and watching Demoiselle Spang patiently fishing nearby, frozen in an expectant gesture, as if made of stone), but his uncle had treated his question lightly, and this gave him much food for thought, and in the end he understood he'd made a mistake in suspecting Nick Fiodorchuk, for Nick had remained loyal to him as before, and could be trusted. Had it not been for this conviction, they wouldn't have met that evening in his room, he wouldn't have listened to Nick's tale, and perhaps that wild notion of settling the Gavryluk affair in his own way wouldn't have come to him on Monday, an idea which he and Nick didn't manage to carry out, but which caused a difference of opinion with his cousin Paul, although perhaps it wasn't that insane idea at all, but Catherine who was the cause of their squabble: later he judged that both were, for when he tried to recall what it was all about, that idea, he couldn't, and his memory brought up only what had happened between himself and Catherine, which didn't have much to do with Gavryluk, and still less with Paul.

Even at that time, however, during that Saturday, Peter only wanted additional information. So he and his uncle were sitting on the dry rocks heated by the sun on the bank of a stream that flowed along the bottom of a greyish-white craggy ravine outside the park, not far from Demoiselle Spang motionless over her fishing line, but far enough away for the conversation and their shadows on the water not to scare her fish; from noon on, just after Peter had got out of going with his grandfather to shoot quail after lunch, and he'd gone to look for his uncle, who was in this very spot with Demoiselle, busy with talk, perhaps concerning Peter, for they awkwardly fell silent on catching sight of him coming down the slope and he caught the conspiratorial glances they exchanged. 'Good afternoon, Miss Spang,' he then said to Demoiselle, 'I'm glad your persistent migraine has gone,' for he hadn't seen her at meals for two days, and then, 'Excuse me, but I have to ask my uncle something,' turning directly to him at once, 'Uncle, did Nicholas and Gavryluk . . .?' but his uncle, as if he had no intention of letting him speak: 'Fräulein Spang would also like to ask you something, Peter,' he interrupted in a tone which normally, had it not been for his indignation and excitement, would have prevented him from asking questions and would have warned him his uncle too (like his grandfather) couldn't treat him like an adult yet; but not at this moment, when he was as it were blind and deaf, and he knew he must find out absolutely everything. At this moment he didn't even hear, didn't want to, forgetting the presence of Demoiselle at once, as soon as he'd told her he was glad her migraine had gone, displacing her from this spot by the stream out of sight, eliminating her, and perhaps she grasped as soon as he began speaking that this partial change had already occurred in him and it was better not to oppose it (in any case she certainly understood this a good deal sooner than his uncle or indeed than anyone else, she'd had a premonition that moment at the railway station when they'd walked past the men marked with the Stars of David that she was taking him not to a place where he might be able to preserve his boyhood, where indeed he might not be able to save anything at all, and was only waiting for that change finally to take place), so after collecting her line and little bucket for fish she moved a few dozen paces away without demur, to facilitate this conversation in which his uncle was a reluctant informant and he, Peter, seized upon details of minor significance, since it seemed to him from the start that all he needed in order to penetrate the whole matter were facts, while his uncle was stubbornly giving him to understand that there were few facts and that they were of still less significance; in a physical sense, after all, no one had done Gavryluk any injustice, though they might have seemed to, judging by his rage (Gavryluk's, of course), but on the contrary they'd done all they could to help him become a worth-while person, and the causes of what he'd done and was still doing had to be sought elsewhere, no doubt in his illegitimacy complex as his uncle defined it, breaking the ice with some difficulty to speak of things which hadn't been mentioned aloud here before, and he, Peter, still unable to grasp all the black magic of blood ties, of complexes, of being alien or belonging which his uncle mistily revealed to him by implications, he only wanted facts, so as to produce for himself an opinion regarding the events which also concerned him, since he was the brother of that man; it was as though part of the other's guilt overflowed on to him, degrading him, but his uncle said: 'Well, and what of it? It's nothing at all. You've invented some romantic little incident for yourself and want to be the leading protagonist in it. Certainly it's not at all bad, but you'd better concern yourself with something else. It really is no concern of yours. Besides, my dear boy, he's no longer any threat to us. That attack on Chupryn succeeded only because of our excessive self-confidence and carelessness. Now he's no threat to us at all, never fear,' as much as to say that all Peter was concerned with was whether something threatened them or not, with no more than a sort of bored but inexhaustible patience, for later on he didn't want to admit that Peter was a man, and certainly thought that since he'd explained what needed explaining, and had assured him he was safe, it was high time for Peter to stop thinking about Gavryluk. No, he really didn't take into account the humiliation that had suddenly come upon him, he now felt it as on the night when he'd found out, except that the humiliation was multiplied by two nights of insomnia, indecision, tension, uncertainty and exhaustion, and shock and stupefaction and (he admitted to himself) fear as well. This was why he tried another approach. It wasn't premeditated, but rather a sort of reflex action in which, however, was rooted the knowledge that by upsetting his uncle's equilibrium he'd start him talking differently, and he exclaimed in a hostile voice: 'How could he do it?' 'Who?' said his uncle, to which he replied: 'My father,' although even a moment earlier it hadn't entered his head to condemn his father, those were long-past incidents and sufficiently vague to be immune from condemnation, he'd learned that he had a brother, and that this brother was wreaking bloody havoc in the district, humiliating him by his very existence and his behaviour, and that alone was important, but instead he exclaimed: 'My father. How could he have done it? How could he have got so stupidly involved as to have a bastard by some country girl or other, and let someone like this grow up? Couldn't he have done something about it before? Couldn't he have wiped the bastard out like a louse, so as to prevent these crimes?' 'What do you mean?' his uncle said. 'I don't understand you at all,' Peter said in his excitement and with hostility. 'I can see you don't,' said his uncle without losing any of his imperturbability and still patient, so Peter once more: 'How could he have done it? Forget himself to such an extent! So many misfortunes from his one act of stupidity,' but his uncle: 'Everything has to be paid for, my boy. And this is how an act of stupidity, as you call it, or forgetfulness perhaps, is paid for. Better not try to condemn your father, however, as you don't know what you yourself may do at some time in the future. I'd only say that you're asking too much if you expect logic and honesty from us. Logic and honesty aren't features of adult behaviour. Of children's, maybe. Some time in the future you'll begin to behave in contradiction to common sense, you'll find yourself yielding to all sorts of impulses, many of your acts will be conditioned by some reflex or other and by nothing else, and more than one of them will come into conflict with worn-out views of morality. But, my God, here we are talking about morality, and Fräulein Spang has already managed to catch almost a whole bucket of fish. What was it you wanted to ask me about, really? I've forgotten.' 'Is there a link between Nicholas and Gavryluk?' Peter recalled the first question he'd come here to ask. 'I don't understand,' his uncle replied. 'Are they perhaps in league with one another? Does Nick belong to his gang?' he defined his suspicion more precisely, seeing a frown of surprise in his uncle's face. 'For goodness' sake! What put that into your head?' his uncle laughed, and this in a way somewhat relaxed the tense atmosphere which had been created by their conversation. Peter sighed: for once, at least, he hadn't been disappointed, but the pressure which was mounting up in him from hour to hour hadn't abated; he felt he wouldn't learn much more from his uncle, besides, he himself wasn't at all clear what he was concerned about; he rose as if about to leave, then sat down again. Only now did he notice that Demoiselle, as if she'd overheard them mention her a moment ago, had turned towards them to tip up the bucket well filled with fish and show them: he shook his head to express his amazement, and they went on sitting there in silence looking at the water as it flowed past their feet.

The wall of dense, old trees interwoven behind them on the summit of the cliff broke the wind which must have been blowing somewhere high up, for the few solitary clouds passed by quickly, and it was breathless, silent in the depths of the ravine, the silver trickling of the streams of water in channels between the stones sounded like a sleepy murmuring, and although the muffled chatter of starlings could be heard up above now and then, as they devoured the cherries that grew along the edge of the park or flew with a timorous flutter from tree to tree as if someone unseen had startled them, yet silence prevailed. Peter asked no more about his friend, but later, when they reverted to the person of Gavryluk (not that he wanted to, he was suddenly reconciled to the fact that his uncle wouldn't tell him any more, answering merely the question 'How?' but not the question 'What?' and that perhaps they no longer understood one another, or he, Peter, couldn't ask or didn't yet clearly know what it was he was concerned with), his uncle said of his own accord: 'It was Nicholas who brought the girl back from Krzysztopol to Chupryn,' and Peter: 'Julia the Second? So she wanted to come back?' and his uncle: 'I don't exactly know how it was, or whether she wanted to. Probably she did. Gavryluk must have debauched her. To him she was only another object on which he would wreak his hatred. So perhaps Nick didn't have to bring her by force. In any case, that would hardly have been possible.' 'But how is it that Gavryluk gets away with everything unpunished?' asked Peter, and his uncle Theodore: 'All his strength and his men are of course in his association with the Germans. For although they're an ordinary gang who murder Poles who favour Poles, attack Polish villages and the less protected manors, they have contacts with the SS-Galicia and Nachtigal's units. The Germans turn a blind eye to their attacks on our people (and perhaps quietly encourage them, who knows?), for they help them wipe out Jews in the country towns, trap partisans, and generally assist in the battles between Ukrainians and Poles; you see, all this confusion is very much to their advantage.' 'I see,' said Peter, and his uncle continued: 'Officially, the Germans don't touch the local manors, but it's no concern of theirs when Gavryluk (or some other gang, there are more than one, after all) burns down one or other of them.' 'But why don't you all defend yourselves? Why not create your own units?' asked Peter bitterly, for the inactivity of the Polish side in this battle for life and death seemed absurd to him, but his uncle went on: 'It's clear from what you say that you still don't know much about the war and the occupation, although three years have passed already,' rather ironically, and even with some contempt, and Peter was about to reply, risking sharp words, when suddenly Demoiselle waved her fishing rod and called in their direction: 'What time are they coming from Gleb? I've forgotten,' and it was this which suddenly drew him back in time.

For a fraction of a second he glimpsed a woman's figure in the dark doorway of the drawing-room, faintly outlined by a shaft of light, he saw this shape in something airy and gleaming which she was holding up instinctively, though with a gesture that looked like embarrassment, around her shoulders, and he saw her glance in his direction as, tired from his journey, he dozed on the sofa, slowly losing the awareness of whether he was really seeing her, and then at once it drew him still further back in time, to that terrible day years ago when cousin Alexei had come for her, and when her waxen face had been sketched like a cameo against the background of the closed door to the veranda, and he, Peter, had stood behind that door helplessly, while they sat inside, facing one another, their knees almost touching, and they had been like this for a very long time already, and the way she was concentrating her entire attention on a little book of poetry from which she was reading verses to Alexei had been so unnatural that she almost deceptively reminded him of those figures in a theatre only pretending to read as they hold the book upside down, asking questions but thinking of something else. The memory was sharp, importunate, it scalded him somewhere in the throat with something salty; unable to get a word out, he waited for his uncle to speak and explain something, but his uncle was in no hurry to speak, and in the entire valley of the stream only monotonous echoes were heard, which were the stifled sighs of stones, gravel, and water; they surged silver in the air, ringing like swarms of insects, and stopped on the very edge of silence, but in the end he managed to ask a question, feeling that when he voiced it his heart would stop. But this was only for a moment.

His uncle waited until Demoiselle had pulled in her line, then replied that there had been a telephone call from the Woynovich aunt at Gleb, and they were coming to supper. Peter at once awoke: 'A telephone call? The day before yesterday Paul . . .' 'What about Paul?' 'He didn't mention any visit,' and he felt on his face and brow a hot brushing sensation, as if the wind had caught him, at once thinking that since his uncle had used the plural, perhaps Catherine was coming too, and this must have been outwardly apparent, for his uncle looked more attentively at him, then turned away his head as if he wanted to give him time to control himself and for the traces of a flush to disappear before Demoiselle came up, if, of course, these weren't merely suppositions of Peter, who had felt himself a moment before like someone caught in the act, since perhaps his uncle hadn't noticed, or didn't want to notice, immersed once again in that characteristic tranquillity and brooding of his, until he suddenly said in a low voice: 'As long as you aren't bitterly disappointed, my boy,' somewhere out of the depths of his brooding, as though speaking to himself and no longer remembering him, then Demoiselle joined them, his uncle awoke and got up from the rock on which he'd been sitting (but he didn't rouse himself in order to explain more precisely what he'd just said and which Peter couldn't associate with anything, neither with their previous conversation about Gavryluk, nor with his own thoughts and embarrassment, but in order to carry on the conversation with Demoiselle, or rather walking by her side merely to complement the conversation which she tried to carry on with him, Peter, bringing up with a dubious brilliance the charm of their recent calm life at K., until it seemed to Peter not only dubious, for it wasn't true, but positively ludicrous, with a brilliance too shallow and artificial for her to be able to say what she was really thinking and what she really wanted to say—so that walking and talking by her side his uncle was somehow replacing the silent Peter, though with indecision and embarrassment, or rather insecurity, as if the mere fact of his having been here in this unquiet land during the last few years had become second nature to him; he'd changed, his uncle, from a dreamer and fantasist who all the same hadn't lost his self-assurance, and become someone who gave the impression he'd lost his way in life and was no longer able to find it), and his eyes had the same expression which had struck Peter a couple of days earlier, when they'd been sitting in the study together and his uncle had tried to interest him in the Cilician buildings in Ayash, an expression of sorrow and guilt which was incomprehensible to him both then and now that he'd resented so outspokenly the tone in which his uncle had carried on their conversation, for it had implied a premonition or prophecy of defeat, and when Peter finally made an effort and managed to ask: 'Will Catherine be coming with them too?' he didn't hear him at all, no, he was certain that he didn't, it was as though he were too far off.

He parted from his uncle and Demoiselle in front of the house and turned into the northern less frequented part of the park, passing the ruins of the orangery overgrown with vegetation where a pond was concealed behind a hedge of cornel, mulberries, and hawthorn, in the English garden—suddenly he wanted to be alone. Pushing aside the branches, he penetrated through a hedge of shrubs and came to a pathway; he thought it would be overgrown, but no, it wasn't, obviously someone visited this retreat quite often. Last year's yellowed reeds, mingled with this year's, screened the view of a tumble-down dam, while closer to him, at the very edge of the water, was a stone bench, moss-grown, placed alongside the path, and over it grew a weeping willow, a mass of drooping branches through which, as Peter sat down on the bench, the blue sky shone here and there, butterflies flew in and out soundlessly, and the misty white heat of the sun seeped in; he wanted to be alone so much that he'd have almost burst into tears if anyone had come. He couldn't understand what was happening to him; somewhere within him everything ached. No one came, it was quiet, and that was good. A kingfisher broke away from over the dam, began circling the water, and its shadow inscribed slow, involved arches on it, everything was completely quiet and deserted, and it was really very good that it was so. The water, not deep perhaps, but darker than in the stream, no doubt on account of its muddy bottom, was of an opaque olive-green colour, its edge filled with the mouldering remains of foliage, towards the centre ripples gleamed as if gently blown upon, the water stood around moisture-eroded posts supporting the tumble-down dam overgrown with rotten reddish cakes of wood fungus. Brown water beetles skimmed nimbly over the pond's surface, a fraction of an inch above it, emitting sparkling reflections, a solitary carp swam about, forgotten by mankind and so spared, while spiders lurked in transparent webs suspended among the stalks of the reeds.

He recollected a sad tale he'd heard in his childhood from his nurse Julia about a beautiful blind girl abandoned by her lover, who'd been pulled out of the water near the dam. The tale was far-off, almost obliterated, but now it returned to him clearly, as if he'd just heard it. He sighed, and his sighing sounded hollow in the cellar-like shade of the willow's arch; it can't have been true, he thought, such tales go around every manor house, and nurses and maids are always pleased to tell them to the children. Nothing disturbed the silence. It occurred to him that he'd stayed here in the gloom and solitude for some time. They were soon to come to Chupryn for the whole afternoon, to sit down to lunch as they always did on such occasions on the terrace under the striped red and white awning, and spend all that hot, stuffy Saturday afternoon there (three days already without a drop of rain, barely a cloud, how long could it last, and what would it lead to?) and perhaps the evening too, recalling—while he, Peter, preoccupied with his torments regarding Gavryluk, forgot, or almost forgot, why he'd come here, what that very powerful, mysterious magnet was which had drawn him back again to the home of his grandparents—most probably recalling his arrival, and perhaps not only recalling it but even believing that their presence would be a comfort to him in the state of mind he was suddenly in. But no, nothing would help him, nothing. He'd remain here forever with the humiliation which had so unexpectedly attached itself to him in this obscurity and solitude that was pulsating with terror.

He felt an ebbing away of sensation throughout his body, and for a moment it seemed to him that the turf his feet were on was shallow, shifting sand, and that he would sink into it along with the bench. So this is how it was: he'd come to Chupryn, yes, to Chupryn, to the house he loved most of all the houses he'd ever lived in, yes, where the various dark paths of the past and present inhabitants of the house came together and mingled, while a man with a black tuft of hair on his shaven skull like a Cossack prowled about the vicinity, a man of the same blood as himself, although not in the least like him, but who, in the end, would find that out for sure, yes, and he was watching him with an envious look that gleamed like the gaze of a serpent, and his eyes were fixed upon Peter from his hiding place, they drove into his chest, yes, and there was his uncle Theodore crazily and insistently turning over dusty old books, papers, reports, looking for notes about hidden treasures which would enable him to buy back the family estate lost in the Revolution, but he'd already lost hope of ever finding them, and besides, what was the use? He'd already lost everything else, yes, and poor, pretty Julia the Second was no longer a sweet little girl but was bearing a hideous fœtus which would at some time be his nephew or niece and the condemned, illegitimate tribe would increase, yes, and Madame Irène had been put to death by his brother (no, not put to death, but tortured to death, they do it to a woman so that afterwards she has to die) instead of marrying his uncle so that the latter wouldn't have been a man who seemed to have outlived his life and would not find oblivion anywhere or ever. And would he, Peter, ever go on a bright

St. John's Eve in August to look for the magic flower of the fern which brings happiness? Who'd want to go with him? No one. Besides, he'd long since stopped believing in it. So why had he come here, was it to learn the torment of knowing that which hitherto had been veiled from him by silence? No, somehow he'd have to concentrate, gain strength once more, think up something, begin doing something, and perhaps in the end this pain would pass him by. But does Gavryluk have to keep pursuing me like this from his hiding place with that envious, sneering look of his? Oh God, if only something would happen!

Somewhere on the far side of the lake a sharp whistle resounded, ducks rose up with a heavy flapping of wings from the bulrushes, and a shot went off. After a while old Cherkvas emerged from the reeds in a small, flat barge, and retrieved a bird that was floating on the water, like an uprooted waterlily turned upside down. The old man examined the bird, tossed it into the bottom of the boat, yawned, got out his tobacco pouch, and began filling his pipe. He sat motionless with his face towards the sun, basking, and Peter felt that if the old man were to notice him, he'd certainly row across and talk: he was talkative, cheerful, and it was he who once had taught him to shoot, how to get in close to animals, and many other useful things, but at this moment Peter was thinking exclusively of Gavryluk's black stare, while grey-haired Cherkvas smoked his pipe peacefully in meditative solitude as motionless in the barge as though he were a block of wood dried up in the heat, and Peter had the impression that his stillness had brought time to a stop altogether. So nothing was going to happen, my God! But then, when he realized they might begin to comment at the house on his long absence, especially now that the expected guests from

Gleb had surely arrived, he rose and set off with a strange uncertainty mingled with uneasiness.

Yes, they'd arrived. Greetings, many unnecessary questions from Mrs. Woynovich about his mother, which embarrassed him (he never could reconcile himself to answering questions of this sort, his mother's life was for him a sphere too delicate and painful to be touched even in thought, and although his father's image had already undergone many transformations, if only during these past few days, he was still on his father's side), questions that barely reached him, which was a good thing, for otherwise they'd have upset him needlessly, like all his aunt's cordialities, he was unprepared for them; then all the formalities at table; and Paul, saying little, troubled by something, nervously gnawing a small triangular moustache which didn't suit his face at all; a commonplace, brief pressure of the hand from Catherine; he didn't meet her gaze and later, when she withdrew her hand, he encountered a cool persistent questioning, and at once felt it penetrate every pore of his skin and confuse his thoughts, for could it possibly be mere chance, or was it encouragement? Or had it, perhaps, some other meaning? And once again uneasiness welled up in his heart that had been lulled to sleep by the moment of greeting. Later everything was as it should be, as he'd certainly supposed it would be; the sun in Catherine's hair, glancing and gleaming, unable to settle, while the rest of her was submerged in shadow, so that to begin with he perceived only that gleaming head (when she smiled, an oval dimple appeared on her cheek giving her face sharpness); and that intimacy with which she said something to his uncle and listened attentively to what he was saying to her, with him, Peter, sitting only an arm's length from them, quite naturally keeping him outside the circle, that was an intimacy for which he'd gladly have been grey-haired, old, and eccentric like his uncle, if only such a similarity would have entitled him to it; their intimacy reminded him bitterly of his own youthfulness once again.

Wine was served and the conversation became easier and more general; gossip about neighbours, about someone's marriage two months delayed, how pretty Maryna Z. had lately been seeing too much of Comrade Bieloserstov, the handsome general of the ROA unit stationed in Kamieriec Podolski, and what little tricks certain people were up to in order to smuggle the pathetic remains of their fortune to Switzerland, and how Vasily d'Anjou had now settled in Sicily, and not knowing what to do with himself, had taken to classifying heraldry, and his uncle talked about the Near East and travelling, while Paul spoke of farming troubles and the harvest, and among the names they scattered in the conversation, Peter heard many which meant nothing to him, he'd forgotten them, and it seemed to him that only with difficulty did anything interesting emerge from beneath the torrent of unimportant or commonplace trivialities, and there wasn't a word about the war. But in the end Peter was glad that all this small talk was going on as it were outside of him, so he didn't have to take any active part in it, and could gaze thoughtfully at the ray of sunlight glancing off Catherine's hair, watching it fade away on the bare nape of her neck, pondering and as though entirely benumbed, becoming nothing but a look plunged into the gold of that sunburned feminine body, not daring to look her in the face, but then this torpor slowly diminished from within, he gained control of himself and even managed to join in the conversation, though without much enthusiasm, because apart from the words he spoke he felt somehow as if there were others he hadn't uttered: spare me your unimportant reality, which you're all trying to crowd into so as to forget other things. What does that reality consist of? It's a pack of superficial clichés and nonsense. Some see it in Maryna Z.'s languid glances and poses, others in the price of wheat. But the true reality is here facing us, more and more dark and threatening. Don't you know how to look it in the face? There's still time, you can still defend yourselves. His heart bled for them.

That morning he had watched the sunrise as it sprinkled the rustling vine outside his window with trembling pink drops, still unable to extricate himself from a warm cocoon of sleep, not even wanting to, as he lay half asleep in that naked pinkness of light; he thought: All will be well, life will somehow settle down, will round off the edges, smooth down the angles; this was the way the sky split asunder by the early sun had acted upon him, had aroused vague hopes, yet later on each step had again brought him closer to the abyss, so that now it seemed to him very unlikely that the hopes born that morning would ever come to pass. The world is terrible, unstable, everything is breaking up, rotting, perishing. As long as he lived, instead of living in harmony, he'd limp and bleed. Hearts would grow dry, words prick painfully, love soon shrivel away, wither, deeds are treacherous and hard, falsehood shuts the door on truth, the gabbling of circus parrots is more honest than the outpourings of people. Would what he'd cherished within himself for years ever come to bloom on the slimy bottom of this dying world? Would that flower ever find its name? It had often changed shape, first it had been the Snow Queen, Alice, Little Red Riding Hood, the Little Match Girl, then the slave girl from the Arabian Nights, still later Iseult and Anna Karenina, but always, no matter what embodiment it took, it had personified that same face, and now, looking at that face across the table, Peter had the impression that it had torn itself from that vision of his which had seemed immutable, and now belonged to a world that was hostile to him, which he still couldn't understand, and which reminded him of a witches' sabbath at the bottom of some volcanic crater that was about to emit fiery lava at any moment. Why didn't they want to see that the ground was falling away beneath their feet? But Catherine's smile suddenly disturbed his momentary reflection, he drew it from her, for she said: 'How funny you are, Peter, you've grown so terribly serious that I'm almost afraid to speak to you. What are you thinking about?' and he'd already come back from those distant regions, was once again among them, in the circle of their mood, of their trivial little ludicrous unimportant matters, for this was what she wanted, and in the end what was his frustration, his sorrow and abstraction, all his fear, in the face of her command? So he yielded without more ado. She was speaking to his uncle, although now she was also looking at him (with some curiosity, even, as if she really wanted to know his thoughts), about some clay pot he'd unearthed in a burial mound near Gleb, probably hundreds of years old—as she said—brought here by merchants from distant Asia, for which she found symbolic associations with conquerors, reminiscent of the monsters of gnostics; a tadpole emerging from river mud and changing into a frog; this seemed to her the image of the human soul unchanged by the mutations of fate which the body goes through from life to death (could it be that she wanted to counter his thoughts with these remarks, no, she couldn't know them), and Peter gazed at her peach-textured face, dry despite the heat, this face out of his own old boyhood dreams and visions—mirroring as long ago all her inner mutability, that life which was going on somewhere within her and to which she was attentively listening, as if the breath of life which fills normal mortals to the brim could illuminate her only with colour, with patches of light and shade, with nothing more, unable to find entry through her skin, never penetrating to the depths of her body—he felt the humiliating impression that he was repeating his thoughts about her of a few years ago, of those terrible days when he'd watched her weaken and lean on the arm of Alexei, when her face and eyes had that same expression as today—strangely turning in upon herself; only he didn't know now whether she was always like this, or was it only in some particular moments of her life? Who was it her feelings lived by, to which she was now listening? Paul approached, stopped behind her as if he wanted to say something but dared not interrupt; she noticed him, but pursued her animated conversation with his uncle. So Peter thought: Who has taken Alexei's place? I should be warned by these experiences, I should not yield to their returning wave, don't let them envelop me in their feverish tide, that's death, don't you remember? The wave then had been the cruel events of late August and September 1939, they'd taken Catherine away, although maybe she'd been happy (if she had matured to awareness of this feeling at that time), but they'd also taken away Alexei and made her unhappy (or perhaps they'd set free through suffering awareness of what had perished?), the wave struck against the shore and shattered everything into particles of dust, into the dust of the earth they lived on and would soon have to die on. No, nothing would be good, nothing.

Paul went on without waiting for Catherine to turn her attention to him. Peter sighed without knowing why, although the stony burden in his chest was making itself felt again. He himself had gone away like that too once, unobserved, rejected, now those images reached across the years to him, and ensnared his heart, no, he couldn't liberate himself from memories and dispel his thoughts (Peter, why have you stopped talking? What's the matter with you? Where are you? You embarrass me, Peter. Have you changed so much?), and why didn't he try to approach her or even show that joy which despite everything he felt as he looked at her across the table and saw her talking to his uncle (but in such a way that it was as though his uncle were merely a pretext for entering into conversation with him directly), reluctant to betray his continually growing interest, though he tried to resist it, but which, if he weren't careful (something was warning him, whispering to him unceasingly and fearfully that this was necessary), she might easily interpret as unusual interest due to the fact that they hadn't met for years, or as something it ought not to be, as a feeling which earlier he himself had feared to give a name to and which, again if he weren't careful, might now dominate him utterly and even—he felt—give birth to something he could no longer hide. Fortunately, however, Catherine didn't notice anything, at least so it appeared to him, as her amused glance rested on him for a moment now and then, and he hoped she wouldn't guess, although at the same time he also felt unhappy because she wouldn't guess, an unhappiness very likely to be reborn as yet another of his mute torments, when he saw the peculiar gaze with which Paul had looked at Catherine, and when he soon realized that Paul had observed his own hidden interest, or what had appeared to him to be hidden interest, and had frowned: in that mute torment which he was soon to know despite everything, he had a chance of being transformed at once, at that moment, at the table on the terrace (when her laughter drowned even the clatter of plates and knives and forks, and had its alluring, familiar sound, somehow too low-pitched not to make him ponder), if it weren't that the torture which Gavryluk caused still smouldered and festered within him, leaving little room for anything else. Then, however, when finally—having for a moment forgotten his previous fears and the promises he'd made to himself to be careful—he wanted to approach her, his cousin Paul unceremoniously prevented him. Nothing happened that anyone would notice, no, but Peter, on catching his sulky look again, already knew what Paul was concerned with. And a fierce suspicion was suddenly born in him, but no, it couldn't be true, and he stifled it by force.

However, Paul hadn't let him out of his sight and something threatening was in his look. He was talking to Grandfather, but it was as though he had bound him, Peter, to his chair by that look, and wouldn't let him approach Catherine. 'It's our own fault. If we don't hurry up and teach the scoundrels sense . . .' he was saying to Grandfather (evidently they were discussing the situation) but in such a way that Peter heard him clearly, '. . . if we don't form our own units exclusively for protecting the manors, I don't know what will happen,' after turning from Grandfather directly to Peter (who rose just then from the table, moving towards Catherine), taking Peter by the arm and pressing him against the balustrade of the terrace he said: 'It ought to concern you more than anyone. For it's due to him . . . you know how . . .' but Peter, interrupting, 'But, Paul . . . Why me of all people?' he asked, seeing at this moment only that almost demonstrative movement of Paul's hand drawing him away from Catherine by whom he wanted to sit down, 'They still don't fully realize the situation here,' for he was only thinking: Why is he taking me away from her like this? Is he afraid, after all? What's he afraid of? while Paul: 'You know better than anyone what's what,' he said emphatically, which might have meant a challenge. 'It's Gavryluk who is the leader of the local Nationalists. They've told you everything, haven't they? I thought that since you know, you must also realize your duty. But maybe you've something else on your mind now? Or . . .' and this was like a sudden blow on the face, he never expected anything of the sort from him, so: 'Or—what?' Peter raised his head, for he was beginning to understand that Paul was not only afraid for her, but was trying to pick a quarrel, and Paul, obviously after reflecting a moment: 'I didn't want to offend you,' he said quickly, 'in the end I'll warn Catherine against him myself, well, and . . . all in all . . .' he made an undefined gesture with one hand, and turned his head to conceal his embarrassment at having given himself away, and Peter: 'Do you blame me for his existence, then? What's the matter with you, Paul? Can't you speak more clearly?' But Paul, evasively: 'You take offence at anything. After all, I wasn't thinking of anything bad. Besides, perhaps Grandmother is right. You're not old enough yet to take any responsibility. Here . . .' 'Have you quite finished?' 'Here, you know . . .' 'Have you finished?' 'What d'you mean?' 'I'd prefer you to stop, Paul. I don't want to have to make you,' and Paul, completely bewildered: 'I don't understand you,' to which Peter replied: 'There's no need to. I've seen through you, Paul. You're behaving as though you were still at the awkward age. I thought we'd talk differently to one another after all these years,' and he turned away and, leaving him alone by the balustrade, walked firmly to the table, sat down beside Catherine, and asked her bluntly: 'Are you leaving today or staying until Sunday?' 'How do you know? You've guessed it. Yes, I'm staying. I'm going to Nikorycha for half an hour. I've an appointment for a fitting,' and capriciously: 'You can't imagine how difficult it is to find a dressmaker now. But I'll be back directly. Would you care to come with me?' 'No. Paul would certainly feel offended,' said Peter, and Catherine: 'What are you talking about, why should he?' and he: 'It's natural that he should, so I'll wait here,' and she, looking at him in surprise but already comprehending, and with an artificial smile on the surface of her lips, a smile which a moment ago had been entirely natural and fresh but had now, as it were, faded: 'Anyway Paul will be coming with me. At present the roads aren't safe,' and as if she wanted to explain this more clearly: 'One can get ambushed . . .' 'Of course, I've heard that my brother is making a nuisance of himself,' he said rather mockingly, and she: 'Peter! What are you saying?' and her eyes grew round, and 'How could you, Peter?' her phrase startled him as though it had betrayed a bodily form, and then he replied: 'Paul remembers, I know. But so do I, never fear. You don't have to remind me.' 'But I said nothing of the sort . . . What has come over you, Peter?' then suddenly she guessed: 'Have you and Paul quarrelled?' but then his uncle, turning from Mrs. Woynovich to Catherine again: 'Perhaps we might go and see the foal now, eh?' he asked, 'It has albino blindness, I assure you. I never saw anything like it before. Well, don't you want to?' and she said: 'But of course, Uncle,' catching with difficulty what he meant, and at once, rapidly: 'All right, Uncle. We might as well, Uncle, I'm eager to see this curiosity, Uncle,' rising at once, although her gaze could not for a moment tear itself away from Peter, as if she expected an answer or explanation, and since she hadn't received one, was trying to read it in his face, and as if too she had suddenly understood that involuntarily (or even despite her own will) she'd hit upon something that was a matter between men, and she'd have to watch from the side line, unable to penetrate it, for they wouldn't let her, nor would they tell her anything. As she was walking away with Uncle through the park, she turned back once more and was already different from before, as if depressed by her own discovery, and tired.

Soon the rest of the company rose too; they gradually separated. Grandmother and Mrs. Woynovich, still talking about Maryna Z., made for the drawing-room while Paul strolled along the patch below the terrace with Demoiselle, giving Peter an encouraging look from time to time, perhaps expecting Peter to join them so that he could smooth over the unfortunate short-circuit between them, but Peter was again rooted by the balustrade, alone now, with eyes only for his grandfather, as he stood bent at the table, rolling tobacco into a cigarette paper, then slowly lighting the cigarette and casting one brief, inquiring look at him over the little match flame, then turning away, and he continued to watch his grandfather until he disappeared through a door leading into the depths of the house, and then for a moment could hear his footsteps, and when at last they faded away entirely, he remained standing at the balustrade, his eyes fastened on the door through which he'd disappeared, and only when enough time had passed for him to be completely positive that his grandfather hadn't changed his mind and wouldn't come back to the terrace, he went after him.

When he found himself upstairs, the silence which filled the entire length of the corridor enveloped him, emphasized by the persistent shadow into which the daylight, filtering through the slats of the blinds, was changed here, and he wasn't entirely certain whether his grandfather was in his study. After stopping for a time at the door of the study, which was not quite closed, he said loudly from the threshold: 'Grandfather.' (But there he was, sitting huddled in an armchair with a high back, a book on his knees, and he didn't even look around when Peter said 'Grandfather' to him, although as soon as he pushed the door and it squeaked on its hinges, and when the threshold creaked as he stepped on it, he ought to have looked up from his book, and with a glance at the intruder, to have frowned: he didn't tolerate anyone interrupting his moments of solitude in his room.) And as he stepped up to him he hesitated and stopped, for it seemed to him his grandfather had fallen asleep, his dry, sharply featured face was relaxed, but once more he repeated 'Grandfather,' and then: 'Yes, yes, Peter,' he said, still not raising his head, although he wasn't reading the book at all, for it was shut, and he had the cloth-bound back of the book before his eyes, where—apart from the price—there wasn't a single letter, and then, still in the same hunched position, his eyes fixed on the cover, he said: 'You had a quarrel with Paul,' yes, he said this, didn't ask it, which would have been entirely understandable, but he actually stated it, as if he'd heard that short exchange of words (though he couldn't have, or at least not much of it), and as if he didn't need any confirmation from Peter, so Peter scornfully remarked: 'It was nothing important,' coming closer, while he, not altering his previous tone and as though to himself: 'I don't understand what's got into Paul,' then at once, correcting what he'd just said, he added: 'I think you surely won't get involved in any partisan venture of theirs. It has very little chance of success in this district, believe me,' and Peter firmly: 'It isn't a question of chance, but of principles,' and his grandfather, now looking him straight in the face, with a sarcastic grimace on his lips, with that grimace which Peter had so often seen on his face since returning to Chupryn that he thought it had become a new, hitherto unknown face for his grandfather, a mask with which perhaps he was defending himself from something, especially since that sort of stiff pride, always impressive in his eyes, had undergone a breakdown difficult to define, as though defeated by time or, if not defeated, then weakened, for in fact it continued to smoulder in his eyes but was veiled by a vague mistiness, such as Peter had seen years ago in his father's eyes, especially when his father had smiled sarcastically as his grandfather did now, as he said with a smile peculiarly characteristic of him at present: 'Principles, you say? What do principles matter now, my boy? Paul is different from you, he may amuse himself with this plan, although everyone knows in advance he won't get into mischief.' 'I'm a Pole, too,' said Peter, to which his grandfather said, 'No,' and Peter: 'No? I'm not a Russian either,' still more sharply than before, and to this his grandfather answered: 'No one wants you to be. You're a Cherestvienski. That's enough,' and Peter: 'So principles are all the more important. That band of brigands has treated the whole district to bloodshed, and no one knows what they may try next,' and his grandfather: 'There's no need to get too excited by tales of atrocities. Perhaps none of this would have happened if the fathers of all the Pauls, well, all the Poles, you know what I mean, had treated the local Ukrainians differently. They've been asking for centuries for today's slaughter. I'd like you to understand that they're none of our business, and that their time is drawing to an end.

Don't you understand? Our, the Russians', time went out in the confusion of the First War. They succeeded in surviving twenty years longer, but now what had to come sooner or later is at hand. Their end, and the time when that . . . what's its name?—rabble will rule, whom you're worrying about unnecessarily,' then Peter: 'But, Mikolai Fiodorovich, after all, Gavryluk . . .' and he, interrupting: 'Gavryluk, my dear boy, is merely an embodiment of this new era that is approaching. Men like him will break up on the way. The Germans will kill him when he stops being useful to them, or the Poles will, when they arrive, or even the Soviets, if they come. I don't know why you should contribute too,' and so in this way, in precisely this way, for rather a long time, as though he didn't understand, or was pretending he didn't, until Peter: 'Do you really not know why, Grandfather?' then he rose and went slowly to the window, and stood there for a moment with his back to Peter, perhaps not wanting to show what was crossing his face, and it wasn't until after a certain time, still with his back to Peter, that he said: 'I don't want to know,' and, in a cold, indifferent voice: 'Gavryluk has signed his own death warrant,' he added: 'he's part of this new world. And it's no longer up to us to settle accounts,' in a voice as cold and indifferent as the one he used in speaking to servants, and not in the least intending to turn away from Peter, but with his eyes fixed somewhere far off, on some view outside the window, or on nothing at all, he said no more, as if he considered the matter closed, and Peter soon realized his thoughts were certainly elsewhere and that if he began talking to his grandfather again he wouldn't hear him at all, for the question of Gavryluk as something separate no longer existed as far as he was concerned, he'd already considered it in those absolute terms of his, terms of the end of one world and the birth of another which was certainly alien to him but which he accepted like anything that was unavoidable, and he felt that he and his grandfather wouldn't understand one another whatever they said, if indeed conversation was still at all possible between them then they'd speak in terms that would have no contiguity, would have no contact, as if they were obliged to speak different languages, and as if they were alien to one another, and he also felt that perhaps his grandfather was afraid for him, not wanting to admit that he was capable of understanding what he, Peter, was concerned with, not wanting to and he wouldn't admit it, and had already drawn back into his armed defence of silence, sarcasm, and brooding on the twilight of his own class, he'd forgotten that he, Peter, was still standing in the middle of the room and waiting, though there was no longer anything to wait for, so, aware of all this and that he was merely wasting time, he turned in disappointment to the door without saying a word and went out.

Then he noticed that early dusk had already fallen; noisy movements in the depths of the house were audible, indicating that preparations for supper had begun. He stopped halfway down the stairs and through a little window into the kitchen almost under the hall ceiling saw an illuminated fragment of stone floor by a table (at which the fat cook Praxeda was cutting ham into thin slices and placing them in a dish), and the corner of an open cupboard with dishes in it: the pane was slightly clouded with steam, but he could see Julia the Second sitting in a chair not far off, saying something to the cook and crying, then, after taking a deep breath, she shrugged nervously and the tears stopped trickling down her face and something timid appeared in their place, not a half-smile nor even a twitch of the muscles around her mouth, and he at once felt again those mingled feelings of remorse, disgust, and fear which he'd experienced on learning of her condition, then he quickly ran down the stairs and opened the door to the porch.

The drive was empty, only the fires of freshly opened tea roses glowed in the dusk around the flower bed, and a heavy perfume wafted from them, flowing like sap, and there was no one in the main drive either. When he retreated through the open door into the drawing-room, he caught sight of his grandmother with Mrs. Woynovich, both deep in conversation, as if they hadn't met in months and had so much to tell one another that they didn't even hear him come in, and when he asked about Paul, he heard their casual reply that he'd gone to Nikorycha with Catherine but would no doubt be back for supper. He stood leaning against the doorpost and wondered what to do: nothing occurred to him.

It was already too dark to sit without the light on, his grandmother lit a lamp and at once rang for Fiodorchuk to bring tea. He stood motionless by the doorpost, already forgotten by them, and tried to catch another sound through their voices: that of horses' hoofs drawing a carriage up the drive, the signal of Catherine's return, and he was aware of a bitter feeling of duality—she was soon to return, to sit down at table with them again and later to stay for a day or two (Paul and his mother would leave after supper, he remembered), and simultaneously he recalled both the conversations he'd had that day, with his uncle and grandfather, and finally everything he'd been worrying about for the past few days and which had prevented him from thinking calmly about Catherine in the way he'd have liked to do. In came Fiodorchuk with the tea things, and seeing Peter as he leaned against the doorpost, he didn't close the door behind him, and when Peter went after him and sat down near the women, his grandmother looked around and smiled, tired to death, evidently what she and Mrs. Woynovich had been talking about wasn't nearly as interesting as he'd supposed, and then the open door squeaked as a draught moved it, and in its oblong frame illuminated by lamplight Peter saw the empty hall, then Julia the Second crossed it in the direction of the dining-room, carrying plates, and after a moment it seemed to him he could also see, as if he were looking through the wrong end of an opera glass, the arched entrance of the corridor and, farther away, in its dark gulf, the diminished, unnaturally lengthened, thin figure of a man moving as in a convex glass, and he recognized Nick, providing it were not merely an illusion evoked by the play of dusk and light: he said: 'Excuse me,' rose, and went in that direction. No, he found no one there, neither in the hall nor in the corridor, but he already knew, unexpectedly finding the decision within himself—the lack of which he'd felt painfully all day—he knew what he was waiting for and what would help him, or rather who would help him, and he also knew who would explain everything to him, and advise him what to do, and he at once ran upstairs to Nick's room, to the north wing of the house, where Nick lived with his father, yes, he ran, suddenly feeling that rapid storming of blood in his pulses, and he ran, there's no other word for it, certain that Nick was waiting for him, and indeed there he was, perhaps awaiting him in fact, and he told him later that he actually had been, but before that he also told him everything about Julia the Second and Gavryluk, and even Catherine too, though her name wasn't mentioned once, he told him everything he knew and had guessed, he told him this as they were sitting in the dark attic room, unable to see one another because Nick didn't light the lamp, but that was just as well, and he even told him that in the end it hadn't been a matter of Julia the Second at all, nor perhaps of Madame Irène, at the time when Gavryluk had attacked Chupryn, but as he, Nick, guessed, it had concerned Catherine, Nick said so without mentioning her name at all, and that was why Peter didn't react when finally, an hour later, he heard the long-awaited rattle of the carriage as it drove into the yard, nor did he go down to supper with them, he didn't react, and even couldn't, it was beyond his powers, he hadn't the strength or courage for this meeting, for he knew he wouldn't be able to look her in the eyes if they met now, and only later, much later, when he heard Paul had gone, did he go down and, as he expected, found them in the park; Demoiselle with Catherine and Uncle Theodore (Grandfather had no doubt gone to bed already, and Grandmother was reading in her room, as always at this time), obviously they'd accompanied the people driving away as far as the gate and then wandered along the paths, his uncle liked taking guests for strolls before bedtime, and Peter guessed they'd already mentioned him and had commented on his behaviour, for they were silent about his absence from table and the fact he hadn't even come out to say good-bye to the departing guests, and there was a sort of tacit agreement between them, though it was full of tactful sympathy. He didn't attempt to explain his behaviour, in any case they didn't expect him to, he merely said he'd been in Nick's room, no one pursued the subject, and they exchanged some casual remarks about the beautiful night, the brightness of the moon, and how they would spend Sunday; Catherine stood on tiptoe and pulled down a branch of acacia and picked the flowers off it as he, standing between them, spoke with a smile and in a gentle tone of voice (hearing his own voice he wondered why it sounded so natural although it belonged, as it were, to someone else), he also spoke of the beautiful summer night and said that Sunday would be intolerably hot, but he was in quite a different place, as though he'd gone away and couldn't get back. Then Demoiselle suddenly approached him and finally uttered the question she'd no doubt been on the point of asking him earlier in the afternoon when they'd met by the stream and when his uncle had said she wanted to ask him about something too, in a tone of voice which had implied that his uncle didn't mean to let her speak at all, although at the time he hadn't grasped the meaning of that tone; now, finally, she uttered the question, putting her hand on his arm at the same moment as though she wanted to keep him at her side, perhaps it was only now that she'd finally decided she must ask, and even now it didn't come easily to her, so that she had to repeat it twice before he understood, and even before he heard what she was asking him about, he was so far away, standing right beside her and all the time distinctly feeling her hand on his arm: 'Would you like to go back now?' Then, having certain doubts as to whether he'd understood what she meant, and where to go back to (of course he understood, just as soon as her cautious voice, full of uneasiness though without defining the causes of her uneasiness, had come to him, conquering the immeasurable distance which divided them), 'To K.,' she added, 'would you like to go back to K.?' but he at once said: 'No,' briefly, decisively, cutting the whole matter off short: 'There was no need to come here at all. But as we did, then no—no,' and she pressed his arm, removed her hand rapidly, retreated and was gone, and so was Uncle Theodore, while Catherine was no longer picking flowers or making a bouquet.

She was standing under the acacia tree, still with one hand slightly raised, as if caught in a flashlight and fixed on a negative, her head turned towards him, and he knew that in a moment she would say something to him and then he'd be out of breath. Nevertheless, he didn't draw back, already feeling that strange twitch coming from deep in his throat, and it would still have been possible for him to go away, but he didn't want to, indeed he couldn't, sooner or later it would have to happen, so he even took a step in her direction, then another, and something must already have been apparent in his attitude, so, dropping the cluster of flowers she was holding, she smiled nervously, artificially, it had little in common with a smile, but was brief and flat, like a sound with a bitter resonance pressed to her palate, and at once, as soon as it broke from her, without that usual resonance in the air so that it might have been sidestepped entirely and not be recognized at all, taken as a figment of his imagination: 'So the boy doesn't want to go home to Mama?' she exclaimed sharply, although not at all rudely, as if she were trying with that word 'boy' to humiliate him in his own eyes alone and only for an instant, and to protect herself from herself, but he, seeming not to grasp her intention at all, didn't help her to do so and, just as a little earlier to Demoiselle, so now he briefly and decisively said: 'No,' and she at once understood, as soon as he said 'No,' that the time was near when he'd become a man and take the Cherestvienskis' affairs into his own hands, or perhaps it was in them now, and in acceptance of this fact—she said submissively, with no introduction or explanation: 'You must be careful, Peter,' as if she'd suddenly begun to fear for him, be sorry for him, sympathize with him, but at the same time not leaving him the slightest doubt that the role which he was to play in his own home was already known to her, and she didn't accept it. He said: 'Oh, it's not a question of your warning me. Surely you know that no one here except me will do it. Obviously they lack the strength, you see? Whether or not I want to—I must,' and she: 'You know already? What? And how?' Rapidly, as if out of breath. 'I haven't thought it out yet. But it's only a question of time,' he said, and that twitch he'd had a premonition of as soon as Demoiselle and his uncle had gone away now dominated his throat entirely and, gasping like a fish out of water: 'Something must be done about it!' he exclaimed, 'for what he's doing and the fact that he exists at all is my responsibility too. Isn't it?' 'Yes,' she said. 'But they obviously haven't the strength to resist him,' said he, and she: 'I know. But if you must, then be careful, don't do anything rash,' rapidly again, as if afraid she wouldn't be in time to convince him and warn him, 'Now the men here have much more important things to do than kill their own brothers. Don't let your first impulse carry you away. After the Soviet deportations, the Germans in their turn are deporting people. There's no one to rely on. The Ukrainians are engaging in more and more pogroms. It's as though we were on an island in the midst of the war. Our partisan group isn't very strong yet. We must keep cool if we want to survive to better times. In short, like Paul at Gleb, you'll have to look after the house and everything else. Peter, I don't want this. I wouldn't survive it if anything were to happen to you that couldn't be put right later,' feverishly and as fluently as a lightning flash, and: 'No,' he replied briefly, stunned, entirely paralysed by the words which had escaped her at the beginning, as though it were completely obvious to her that the situation being as it was, he must do it, must kill him, and as though she knew that he also already knew, although he'd say

'No,' and even when he'd said it, that 'no,' exactly as if she'd known and hadn't had the slightest doubt about it, although he still had that 'no' on his lips, and was still looking her straight in the eyes, but all of a sudden he lacked his previous certainty and at once longed to take his eyes away from her, so false did his own look seem to him, and then he felt some incomprehensible power tensing Catherine's body, so that she became rigid as she turned uneasily in his direction, she couldn't straighten her arms or hands, which were stretched forward, nor could she draw them back, and 'No,' he repeated very weakly, and: 'Was that all you wanted to say when you came to Chupryn today?' and she: 'No. I don't know,' and there was such helpless sweetness in her voice for a moment when she said: 'No. I don't know,' that he sighed with relief, and she made a tiny gesture, as if she wanted to draw back, perhaps she really did but couldn't, for that power which a moment ago had begun to dominate her had surely become stronger than she, and 'Touch me, Peter,' she then whispered, 'please touch me, Peter,' she whispered just like that, as he stood there unable to take his eyes from her, although he wanted to shift his gaze away, and again it was as before: an iron pressure in his throat, he was breathless, but that force from her poured relentlessly into him as soon as he touched her arm, and at once he felt her, and her hair with its scent intensified by the damp dusk air, and the timid movement of her lips, which were quite cold, pressed together, penetrating into him with a mortal chill, and she at once drew away and even held away from him with a sort of still movement of her entire body and, without looking him in the eye, turning quickly away, she said: 'Be careful, now you'll be an animal he's hunting, as I am,' except that in her voice there was no longer a hint of her previous fear for him, or of mercy and sympathy, or warning, or persuasion, or consolation, or sweetness, or even a drop of warmth, only something which might be both mockery and challenge, or both, mingled with a concealed threat, and she left him alone, disappearing around a corner of the drive.

For a moment her scent remained with him, the scent of her hair intensified by the dusk, perhaps of the acacia flowers too, a handful of which she had tossed to the grass and which he now automatically picked up, but then even that scent dissolved, the darkness seemed to thicken and the stifling sensation almost started again, as if there weren't enough air in the whole park for him and the air itself wasn't sufficient for breathing. Then he set off after her, although he had long since lost her from sight, and her footsteps had died away, he went directly to the house and upstairs to his room, stifling all the time, gasping for the air that was insufficient or which, perhaps, was suddenly lacking altogether now, his mouth wide open, then in his room he threw himself on the bed without closing the door, so that a draught began blowing from the corridor through the room towards the open windows and, after a while, blowing back from the windows to the corridor (lying face down he could feel this different, bitter breath on his back and how it chilled him through his sweat-drenched shirt), yet he was stifling and couldn't cope at all with his choking breath, and then on the border of sleep and lassitude he was in his grandfather's study again, he heard his grandfather saying that no matter what happened, Gavryluk wouldn't escape his shameful fate, the Polish partisans would deal with him, he owed them his skin, or the Germans would, he'd soon stop being necessary to them, or even the Soviets would, when they arrived with that new order of theirs, when the map of Europe would change, and the only thing still worth the candle would surely be to survive honourably to the end of one's own era and to prepare him, Peter, to adjust himself to existence in the new era, all this with a sarcastic smile, as if he were quite certain that his world was fading and he saw no need to search for a place for himself in another one, as he had already had to do once, after the Russian Revolution, and he was only concerned with him, Peter, not with Gavryluk, certainly not, that was a matter of no consequence at all, since his own old world was fading and even he himself was fading, the oldest of the Cherestvienskis, along with it, and Peter couldn't accept this, at least not in such a way as to have to disclaim certain principles according to which his grandfather had brought him up and with which he'd imbued him, and he heard that surprise in his grandfather's voice, no longer hearing what his grandfather was saying or, more precisely, still hearing but deliberately not listening, not wanting to understand the content of the words he uttered and thinking that no matter what happened, he wouldn't want to help him, he himself would decide what had to be done, knowing that his grandfather's surprise was caused by the discovery that for the first time they'd been unable to understand one another properly, he himself being no less surprised that they couldn't, for at one time they had understood one another even without speaking, and feeling disappointed: then again he was there in the attic of the north wing, still stifling on the borders of lassitude and sleep, gasping for breath with his mouth open, and he was sitting opposite his friend, separated from him by the darkness which was a good thing then, for it erased the frontiers of time which might have separated them, so it linked them, even before he realized that in fact those years were unimportant, at least in the situation in which they were meeting again, and a pale ray of the new moon poured through the window into the room (it hadn't been there when he ran in and when Nicholas told him to sit down and he had done so obediently, but later on there it was, and it moved around the room slowly, not illuminating it at all, so they could barely see each other's outlines, nothing more, and that was a good thing too, because they didn't have to search for that peculiar stamp which had been impressed in their faces by their separate experiences), that ray slowly moving over the floor finally reached the edge of the carved chest Nick was sitting on, as if to extricate him from the darkness and thus conclude its wanderings, for soon it began to grow still paler, evidently the new moon over the park was veiled in clouds and again he heard Nick saying that in the end Gavryluk wasn't of any greater importance than the other pogrom bands disturbing the neighbourhood, his band didn't even differ in numbers, only he was more intelligent so that his band was rather more harmful than the other bands of local Nationalists, and it was true, he'd heard your uncle tell you so; Nick said that his own father had said the same, and still better-informed people from the little town too, well you can believe me, I know a lot myself, so his, Nick's belief was the same, that Chupryn, at least officially, wasn't threatened by Gavryluk in any way that couldn't be forestalled easily enough, some surreptitious sting at most, he'd revenge himself like a dog that had previously eaten from your hand but that had gone mad and wanted to bite the hand, this is how it had been with the attack on Chupryn over a year ago, it's because he wants your land, your houses, your women, but as he can't get them he must destroy or do no matter what, providing it's against all of you, and that's how it was with Julia; Peter heard Nick speaking calmly in that darkness surrounding them, cut in two by the moonbeams, well perhaps not quite calmly, but to some extent, as if he wanted him, Peter, to be able to treat these events in a detached way, as something comprehensible and logical in the situation which existed in this country of theirs, because they have to do it, he heard Nick saying, they have to do it, and one can't talk about Gavryluk without talking about his compatriots as well, and all that hatred which has smouldered through the years under the façade of apparent tranquillity between the two nations inhabiting this land together, Poles and Ukrainians, and which had to find an outlet in fratricidal murders; one must speak of all of this if one didn't want to distort the whole picture, and it concerned more than merely what one Ukrainian bandit had done and would do. Surely that's how it was, thought Peter, because Nick was speaking the truth, he knew this truth from that September day in 1939 when they'd been at Gleb just before the evacuation to take a letter from his grandmother because the telephones weren't working, and on the way back they'd cut down from a tree the body of the Polish schoolteacher, whom the Nationalists had hanged at the mouth of a ravine behind the Motren Forest, and Nick's father had said they were only just beginning the massacres, at least something of the sort, and soon it turned out to be so: and when the Soviets came, and afterwards when the Germans came, yes, he knew this truth and knew the inevitability it expressed, thought Peter, as he tried to control his gasping breath, gulping it as though he'd swallowed a foreign body of some kind, and although the draught was blowing cold air from the door to the windows and back again, from the windows to the door, he felt there was less and less air, and he was plunging more deeply and swiftly into lassitude or perhaps into sleep, he didn't know which, it didn't matter, he was still sitting in the darkness opposite Nicholas and heard him unfold the whole confused story of Julia the Second, and even saw her as Nick spoke, for it began to seem to him that it wasn't Nick at all but Julia the Second herself who was speaking, he saw her as though in that beam of pale moonlight which illuminated nothing though it gleamed like sweat, and which, after moving around the room, had stopped on the chest carved with griffins where Nick sat; Julia the Second herself was walking, in that Sunday dress of hers with white and green stripes, and then she was going where she'd said she was going that evening from the church, coming back not by the road but by a short cut through the fields, to get home faster, and it had happened then, not far from the bridge, when they'd jumped out from under the bridge like black, maddened stallions, and she'd wanted to run away through the water, but they caught her at the very edge, turned her over on the dry bulrushes, there were four of them, with Gavryluk among them, she'd recognized him by the quiff combed up on his head, as they overturned her, twisting her arms, and then they held her feet so that she was conveniently straddled, and they tore everything off her with laughter and, one after the other, like black, breathless stallions from the pit of Hell, they set upon her, closing her mouth so that she couldn't scream, although she wouldn't have screamed, as helpless as a whipped animal, humiliated to the very depths, for they spared her nothing, then afterwards they'd said: 'You bitch. You're your master's bitch. You're a bitch brought up for your master's bed. If you weren't of our faith, you'd be hanging in strips on a tree, you bitch,' speaking to her like this when they'd finished and were fastening their pants standing over her, and later they'd left her as she lay when they'd finished, in all her total humiliation, stupefaction, and pain, under a sky which had certainly seen it all but was more dumb and helpless than she was, and no one knew what had happened after that, Nick couldn't explain it either to himself or to him, Peter, for she'd never explained anything to anyone, perhaps she didn't remember at all later on, or without knowing from the start what had drawn her back to Gavryluk again, not realizing at all the meaning of those dark, feverish, and incomprehensible powers, stronger than she was, stronger than her shame and humiliation, or perhaps it had been slumbering deeply hidden within her, that force which drew her to him, in her instinctive, half-religious, and erroneous belief that she belonged to the Cherestvienskis and he was one of them too, so she must yield to him whether she wanted to or not, escape or not, or perhaps, for it was not at all out of the question, perhaps it was beyond her, in some arrangement or other of blind Fate, in some catastrophic circumstance, no one knows, for the mechanism of events remained forever hidden, so Nick could only say that it had happened over again when she went to Krzysztopol where he had quarters with his band, already firmly established in German style and incorporated into the Hilfspolizei organization, one evening she'd gone to their barracks in Taganrog Street, and Nick said she'd stayed there with him so that, after he had got rid of the other women and his comrades who, like dogs sniffling a bitch, had tried to set upon her again, he'd driven them away and taken her for himself, and later he had her for himself alone, and became infatuated with her, so that later on she could do whatever she chose with him, perhaps forcing this upon him by her insane devotion, or by devotion that came from madness, that madness which enabled her to endure anything from him and to forget her own shame, surely some elemental force must have been ruling her, for there was nothing rational in the influence, and he too must have yielded to this force for a short time, although perhaps even then he was taking in her body the body of an entirely different woman while she, Julia the Second, was merely the passive embodiment for him of the women from the Cherestvienski family whom he'd desired all his life entirely unobserved by them, or even the quite concrete embodiment of some particular woman, Nick didn't say who, and Peter didn't ask, that question refused to come from his tense throat, he was already feeling for the first time that iron pressure in his throat, and he would at once begin to suffocate, as he was doing now, suffocate, half fainting, plunged into some swampy, bottomless slime, lying fully dressed on the bed, half in a feverish sleep, yet at the same time hearing Nick saying that something of this sort had happened to Gavryluk at that time, so that for a while he'd even neglected the contemptible duties of a Ukrainian leader, he almost stopped going to the 'pacifications,' the lootings and military actions, for a time the district had breathed again, although this couldn't last very long, after all the Gestapo had their requirements, everyone knew what and how, and that band of his wouldn't tolerate such an arrangement, for if he brought women into his place for the night and sent them away next morning, that was a common enough matter among them, but that one of them should gaze into his eyes every day like a dog, and that he too should have eyes for no one but her and drive away the others, this must have been too much for them, and at once Peter could see that couple who filled him with horror, disgust, and hatred, not taking their eyes from one another, she in her madness like a dog which, after being kicked, will crawl back to the feet of its tormentor, writhing in devotion full of slavish humiliation and loyalty, without making any demands that its loyalty be reciprocated, and he in a sort of insane stupefaction, in which the women he desired and had never had, pupated in her body which, by an incomprehensible arrangement of fate, he had whenever he wanted; he could see how they looked at one another with a heavy gaze that evoked desire, how they were isolated all day long by that dark, mysterious power which had suddenly enslaved them and wouldn't let them go, and he saw what they did later, when that power drew them together at night in a corner, on one of the makeshift beds on the barrack floor in that hall saturated with sour male sweat, breath, and fever which the band used as their quarters, full of looks enveloping them like slippery worms, and how that crowd of drunken murderers, stinking of alcohol if they couldn't stink of blood, slack for want of action and furious, how they stalked after them, watched them, and commented on what they were doing, as they, forgetting they were not alone or perhaps being alone despite them as a result of their mutual madness which lasted from that winter day when she'd come to Krzysztopol until early spring, and how the band felt cheated, rejected by them, robbed of their leader, and what was going on between the pair of them was outside the scope of their understanding, both of the band as a whole and of each of these men individually, Peter saw, listening as Nick spoke to him from the very heart, from the bottom of the darkness which was so deep and wide, and Nick's calm, level voice, seemingly deprived of tones of excess emotion, didn't concentrate but spread, flowed lengthwise as it were, and only now did his, Peter's own memory concentrate it and elevate it so that at moments it seemed as though Nick were screaming, although, there in the attic in the north wing, as they were sitting face to face, this didn't happen once, and it gave his voice a sort of stifling, hurried, impatient sound, in this darkness which now was deeper than before, the moon had gone, and which was suffocating him as he heard Nick speaking again, and again he saw this girl, just as Nick wanted him to see her, now on the very brink of the time when she underwent final defeat in the contest with all that band into which she had thrown herself, seeing her alone and lost among them, no one knew what she was waiting for, what she was counting on, on nothing maybe, for that stupor of hers must have paralysed any reactions of reflection or instincts of self-defence, so unprepared to accept defeat, not expecting it at all; this was precisely how he was seeing her, faced by the enraged band who had had enough of it for a long time, and that evening too, seeing as he heard Nick speaking, that it was an early evening in March, between winter and spring, how they had evidently reached an agreement and appointed five or six of the most daring among themselves, they'd gone up to him in that corner of his and hers in the room, no doubt in order to have some basic talk unambiguous in its final effect which, in their opinion, would give them their leader back or force them to have to choose another one, their eyes showing their criminal intent which he must have discerned right away, as soon as they approached and stood in a circle, and also what the stake was, and how in silence, after delaying a good while, their breathing finally intruded, although it must have been growing more audible earlier, but it broke out suddenly and everything was filled with it, for the words that were to be uttered, perhaps prepared in advance, weren't uttered, their looks were too clearly eloquent, this decision must have come at once, for they demanded it with their eyes: he and all of them, and only they didn't yet know how or what, neither did he, nor they, and the breathing rose into a feverish hissing that erupted in the stagnant silence like the taut springs of a broken clock suddenly set into violent motion, and they emitted, perhaps wanting to stifle them, some sort of sounds, as if their bones were coming out of their sockets, insistently searching for the solution in his eyes which from the start had been shallow, glassy, as if drunken: what and how, that sign, an answer, a phrase, whatever it was to be or what it was called, it was unavoidable, and seeing her too, seated cross-legged on the bed in the furthest corner, motionless, like a life-sized wax doll, her attention fastened on one point in his face, centred in his eyes, also no doubt waiting, as soon as she began divining, if in fact she ever did, what the game was and what the stake was in this game, if she were at all capable of divining, waiting for that sign, answer, or phrase, whatever it was it would have to come from him, parting her waxen lips which were as pale as her face and parched with her breath, although she was hardly breathing at all, she alone, for they had already for some time now been breathing with intolerable whistling and hissing noises which they themselves had surely had enough of already but were unable to curb, and he saw Gavryluk finally shudder, stretch out a hand stiffly in front of him and snap his fingers, and that evidently was the sign, for they at once came closer, and when he quietly said to her, Lie down, in a strange wooden voice, himself moving aside, they all rushed forward instantly, halfway through her shriek, elbowing one another in their haste, and already Peter could only see her eyes in the fleeting gleams of light, turning back in their orbit towards Gavryluk, for he was standing at the head of the bed, her eyes with a dull gleam and as motionless as if she'd suddenly lost all feeling, and he sensed the odour of their sweat and sperm worming its way into his nostrils, he heard the bed squeak, the mattress rustle, and their breathing as it drifted slowly to the very edge of silence, and then again the wooden voice of Gavryluk as he said, Now get out, you bitch, and again a twitch caught in his throat and he started suffocating out loud, and his own choking breath grew so loud that after a moment it stifled even the memory of all those disastrous sounds, and again he heard, as then, the carriage driving up to the house, already he knew it was Catherine, because this was just how it had driven up with Catherine, and there was Fiodorchuk who, as he helped her out, said something to her and she replied in a few words which admittedly he didn't catch, but he had recognized her voice and rushed to the window, exclaiming in Nick's direction that he could not go down to her there, and asking him to let him stay longer, for he didn't know whether he could look her in the eyes after what he'd heard, although it had had nothing at all to do with her, but all the same it might have had, if it hadn't been for sheer chance, and she couldn't help knowing that, and Nick insistently reverted to this same narrative of events and he, hearing his voice, also had to go back to the place he had just wrenched himself away from, back into that rainy night on the border of winter and spring, hearing once again their whistling breath as it drew closer to him from out there, and Gavryluk's voice as he later said quietly, Now get out, you bitch, and suddenly he began shouting at Nicholas, No, stop it, stop it for God's sake, you know I'm not to blame, what do you want me to do? and then the silence, closely surrounding him, full of those distant sounds, burst, split, and fell apart, and he heard his own cry in reality, real, reverberating in his eardrums, splitting his skull: he woke up.

He was lying, drenched in sweat, on top of the blankets, still not sure where he was, having forced that shout out of himself, he could still hear it on the edge of his awareness, but it was already dying away, he lay completely helpless without moving or opening his eyes, unable to feel anything except terror lest it return, and that it would return if provoked by anything and would catch him by the throat again, really hearing only its distant echo, he slowly returned to the spot where he was lying and to awareness of this place, and later, when he had gained assurance that it wouldn't come back, he opened his eyes and in that marshy darkness of the room against a background formed by a few gleaming blotches on the wall, he perceived the oblongs of pictures and the Dutch clock, and there, between the cupboard and desk, in this silence which had swallowed up the sound of that shriek of his which was now merely pulsating with the gentle rustle of greenery just outside the windows, against a background of one of them, illuminated from behind by a flickering gleam was the silhouette of his uncle Theodore, who leaned over the bed, entirely faceless in the dark: and, as if his uncle had already known that he, Peter, had just opened his eyes, he heard his uncle say gently: 'You were screaming.'

Not for a long time did he reply: 'Yes, I was,' and his uncle: 'Were you having a bad dream?' and he: 'Yes, you know I was,' and his uncle: 'Yes,' as if he really had known it and had accepted the fact that he must have been dreaming, and then when the cool breath of the draught took the last faint traces of sleep from Peter's face, he asked his uncle: 'Have they all left?' His uncle, however, without any surprise in his voice, said: 'No, of course not, Catherine stayed behind,' and he: 'Ah, yes, Catherine stayed, of course,' with a touch of relief, 'That's good,' and his uncle: 'Well, I don't know. I'd like to . . .' and then a foolish, unhappy thought came to Peter that ever since he'd come back to the family home, not a single step of his, nor any of that struggle with contradictions, nor, finally, any of his secrets had been unobserved by his uncle who followed like a shadow behind him all the time, penetrated like a shade into his thoughts, and that he was a very good man, but what would happen when he wasn't there any more? He thrust away this premonition with distaste.

The greenery outside the windows was rustling as a light breeze touched it, the sky had begun to gleam far off, the moon appeared out of the depths like a solitary boat emerging from a bay veiled by the horizon into the depths of an ocean, then sank into the clouds again. Peter lay sober, awake, the iron pressure of sleep had irrevocably passed, leaving him free of nightmare but with his heart strangely chilled: now he slipped into his own warmth: the pleasant abyss of the bedclothes promised security and peace. His uncle contemplated him in silence, then asked: 'Can't you sleep?' 'I was asleep,' 'And now?' 'I don't want to sleep any more. I'm all right now.' 'I can't sleep either,' said his uncle, 'and then I walk about the house and search.' 'What for, Uncle?' 'What used to be here once, my boy. Her.' 'I know, Uncle. It was a long time ago, but I remember Madame Irène as though it were yesterday.' 'I can't believe she'll never come back,' said his uncle, and he: 'Did you love her very much, Uncle?' 'It is still alive . . .' said his uncle almost in a whisper, and for a moment they looked at one another across the darkness.

The breeze rustled again, blowing from outdoors the various silken perfumes of the night, and among them came a sort of sweet scent which reminded Peter of Catherine standing motionless under a tree in the park, and those brief, shifting movements of her hair as it hid her face from him, and what had happened then, but his memory at once and violently fenced him off from that picture by recalling the words she had said earlier (they sounded in his ears now less sharp and brutal than they had done then, and he thought: Oh God, she knows I must do it, she knows . . .) and at once he longed to be in some distant place, so far away that he could forget her and her words.

The long, lean aesthetic face of his uncle which consisted entirely of haggard flesh had lengthened still more in his concentration and, as if he had guessed what he, Peter, was thinking and what he desired more than anything else, he spoke of himself, directing his thoughts far away, as far away as possible from the places Peter didn't want to think about, he spoke quietly but clearly and without a trace of sentimentality: 'I must tell you that I loved Irène not in the way you no doubt believe. Perhaps you're still innocent enough to believe in feelings like thought, like the air that fills the area around the object of our love, which doesn't seek to fulfil any dreams and desires, and doesn't even produce these desires, but stops, as it were, on their border and lives on by the mere fact that this marvellous being exists who has aroused love in us, that she is present and that one can meet her daily, talk to her, look at her, be seen by her oneself, though this isn't necessary. Yet at the same time you are not innocent enough to believe that such love exists outside of pure imagination, outside of abstract notions and literary fiction, if indeed it ever happens in real life to last beyond a moment only. Yes, for life is stronger, my boy. If a man loves, he at once wants to possess. He sees in what he loves the embodiment of himself. And is it possible to separate from one's self? You have fallen in love with some country, you'd like to call it "my country." A house—

you'd like it to be your house. A woman—you want it to be your woman. Feelings are eager for conquest, and even if this is not so at the start, yet they soon become so. They drive us on to fulfill the promise, they want to lead us as rapidly as possible to the moment when, in the eyes of the beloved, as though in convex and magnifying mirrors, you see that paroxysm of delight bordering on pain, or that which is both delight and pain simultaneously, your own face which is the only face for her now. I wasn't Tristan, Peter, and she wasn't Iseult. But is that a bad thing? Neither good nor bad. Perhaps this is spoiling yet another of your fine boyish notions. Or perhaps it isn't?'

Not knowing whether his uncle really expected a reply from him, Peter quietly said: 'No,' for not only did it seem to him that he'd been prepared for this confession, but that it corresponded to some of his own questions and doubts barely realized hitherto, and to which it was in fact necessary to say 'No,' and his uncle (Peter wasn't sure whether he'd heard him at all) went on: 'It's impossible, my boy, to love for long without wanting possession at the same time. And although what I'm saying may seem to you brutal today and, as it were . . . unclean, yet you will at some future time remember that I'm right. It was six years before the war, during my fruitless stay at Sidi-Bou-Zid, where I'd been excavating for six months or more with Beule's expedition in the ruins of a supposed sanctuary of Baalhamon (nothing of interest, I assure you, more of an academic squabbling among the participants than real work), and the region had sickened me for good and all. One day I dropped the entire job and the devils too, and set off for Tunis in the first car that came along. I didn't intend to stay in the town at all, just shave, eat in a decent restaurant, bathe for the first time in months in a real bath, and on that same day I was at the El Aina airfield thinking of nothing but Europe. And yet she was waiting there for me, she'd been waiting several years, and I'd been waiting too. Her name was Irène. To the Greeks it once symbolized peace, but doesn't it also symbolize tranquillity, calm and equilibrium?' He pondered for a moment, then took up the thread again: 'Life, you see, is a single unbroken chain of accidents: usually we're unable to discern their meaning. Only occasionally, when they affect our future destiny in decisive manner. Then we talk of "a miraculous accident," or a "providential accident." Never mind what we call it. I was taken ill at the airport. Perhaps it was a touch of the sun, perhaps the sudden lowering of air pressure. An ambulance took me back to the hospital, which I left next morning. But my desire to leave at once and at any price, which was equivalent to escape, had left me. I stayed on in Tunis (I even considered idly whether to go back to Sidi-Bou-Zid), I wandered about the region a little with no special purpose, on the seashore I made the acquaintance of a few dark-skinned porters who supplied the city with all sorts of sticky, juicy fruit: those were sleepy days, which have left no memory. And then I met her. It happened in the cemetery near the Goulette valley. No doubt you can picture to yourself those old necropolises on the cliffs where dead bodies, religions, and nationalities have piled up over the ages, where conquered and conquerors lie, and new conquerors and new conquered as well, and so on endlessly, in shallow flat layers one on top of the other, made brothers by death and yet alien, so that if one day they rise again, they will have trouble understanding one another (a tower of Babel, you see), and if one pushes a spade a little deeper down, it's quite easy to uncover Roman layers, and perhaps earlier, Punic ones, too. Those are the most silent places in the world, the tombs of entire humanity, the rise and fall of civilizations: even the latest graves, vulgarly rich and well-kept, screaming to the passer-by with their still unobliterated gilt inscriptions to stop and offer a sigh to the Lord for the soul of the departed, even they seem more modest and their vulgarity extinguished in this eternal environment.

'She was standing amidst date palms, by a slab of more than modest grey sandstone, and that barely perceptible though definite attitude of waiting in her silhouette struck me at once, as she stood there with her eyes fixed on the gravestone, as if she had just a moment ago said something extremely important to her dead and wanted to hear a reply. Passing, I glanced at the inscription, and it was in Russian, in the old orthography, under an Orthodox double cross, and I must have stopped then and she had something in her glance as she turned to me, so that I had to say something too, I spoke in Russian: we were never able to remember what it was, nor what she replied, but she replied in Russian also, though with a foreign accent that sounded Gallic. And we already knew that this meeting had had to take place, that we were both prepared for it, although we didn't know each other, yet we'd been close to one another for a long time already. And later we stood for some time by that grave from which—beyond the trunks of the date palms—could be seen a wide region bathed in sunlight, yellowed and parched: higher, in the direction of the Byrsa fortress, the outline of the overloaded neo-Byzantine cathedral of Cardinal Lavigerie, and below the beach, a point of land jutting out, overgrown with poverty-stricken native gardens, old ditches, and in the lagoon behind the peninsula were reefs with the ruins of the Phoenician *choma,* and an artificial dam where at one time Scipio's soldiers storming Carthage had established their first bridgehead. We didn't speak to one another, or hardly at all, but that didn't matter. Lovers understand each other by the misty light in which eyes meet, by a vague gesture of the hands, a glance escaping into space, a defensive flutter of eyelids, monosyllables in place of words, a quickened breathing, a landscape fixed permanently on the pupils, some recollection or other without relevance, voices, a sound that evokes an avalanche of memories which at once become shared—everything that can happen in the limitless expanse of a moment, but what's time if not a moment capacious enough for two people, like eternity? And from that day on we went every morning to that place where the sun burned with peculiar intensity, while the air hadn't yet taken on that irritating opacity caused by the steaming beaches, or the dust raised in the interior of the wilderness. We never said much to one another, facts and that was all. She was the granddaughter of a French tutor and a Polish woman, she was the daughter of their son who made a living too by tutoring, and married a Russian: a childhood somewhere in the governmental district of Orlov, followed by exile: her mother was buried here on the African coast. I understood at once that she was a person who from her birth had been without a country, without a homeland, condemned by fate to eternal wandering and vague yearnings for a home, but by her very nature incapable of finding one, continually torn by desires which were the result of a mixed bloodstream, a person the language of whose thoughts was a linguistic mosaic, and the language she used in speaking wasn't her native tongue. 'Do you know the growing process of genuine, mature love?' his uncle asked, then replied to his own question: 'When we realize our desire to possess but at the same time understand the harsh necessity of resignation, not complete resignation, perhaps, because of a desire for exclusivity (all the less so because love always breeds hope), but if we can make do with that and don't go away at once, that is love. I knew it two or three weeks after our first meeting.'

He stopped a moment and thought, perhaps evoking for himself that day when Madame Irène came to the cemetery which was the place of their non-accidental meetings, in the company of her husband, fifteen or perhaps twenty years older than she, a stout, short, jolly little man, kind-hearted, a provincial booby—so Peter had described him when he first met him at Chupryn—an artist misunderstood by the rest of humanity, with an operatic, Italian soul in his French body, a teacher of music and dancing for a few francs (paid monthly by the student), cast up from Europe on the sun-baked, opposite shore, perhaps so, but perhaps he was only thinking of his own resignation which seemed to him an inseparable part of his feelings, for in the end he said: 'At your age, some subtleties are still quite imperceptible and no doubt it seems pitiable to you that I could accept his existence and not want to take her away from him, since I was in love and knew from the first day, almost from the first glance, that I was loved too. But, my boy, there are bonds which aren't really based on the ordinary love between a man and a woman, but which, for all that, are lasting, what's more are totally unbreakable. Perhaps precisely because these bonds lack the passion which attracts but also repulses, the force which unites but can also be disruptive, the force lovers submit to, the game they constantly maintain. He was like a father to her, and at the same time I found in her those inexhaustible maternal sources which sometimes characterize women who for some reason or other are childless. And another thing: she didn't seem to be capable of surviving another shock such as my violent and unceremonious intrusion between them. She'd never have forgiven me that, she'd have felt guilty, and no doubt in the end would have blamed me for it, and forced me to leave her. If I wanted to conquer her, I had from the start to renounce any struggle with him. So, as you see, my resignation wasn't without common sense forced upon me by a knowledge of the situation, and it also derived from despicable calculation. This absurd little man who'd once found her almost on the streets, had extricated her from the depths of poverty, guided moreover not by pity at all, but by a charity of which he was unaware and an innate simplicity of soul, he'd bound her hands forever, chained her to him, bought her for a song, but at the same time he'd become as necessary to her as the air for breathing which isn't to be had in the defiling effusions of gutters and the filth of all those vile drains above which contemporary man lives out his peacock-like existence. She belonged to him as obviously as a leaf to a tree, heat to a flame, a mother's voice to a child, perfume to a flower, the blue to the sky, or like air to our lungs, for that naïve, conceited, honest little man with the heart of a child, whose limitless goodness answered to some part of her being, was a rampart behind which she could always find shelter. There was trust in their attitude to each other, and although there was something unspoken and unfinished too, some total lack of any need to communicate by the physical touch of words, gestures, looks, or bodily contact which are, after all, an inseparable part of an association, I was far from drawing any conclusions advantageous to myself from this fact, since that meant perhaps only a kind of calm equilibrium acquired in an ideal understanding. And yet I loved her despite this peculiar, unnatural division between the two of us, and although at first he aroused hatred and instinctive rebellion in me (the fact that she belonged to him as well complicated our relations with each other), I understood that my voluntary surrender of any exclusive rights was only that mature love which comes with the twilight of life, a state I was slowly reaching. Although, to be frank, I never much liked him. The obstacle to this wasn't that she belonged to him as well (I say "as well" because primarily she belonged to me), but the fact that she also belonged to him only, that their association was completely permanent despite the fact he never did anything consciously to maintain the bond, while towards me—he was uncertain. But I didn't realize this until much later, in Europe (for at first I was still deluding myself, though later I didn't at all), to which I took them with me as one takes baggage or household pets; I in turn bought them for a song and paid for them, moreover, with the fake small change of friendship, and I dragged them (as their owner and servant, living in the fear that one day they'd leave me, and spreading the fear that I might jettison them on the way like sucked fruits, to suffer humiliation and humiliate myself) around all those nightmarish little hotels in Sicily, Albania, Yugoslavia, the Levantine coast, as far as Constantinople and later Turkey, and back to Constantinople, anywhere where there was something to excavate, a wall, a graveyard, buried pottery or bones which by their eternity had ceased to be human and become merely an indifferent exhibit, around all these nightmarish dirty little hotels which profaned life, so full were they of solitude, the brother of death, around all those rented rooms which gave the impression a suicide had just been cut down from the chandelier, rooms in which hearts freeze and despair reigns, I dragged them with me, and I dragged them for a whole year, in order in the end, however, to find or perhaps I ought to say to "gain" a marvellous equilibrium, also called happiness by some, in that vortex of contradictions.

'I recall a wretched village somewhere in South Rhodes, at the entrance to a valley, the terrible heat, nets across the windows and an entrance cavity which merely distilled the light, and the heat burned even from the clay floor: tormenting implications and the pain which we give ourselves against our will, all were devouring me. A pain in the heart at the sight of her eyes narrowed with fatigue. Ears full of this chatter as he admired everything, he was inexhaustible in his enthusiasm, chattering, humming, whistling, and telling jokes I never laughed at and never listened to, and perhaps she didn't either. We had just finished cataloguing a small find of coins of the Isaurian period (these regions had been little investigated, being inhospitable and inaccessible, and although I got an additional grant from a New York museum to continue my search, I wanted to move on as fast as possible: something was happening to me, so that I couldn't stay long in the same place), and he went out of the hut with that rather duck-like gait of his by which I usually recognized him in the distance, though he moved uncertainly as if ill and weak, and he stood there in the sun to gaze around at the cliffs, he gazed for a long time at the reddish, naked cliffs which looked like badly baked bricks, unnaturally pale, and then he suddenly staggered and fell unconscious to the ground. I remember the blaze of anger in her eyes when I ran out of the hut and leaned over to lift him and carry him into the shelter. She didn't want to let me, shrieking: "You'll kill him," but she herself hadn't the strength and in the end I carried him, then at once however she thrust me firmly aside:

"Go away," she said, "go and get some water," and she sat by the plank bed until he opened his eyes, staring into his face with eyes that gleamed as though with tears and abstractedly. It was only a slight indisposition brought on by the lowering of air pressure before a storm, and though that evening she said: "Don't be angry for what I said, I was upset. I know it wasn't your fault," she at once added in a tone which brooked no denial on my part: "We can't stay here. He's stout, he has a weak heart, he can't bear this climate and altitude," and she waited for me to agree, though firmness and resolution tautened her face. In a second everything that bound and divided us stood out like a lightning flash in my mind, and I thought over all that year of ours. I had no idea whether she was thinking of him or of me when she said we couldn't stay there, or whether she was thinking about the three of us, but I preferred not to risk asking, I don't know what she'd have replied: I remembered after all that she didn't have to be forced to make a choice, and I said quite eagerly: "Of course, we'll strike camp tomorrow," but she said nothing to this, only the tension in the muscles of her face relaxed, though her eyes still gleamed forcefully and strongly. But that night again, as often before, she belonged to me, to me alone, I don't hesitate to emphasize this, and it was as though for her I constituted an indivisible entity with him. A storm was raging outside, the bluish light which smelled of ozone pushed the walls together then apart, and the ceiling was as high as Heaven. With her head on my shoulder she said: "Youth is inhuman, Theodore. Confident in its powers. But we, after all, aren't as young as that. We can give others only a part of what life sends us. Our supplies are greater, but our strength is less. And so, in return for our generosity, perhaps one day when we're weak, others will support us with their strength," and then, after a moment of silence, she said she loved me, and her voice was timid but at the same time aggressive, sleepy and vigilant, yielding and tense, and already her breathing had risen into that sort of total forgetfulness of self in which it resembles a sob, and that very night I realized for the first time quite clearly that I was really free and yet wasn't at all. I yielded to all these feelings, ruthless in their consequences, which arouse in us a lack of control, greedy passions, and later on we suffer so much for them, those feelings which we allow to grow in our own hearts like weeds, despite ourselves, against our better judgment, feelings from which we dust the mildew and feed on in order to poison the pure and sweet taste of happiness, all those feelings which in fact bear the common name "jealousy," which I'd suffered from hitherto though without always knowing it. But then I was really free, that night and ever since.

'Believe me, love can be natural and beautiful, no matter who was or is fed at its source apart from ourselves, if only we can concentrate, as ruthlessly as I did then, on our own feelings, surrender to and understand some other being. That was our best year. If I say "best," it's not because the later years were worse, but it was our most shamelessly open year. No, he never noticed anything, though later in Chupryn we had to be careful. It was the best and briefest year. I can still see us riding on pack donkeys into the valley. Irène's donkey began limping, she laughed and said to her husband: "You're too fat, *mon cher*, it won't carry us both," and she carelessly changed places to sit behind me. A train journey, like something out of the last century: she dozed, leaning against his shoulder, but her hand in mine. We went to visit the Hagia Sophia, on the way we bought roast chestnuts and burned our lips as we ate them. We bathed in the Bosphorus, and never knew why a policeman fined us. Irène quarrelled in a market place with some dwarfish Greek who thrust slippery creatures resembling small octopuses into her basket instead of fish. Our protests led to a diverting squabble, and we fled. I heard her in the night creeping from her room to mine. I was afraid: why was she treading so loudly, yet it wasn't her footsteps at all, but my own heart beating. A tipsy wedding in the country. A trip by steamboat full of tourists loaded with money, and when some Sudanese sheikh as brown as a berry asked Irène to dance, she shot us a look over his shoulder as we were sitting by a door to the deck with cool drinks. Then again, New Year's Eve in Trieste, the streets exploding with lights, bells ringing, silver rockets dissolving with a bang, processions in fancy dress winding across the squares and singing, and we fled a boring reception at the Polish Consulate, got lost in the crowd, and met again in the morning by a fountain near the harbour. Irène, carrying her shoes, sat on the stones with her feet in the water up to her knees, as we came up each from a different direction, driven by the same impulse. She was delighted and wondered whether, if we bathed, a whole mob of policemen would come running up, this became a problem of almost metaphysical significance. A fray with some Brazilian sailors which ended with mutual back-slapping in a harbour bar. Then at once a long boat journey around the Continent. It grew colder, the sun was like a red mass of iron in a pallid sky, but icy, with white flowers on the window-panes in the mornings, and a wind trying to freeze the hot blood in our veins. All in vain. So our next year began. In fine shifting snow, a sledge harnessed to black horses, white hoar frost on the trees, a stream and the marshes fettered in ice, perpendicular smoke from chimneys visible in the distance, naked branches of plane trees like bronze pipes reaching towards a livid arch of sky, the smell of pines, barking dogs, Ukrainian beetroot soup with noodles on the table, this was Chupryn.'

He stopped and turned his head to the door that was open to the corridor: he listened. No, they weren't steps, no one was walking or coming, it was a monotonous and continuous sound, as though out of the depths of a pot filled with boiling water: the creaking of stairs, tick of clocks, wafting of curtains, the monotonous echoes of chairs rising to and fro on rockers, the grating of shutters and the groan of wooden panels drying out. In the park, nightjars were still singing, but a thrush was already trying its dawn song. A single, extended, long-drawn, ringing note sounded from the foundations of the deserted expanse. His uncle leaned over to Peter to see whether he had fallen asleep, but he was still awake. 'And spring came again,' he at last said quietly, 'then summer, autumn, and winter. You know everything that came later, really. I felt I possessed forever that much-desired tranquillity which happiness brings. I could see our association clearly and without distortions. The woman who had fallen to my lot was mine, while he existed merely in those distant, misty regions from which, if I didn't attempt to penetrate them, nothing threatened me. He was nothing. She told me so once, as far as I remember it was towards the end of the following summer. He often went away, he gave lessons in neighbouring manors, conducted a parish choir in the little town, and, all in all, wasn't much at home except in late autumn and winter. She didn't say so directly, but I knew she was thinking it: "You see what he's like . . .? Yet not so long ago you wanted to change everything. It wouldn't have been a good thing, it would have destroyed us. We don't ask too much of each other, and that's what is so good." We were lying side by side: one of those rainy, chilly nights in the second half of September. Her bright golden skin, despite its delicate chill, radiated warmth. She put her hands under her head to listen to the rain spattering noisily against the windows, and to the wind that was muttering confusedly in the chimney no one knew to whom, or why. She looked at the ceiling. Sprawling with a sort of innocent freedom on the bed, motionless, she was perfectly beautiful in her nakedness and as perfect as classical marble statues seen in solitude by the gleam of night. It occurred to me that everything that was going on between us would never weaken, it was rising within us like a storm full of opposing forces, and then it would die down, with the mildness of a child falling asleep, it enabled us to feel aware of ourselves in the most penetrating and total way, and then to be lost in an association which simultaneously thrust us from each other and hurled us together—it was of the purest golden ore which people search longingly for all their lives but rarely find, only to die in the end unsatisfied and in mortal weariness. It meant nothing that I wasn't the only one who had her experienced and yet at the same time virginally inexperienced body, resisting and yielding, a body awakening frantic and yet at the same time tranquillizing madness, and that after all he still existed, he who possessed her in consequence of all those various bonds which laws, customs, religions, beliefs, our own habits, incomprehensible complexes and repressions, pity, laziness, fear of change and the unknown lay upon people. None of this had the slightest meaning for me, nor did whatever he did with her those nights when I was alone. Even the fact that autumn was at hand, and he wouldn't be going away so often and perhaps for weeks at a time, even months, he wouldn't leave this house and she wouldn't be able to come to me so easily: that once again we'd have to play hide-and-seek for whole days, to lie or remain silent, and I'd admire her instinctive, almost animal skill at surrendering herself at the least expected moments and places, and I would be tremendously grateful to her for it. I only felt that I was very much in love with her, and it was that sweet purity of life, one and unchanging. That was good. Never before had I thought of what I'd do with a woman or girl as being a good or bad thing. I never considered for long the good or bad aspects of associations with women. I thought of them simply as of something which happened, which I could afford, but if I couldn't afford it, I never thought of it at all. But then for the first time I realized it was good. But it had to end, Peter. If I'd known I wouldn't have come back, I wouldn't have brought her to a country where someone had long been awaiting her with desire in his eyes and a knife in his hand. In this country, that is the way everything ends and is extinguished. Here the past no longer interweaves with the present. At some time the future will begin to build its own world completely anew, though not for us. Don't take what you see around you seriously; it's only the malice of fate prolonging our agony. It confuses and horrifies us. The setting sun will no longer warm this house, nor will midnight cover it with a gentle mist, day and night have become the same, but the years aren't passing, for they have already passed. Soon we shall all die and wander here only as some vague memories in the cold blood of darkness, until our house falls into ruins, is overgrown with grass and weeds, and time will patiently level this collective tomb with its equally mortal surroundings. This is the absurd last act of our proud history as the masters of this land. The days are passing now faster than snowflakes in a storm. Somewhere on their border only a long winter is waiting. And that, you see, is why I wander in these sleepless nights through these rooms devoid of life, so as to catch for the last time perhaps the echo of the fleet and feminine steps of her who once walked here: loneliness, like temperature in a fever, intensifies at night. You needn't have come back, Peter. Don't try to make a life for yourself in this house. Light is necessary for that. But it has gone out within these walls, burying everything in darkness. Let this be a warning to you. Don't enter, Peter, in our house darkness is death.' But perhaps those were no longer his uncle's words. Some shadow merely resembling him was whispering to him in the gloom, maybe death?

Peter was lost in his thoughts, his head rang. For if he were to believe his nursemaids and old country-women, death rarely appears in its own shape. Sometimes it takes upon itself the body of someone near and dear. So this certainly was death, if everything Peter had heard wasn't a lie. Yes, the world was frail and impermanent, something is always being destroyed then recreating itself. The green of summer is turned grey by winter, the white flowers of hoar frost are melted by spring. Cares and unfulfilled expectations soon blight the freshness of a mother's face, one can see today in the childish outline of a sister those sad resemblances to all the old women in family portraits. Could it be that nothing of what Peter loved could be saved? What would happen to Catherine?

His uncle one day had found Madame Irène dead among the ruins of the orangery. She was white and distant, as if she had taken refuge in sleep from violence and her own terror. The myrtles and spruces had given their scent later as she lay on a catafalque, calm and safe in sleep which no one could disturb. His uncle's head sank and Peter noticed that his lips were moving soundlessly, his eyeballs sinking into the depths of their orbits, reddened, in limitless fatigue. Catherine emerged from the mists of memory and said in her insistent, silver-sounding voice: 'You'll become an animal to this Ukrainian bandit, Peter, which he'll hunt down as he hunted Madame Irène and me.' Soon, amidst the emptiness of the room, perhaps as a result of what she had said, the eyes of Semeon Gavryluk gleamed like phosphorescence. Peter thought that sentence on him ought to be carried out by himself, without the help of Paul or Nick. He tried to rid himself of that weight on his legs which was holding him to bed, so that he could get close to him ('How often have I told you you're not going to Chupryn? That's not the place for you, among your father's crazy family.' 'Don't say that, Mama, it's only for one summer. A perfect holiday, Mama.' 'Stop joking. When you smile like that, it's as if your father were smiling. I can't bear it!'), but the burden was as heavy as though someone had sat down on his shins, although no, there was no one there, his uncle had gone too, surely only just now, for the door was still moving, as if pushed by an arm ('I can't understand why you dislike them so much, Mama.' 'You'll find out for yourself one day.' 'Are they to blame because you didn't love my father?' 'Don't try to pass sentence in matters you don't know anything about. He was a bad man. They're the same, and you don't belong to them.' 'I do, Mama!'), finally however he succeeded, he crept out of bed, and when he stopped, facing Gavryluk, all his powers suddenly came back to him, he gave him a blow, the greenish glow of those eyes glittered once, then died out forever: so it's as easy as that?

Then there he was back again in bed, the bed was old

Cherkvas's boat, the floor was a stream rising with the spring tide, Nick and Julia the Second sat at the oars. The water was bearing them in the direction of the mill in the forest. Here's the path and the mill. The mass of the toothed wheel was revolving, flip-flap, flip, flap, and this monotonous sound again rose as a painful echo inside his temples. It had been like this once before. Again the ball was rolling off the path and falling into the pond. Who would fish it out? But Gavryluk was standing there ready, leaning against the handrail of the bridge, although a moment ago there hadn't been anyone in the vicinity. 'Who're you?' he asked. 'Cherestvienski,' said Peter. 'Who?' the question sounded like the echo of a question uttered God knows how many years ago, and locked into ice, and now unfrozen, like the word in Baron Munchausen's tale. 'Who?' And Gavryluk made a violent gesture as if he wanted to hit him, Peter. But the image faded, now the wood's edge. They were sitting in a clearing in pine woods overlooking a steppe landscape. Madame Irène was kneeling on a tree stump and gathering mushrooms. She threw away the worm-eaten ones, put the good ones in her basket. 'One has to be careful with mushrooms, children, the grubs go from a worm-eaten one to the good ones if they're left.' Monsieur Philip, her husband, was coming along a path, as merry as a young cockerel. 'I've seen a ghost,' said Peter to Monsieur Philip. 'Ha ha ha,' Madame Irène's husband laughed tolerantly, 'such a big boy and he still believes in ghosts. There aren't any ghosts in the world,' but he was gazing with the eyes of a disillusioned man. Or perhaps he himself was deluding others? Who could tell? Snow covered the footsteps on the meadow. The road disappeared into a white haze. Julia the Second had gone that way, seeking humiliation in the little town. He tried to shout: 'Don't go there, don't go, you fool,' and Catherine's old nurse Parashka (how had she got here? Since Catherine's unfortunate marriage to Alexei, she'd been living with her at Gleb), mumbled curses in her toothless gums as she whispered into his ear: 'Oh, your clan is bad, bad. Even God can't count how many injustices you've done to people. And now the young lady will pay with that bright head of hers.' But now, in some spiral vortex of the earth, he began falling into an expanding depth, down, down, and he could taste rusty iron in his mouth. His uncle Theodore's face emerged out of the spongy mist and said: 'I felt I was very much in love with her, and it was that sweet purity of life, one and unchanging. But now the light has gone out in our house and everything is being plunged into darkness. Don't enter, Peter, darkness is death.' Then, however, instead of his uncle's face, he saw the burning globe of the sun and brightness dazzled him for a moment. He shouted it wasn't true, sweating violently: he awoke.

The room was full of the pink light of early morning, it was empty, the door shut, although something indefinable still wafted through the air, as though someone had just gone out. A stream of birds' chatter poured through the open windows, there was no trace of the nightmares and horrors, evidently daylight didn't favour them, and Peter, shaking off the last vestiges of his nocturnal ramblings, sat up in bed. He looked around, slowly coming to himself. His breakfast on a tray stood on a small table nearby. Milk in a little jug had formed a skin, but when he touched the porcelain it scalded his fingers. And so Julia the Second has been here, he thought, and all that was only a dream. But no, his memory, like a sensitive photographic negative plunged into a chemical mixture, repeated like lightning a few images and he thought that after all . . . after all, it hadn't been merely a dream. He thrust away this thought quickly and jumped out of bed and then, rejecting even the recollection of her, he plunged his head into a basin of cold water. He sobered up completely.

When, after a bath and breakfast, he walked down the corridor an hour later, the house was still in its morning repose. Without thinking, he stopped at the door of Catherine's room: he had just been playing with the idea of a stroll, but now, surprised at himself, he stood with one hand outstretched to the latch (the door wasn't shut, through the crack came the sound of quiet footsteps within), and unable to understand why he was doing this, but unable to resist, he tapped. 'Come in,' he heard Catherine's voice, as if she had guessed it was he and no one else, and at once, 'Stand by the window, be good enough to turn your back. I'm not dressed yet.' He did as she ordered and everything at once revived within him: the previous evening, his nocturnal dreams, his talk that night with his uncle, the dreams again, but only for a moment, for he made a great effort to rid himself of it all, even though only for a moment: he succeeded with unexpected ease, and plunging into that tranquil, scented intricacy of this room, in which he could hear the sounds of her breathing mingled with the rustle of silk, and the light touch of bare feet on the floor, he suddenly felt like a man who very recently, yesterday or the day before or hardly a moment ago, had had something to attend to, many indescribably important things which he'd now put aside until later (it happened outside his own volition, that's true, the things were further away, they were making themselves felt beneath a misty interior veiled with fever and dreams inside his skull, which the night had left him, but they'd retreated into its depths and it was enough for him to know he wouldn't forget them for them not to be intrusive and stop requiring immediate solution), so that later, thinking, later, later, the proper moment hadn't come yet, though it soon would, but now there was no need to summon them up from behind that veil, let the day which was beginning calmly pass in the same way, this was certainly a reaction against all the struggling of yesterday, let Catherine say nothing of the sort, no, she said nothing, the rustle of her silk underwear stopped behind his back, and he heard the electric crackling of her hair being brushed. He felt that prolonged sound fall with a brief shiver into his interior. In order to say something, he hastily said: 'It's Sunday, have you any plans?' 'So it is,' she said, 'Sunday, I think we ought to go to church. The late Mass will do. And you?' 'I haven't decided yet,' he said this rather drily, and involuntarily: 'Won't Paul join us after Mass?' but, as though she saw his question was only too justified, 'I don't think so,' she said, 'if he goes to church with his mother, it'll be much earlier. Now, too, he has a lot of farm work, even on Sundays,' and then she fell silent, and now he heard only that regular movement of the brush in her hair, which he felt as though someone were stroking his skin, and without turning he stretched out his hand, pulled up one of the soft old chairs standing by the wall, and sat down; the springs creaked as though in delicious pain, and Catherine stood behind him, stretching her arm to the window sill for a box of cigarettes, she lit one and puffed out the smoke; it was like a sigh, it breathed on him along with her perfume.

From the first moment, as soon as he'd come into the room, or perhaps even earlier, when he'd involuntarily stopped at the door, a thought concerning himself and her had revolved inside his head, a thought which he still feared to define and which even yesterday, when he'd been observing Catherine at table, had given him no peace, but yesterday he'd thrust it away not only with fear but also with dislike, feeling what it threatened him with, but now he only feared making it more precise (this change had occurred almost unperceived; perhaps it was a result of the memory of that evening incident in the park which lingered so mistily in his memory, so that he wasn't at all sure whether it came from a dream or had really happened to him), and he was stunned by this thought, taken aback and even a bit unnerved, like a man who has for long been carrying something heavy in his pocket and never puts his hand in to find out what it is, then suddenly learns he's been carrying a million, since slowly, very slowly, the thought grew more precise and took on a completely objective form in his head, as though he were observing the state of quite another person: I'm in love.

But she went on brushing her hair, and it murmured electrically, somnolently, and sweetly; it really was as if someone were gently stroking his skin. The whole room was perfumed by her, her breath pulsated in the depths of that warm scent almost inaudibly yet clearly, and he had the impression of shifting away into unreality along with this scent, the sounds, the whole room, into distant parts, where no intruder could penetrate; he wanted to keep this moment to himself forever, he very nearly succeeded, but then he heard her voice, although in fact he'd been hearing it for some time already, for all the time her voice had been echoing through that floating layer of scents and sounds, obviously she was speaking without expecting any answers; suddenly, however, the tone of her voice deepened, and the phrase she uttered was suspended, he understood she was questioning him, he replied after realizing that it was so, he tried several times but fortunately to no purpose; she laughed gaily. He said: 'You know how it is, one must try everything at least once. And once my mother caught me, and made a terrible scene. She didn't really catch me, but smelled the smoke. Do you smoke a lot? I don't remember you ever trying before the war.' 'No, for a year or maybe eighteen months. But one can hardly call it smoking,' she replied carelessly, 'well, you may turn around now,' he did so, she smoothed the material over her hips with swift gestures, put on her shoes, then straightened herself.

I didn't know she'd do it like that, he thought involuntarily, not at all realizing what he was concerned with; whether it was the way she straightened herself with a gentle flexibility, or the way she put her shoes on, he was to remember it very well and later on he often recalled that he even repeated that thought: I didn't know she'd do it like that, this was exactly what he slowly repeated with a sort of brooding, like a man startled, feeling simultaneously that the blood was ebbing from his face, and his tongue turning into ashes in his mouth, for he didn't understand and never would what it was in her that so startled him at that moment; it's true that certain situations strike into our memories for no good reason, for example the position of a leaning body, its weight resting on one foot while the other leg is slightly bent at the knee, those delicate, soft lines of a triangle emphasizing the perfect equilibrium when one might expect the body to totter, or some gesture of a hand cutting the air and grasping at emptiness, as if caught, something of that kind, in any case he saw nothing like this in Catherine's attitude at that moment, no detail he might have caught and said: 'How strange that is. How does she do it?' perhaps only that statue-like equilibrium of her body was enthralling, but he clearly felt through his surprise that strange dryness in his throat and the blood ebbing from his face, and then she said in a voice slightly lower than usual and rather hoarse: 'Why are you looking at me like that?' and he shivered and said, 'No special reason,' suddenly feeling in himself something like a continuation of that thought which had crystallized in him before and which now surprised him as it had done earlier: he felt he was a man. She said in a different manner: 'That's all right, I just thought . . .' and she broke off, and he quietly repeated: 'No special reason,' 'That's all right, then,' she repeated.

She stood against the background of the cool, shadowed white wall, in her pale blue, fresh linen dress, with her long olive-tinted slender arms hanging against the pale blue material, and was looking at him openly and with curiosity. 'You seem tremendously interesting, young man,' she said, as if she had only just noticed him for the first time, and now the outer corners of her eyes quivered with a smile, 'You look as though you were wandering goodness knows where all night. What's happening to you?' 'I don't understand,' for indeed he didn't. 'Look in the glass,' so he looked, he had a livid, unhealthy face, eyes deeply sunken. 'It'll pass,' he muttered; she at once grew more serious. Now it was clear that she too had decided to forget something: the previous day, the previous evening, and although he only wanted to forget what had had its epilogue in the shock caused by Nicholas's narrative, no, not even forget it, but merely postpone it until later, when the decision as to what he should do about Gavryluk would ripen in him of its own accord, yet she had evidently decided to forget everything (if, indeed, what he'd been thinking of when she grew more serious and what she was certainly thinking of when incautiously that 'What's happening to you?' had burst from her was real and not only a dream: he must have had this question on his face, for she looked away) and she abruptly asked: 'Well, then, shall we go?' and without waiting for an answer, said: 'I must be crazy to have stayed here. My mother-in-law will grumble for a week. I've left the entire house to her. But I couldn't deny myself these few days and Sunday. It must be three years since we met, isn't it? The last time was in September, wasn't it? No, there was one time later. Early in October. You were splendid then. Remember how we crossed the San bridge in those awful disguises we wore? The Soviets were on the east bank, they inspected our faces and hands. From time to time, they fished someone out of the marching column—because his hands were too fine he was packed off to Siberia. And the Germans were waiting on the west side. Their stony faces above field-grey uniforms, the great unknown. You took me and Grandmother across the bridge, then you went back to the east side again,' and he: 'Why are you talking about all that? Must you speak of it now?'

They went down to the main hall without meeting anyone. The passage beyond the spiral staircase was open to the park on the opposite side of the house, full of warm breezes from outside, and on the terrace Grandfather's dogs were lying in the sun; without stirring from their places they lazily wagged their tails in greeting. 'Don't you like memories?' Catherine asked after a moment, as though reluctantly, blinking and turning her face towards the sun, but she stopped still when he feebly replied: 'No, not now.' He could feel that already familiar twitch in his throat. 'Everything here is memories. Each is associated with some atrocity. Whatever one touches,' he said painfully. 'Yes,' she said, 'whatever one touches,' and then he burst out laughing bitterly, while she looked at him with cool attention. She turned back to the door, pulled the bell rope, and then they sat down at a small table near the balustrade around the marble floor of the terrace. The fountain in the centre of the flower bed threw widely scattered streams of water upwards in feathery drops, and their delicate dust, silvering in the light, rose into the air like little clouds: they breathed deeply. 'It seemed to me to be the other way round,' said Peter, 'from the start I noticed that not a word is mentioned here about the war or about everything that's happening now. It was as if I'd come to some island isolated from the world. I was mistaken,' but she replied: 'What do you expect? We live with it every day so there's no need to say much. Everything is known. And you thought that "the steppe winds will rock, the wild echoes blow, and the limitless distance lull with its silent melancholy," ' she quoted ironically, 'the plain fact is that you haven't lived here three long years, so it's all come upon you at once. I know it's hard to bear. I suppose you are all having an idyllic life over there, aren't you?' and he: 'You don't understand at all. I'd like to have at least one day. One day, d'you see? One day as they used to be. Yesterday a great many things happened which you don't know of, and there would be no point in my telling you about them. I thought I wouldn't rid myself of this until I did something that a man in my position ought to do. But this morning I woke up free from nightmares. Of course I felt that this was a brief, borrowed freedom, perhaps only for one day. But I'd like to live that one day as before. I don't know if you understand . . . So that it . . . How should I know? Good . . . As ordinary as possible. In a word—good. Before all that starts again and I have to live with it, as the rest of you do,' and she quietly echoed, without looking at him: 'Good. Ah, I understand you, Peter,' and she put one hand on his arm, leaving it there for a moment. 'You've no idea how I long for that sometimes,' she then said, 'for it to be good even for a day. As though nothing that has happened had happened. For me to be . . . as I was years ago,' and, as though ashamed of her confession, she turned away her face; he followed it with his gaze, she was staring without seeing, although her eyes were wide open.

Fiodorchuk came on to the terrace, to ask what they wanted. Catherine asked for something cold to drink, and they waited in silence for him to come back and place a dish of chilled stewed fruit on the table. 'I'll serve it,' she said to Fiodorchuk. The air was growing hot and terribly white. Peter furtively wiped the damp from his forehead, and thought of bathing in the stream, but he at once remembered that Catherine had appointed him her companion to church. The dogs Hook and Pook got up, stretched till their legs quivered, then moved off towards the steps. A moment later he saw them, noses to the ground, wandering in the direction of the pheasantry; obviously Grandfather was walking somewhere near there. Glancing at Catherine he noticed her face was dry, without a drop of sweat; they kept silent. Later, the gravel gritted on the path by the wall of the house, and Peter leaned over the balustrade to see Julia the Second with her hair loose about her shoulders, like a theatrical Ophelia, gazing ahead with a rather confused, unseeing look and singing in an undertone: 'I lost my corals, red, cherry-red . . .' and then Catherine put her hand on his wrist, her cool dry fingers pressed, and when he didn't understand, she pressed still more tightly: she pulled him back delicately but firmly, 'Let this day be really good, as in the past,' she said quietly, 'don't look at her,' and she kept hold of his hand until Julia the Second had passed the bottom of the terrace and disappeared somewhere around the corner of the house. For a certain time he could still feel the touch of her fingers, and how they warmed him, until she finally said: 'We might go now.'

Thus that wonderful Sunday morning passed in silence, in meditation, in the air full of something mild and soporific, although perhaps it only seemed mildly soporific: it was what they needed it to be, as they wished it to be, it was good, and all the time they were stylized in their attitudes, very nearly inappropriately for two contemporaries linked in unbreakable friendship, so that when Peter looked at Catherine he had the impression that the air was drawing all the natural details of her form into itself, was changing her outline: the woman he could see wasn't the real Catherine, but someone his own imagination had created, and perhaps she too sensed him in the same way. But it was good. He'd understood this when she put her hand on his wrist and tightened her fingers, not letting him look at Julia the Second, because Julia the Second recalled 'that,' then, when they were sitting on the terrace, not speaking and not even looking at one another, not even hearing the quiet rustling of the vine leaves hanging in garlands on the wall, hearing, as it were, only their own thoughts. They didn't hear the rustling until later, or rather, he heard it: a quiet, soft, damp rustling, and he caught a bitter-almond scent, yes, only much later, when he'd gone upstairs to his room after lunch and was lying down on the made-up bed did he wonder in despair whether it had been good for them simply because it had been good, or was it perhaps only because once, long ago, when they'd still been children it had been good for them? Perhaps their tranquil morning joy was only like the false light of the moon which, not having any light of its own, shines with a gleam reflected from very far away? But when the morning was passing he hadn't thought of this for a moment, nor even when it finally passed.

Then noon came and he rode with Catherine along the highway towards Nikorycha in the dry, suffocating heat. They were sitting side by side in the cramped little carriage, old Cherkvas on the box was flicking the horses' rumps with his whip and Catherine smiled at him, Peter, with that girlish smile of hers, a smile that seemed totally innocent of everything, across the vast impassable distance between her arms and his. But even then it was still good for them. And then Nikorycha greeted them with its colourful crowd after service at the church, and several carts were moving along the street down which a few groups of Catholics were walking slowly to the Benedictine monastery. And so the second part of the day started: in the cobblestoned yard in front of the gate, with the sudden, shadowy, stifling coolness that was imprisoned as if in a well between the high walls, as Peter got out of the carriage first, he took Catherine's elbow to help her down, and she, after being suspended for a moment in his arms, turned unnaturally pale, and then he asked: 'What is it?' She said: 'Nothing, it's hot,' and with awkward, stiff steps she crossed the yard, preceding him a little, as though in a hurry, and went into the church.

Mass had already started, and Catherine was sitting on a bench, frozen into immobility and very straight. She was already sitting there, it seemed to him, before he had passed through the dark porch and managed to make his way between the people kneeling by the choir, so that when he finally found himself in the aisle he had to look around for a moment before finding her, motionless and erect, her eyes motionless too, somehow too bright, but unnaturally clear in that artificial half-shade of the pillars supporting the Renaissance vaulting, but she wasn't praying, that was the first thought which Peter managed to grasp as he sat down and looked at Catherine, the first thought to distinguish itself by its comparatively logical structure from the fragments of thoughts which, as he recalled, had begun to surge in his skull at the moment when he had helped his companion out of the carriage and she had turned unnaturally pale and replied: 'Nothing, it's hot,' and then she had gone with that surprisingly stiff, unnatural step across the yard and into the depths of the church, though now, however, she was already sitting there as if in a trance, not praying and surely not thinking of anything either, so he thought, when this first comparatively logical thought emerged from the fragments of those other thoughts, and at once he touched her arm and whispered: 'Did something happen to you? Do you feel faint?' but he got no answer, she hadn't heard. But all the same something had happened, he didn't dare give it a name even in his thoughts: it had happened in that fraction of a second between old Cherkvas's last flick of the whip as he sat on the box, the creak of the wheels coming to a halt on the stone pavement of the yard and Peter stretching out his hands towards Catherine, as he'd taken her by the elbow to help her get down, in that sudden, stifling, stagnant chill which oozed into the scorching July heat out of the old, lichenous and mossy walls, and Peter understood this at once, for it had happened not only in Catherine but in him too.

The sun, shining through the stained-glass windows into the church interior, burned the back of his neck and he felt it through his jacket. Then it seemed to have moved away (a good deal of time must have passed since they had sat down on the bench) and was staring into his face. It was unnaturally bright, it blinded and stupefied him. People were singing something and through their voices and the stifling incense he kept hearing, as from a great distance, the tinkling bells of the choir boys serving Mass at the high altar. The brilliance of the light falling from above in biting rays confused his thoughts again, and again they were merely fragments, brief and dissolving in his stupefaction, fleeing before the next ones, but he knew one thing for certain: they concerned Catherine. He could not tear his gaze from her (now she was kneeling, her head slightly bowed, her arms somehow imploringly bent at the elbows, hands before her face: he didn't remember noticing that as she knelt down this position tautened the material of her dress and unintentionally changed her figure, accentuating it and as it were betraying her body) and suddenly he thought, or perhaps it seemed to him he was thinking, that she was a woman, yet surely not, surely he didn't think that at all, for if that was what he was thinking, it was meaningless in itself, he might have thought it sooner or later, and he'd even thought it many times before when he'd been a boy still, years ago, and it used to sadden him, the thought that once they'd been equals, while later she'd become a woman while he had continued to remain a boy; now, however, he felt no sorrow at all, only that light exploding his brain, the light which in fact was glaring straight into his eyes, but it was as though the light had penetrated into the very centre of his skull and was distending it from within, so that it couldn't be the thought, at least not in the logical sense of that concept, maybe it was only the reflection of a thought, anyhow, whatever it was, it meant nothing, for afterwards, although he didn't move his eyes from Catherine for a moment, he began to be completely immersed in those stifling perfumes of incense, of the monotonous singing of the congregation, like a long-drawn-out groan, into the hot light which smelled of dust, and although he was still sitting on the bench, he felt he was plunging deeper and deeper into all of it: and his thoughts, which a moment ago had been able to react to certain impulses from outside, now became entirely deadened, and as though turned to stone. And it wasn't as it had been before noon, it wasn't good, not a trace remained of that mood, there was no knowing what it was at all, since he couldn't even think of his own state of mind.

Then they went back to Chupryn in a tunnel of transparent, vibrating heat, or rather on the edge of it all the time, pursued by a grey spiral of dust rising in clouds from beneath the wheels, and the horses pulled ahead as though with the deliberate purpose of pulling the carriage out of it and into that clear tunnel of air which stretched to the horizon, in vain of course, and they talked about this and that, they even talked a great deal, although he didn't remember what, the conversation had no significance, it didn't betray anything of what they were both thinking, nor did their faces; in any case, on their way out of the church, Peter had already noticed this stiffening, this sort of contraction of the muscles of his face, which had been happening to him more and more of late (a mask that helped him conceal his feelings, but sometimes he just didn't feel anything at all), then there was lunch and more conversation of some kind, a great deal of it, for both his uncle and his grandfather said something to him, while Catherine exchanged culinary notes with his grandmother, and Peter didn't recollect these conversations either, didn't even try to, although he certainly took a lively and apparently natural part in them, and later Catherine went with Demoiselle to sun-bathe by the stream, while he went to his room upstairs and lay fully dressed on the bed and avoided thinking of the few hours separating him from the morning as if they'd never been, for he knew he'd have to go back to them willy-nilly, since they existed, after all, and meant something, he even had a premonition of what they meant—he thought about the morning and the whole afternoon; why had it been good for them then, and at first he couldn't find the answer, but then he understood that it was only because they had briefly forgotten what they'd both become over the years and because they'd been able to be as they'd once been, and as he thought this over he managed for a second to float away into his distant, happy, and carefree childhood, presided over by his mother's laughter as she sat in the drawing-room full of friends who came calling on foot or in carriages from the neighbourhood, of ladies' men who flourished on Sundays, idlers of the Polish Kingdom, lancers in retirement who had never lost anything, sensitive plants willingly dancing attendance upon her, attracted no doubt by just that silken laugh which he too heard, breaking off so unexpectedly low that when he heard it his throat dried up, and he also saw Catherine there with his mother, still with mousy comical braids hanging down beside her face, yet already she was able to arouse embarrassment in him and an incomprehensible desire to protect her from them all, so that she should stay with him alone; but he immediately left this image behind, and her too, and jumped a year or maybe two in his thoughts to summon up the image of K., with Catherine no longer there but only his mother and her laughter which caught him by the throat; at once, however, realizing with amazement that now he couldn't think of her as he wanted to, he thought (so as not to return to reality but to remain in K. for a while longer) about various different things which were associated with that period of his life but which had little connection with the state he was in at present, for example about the streets in K., cool, full of shadows, crowded on a Sunday afternoon by rather haughty girls strolling idly along who, in order to overcome their shyness, behaved defiantly, whom the boys followed in twos and threes, casting importuning, mocking comments in their direction which the girls echoed with shrill laughter, and then they'd be walking along together, holding hands, in the evening they'd disappear into the wood beyond the lake: he thought about the lake on which he had floated on a raft made by himself with rushes, and about the beach burned to whiteness where in the sun, within the reach of an outstretched hand but painfully unattainable, the golden bodies of women lay on the sand, and they got up satiated with the heat, sleepy, put on their parrot and peacock-coloured dresses that were hanging not far away on the bushes, and rode on their bicycles along the road to the little town: about some bicycle trip or other down a country road amidst hawthorn and wild pears growing by the ditches, and when they came to the moor how the wind had snatched at the girls' dresses for a moment, sculpturing them delicate and graceful with its breath, while the round apples of their knees twinkled faster and faster, and suddenly Peter felt a tumult in his head and his mouth constricted, still full of that wind caught as it rushed, and he jumped off the bed, rubbed his eyes, still feeling the tumult in his head, not yielding at all when he got up, and thinking: What the devil's coming over me? He went to the washstand, reached for the jug, poured water into the basin, plunged his head into it up to the neck (no, it was warmish, it didn't help) and he thought: It's nothing, it'll pass.

Then in the afternoon, or rather towards evening, for the heat managed to decrease a little, perhaps it was already after supper or if not then surely it was just before, because he hadn't wanted to eat with the others or to see Catherine talking to his grandmother, grandfather, uncle, or Demoiselle (who no doubt imagined that it was only for their sake that she had stayed at Chupryn), never mind whether it was before or after supper, no doubt it was towards evening, for the sun was sinking and soon disappeared altogether and gleamed with a pale glow rising from beyond the horizon; he went into the English garden and wandered aimlessly around the lake until under the influence of some powerful drive he returned towards the house and, finding himself near the old orangery, plunged into the thicket growing around its ruins (ivy and convolvulus had interwoven closely over the iron skeleton, making it something like a summer-house: there were still mushroom-shaped benches and the table with a marble top, now overgrown with moss), and he sat down in a corner where a pedestal with the remains of a plaster copy of some ancient Greek figure still stood, without, or so it seemed to him, any special idea in his mind, even without what he might later have called a premonition, but simply under the influence of a sudden and powerful impulse, he sat down in the shade that had been steadily increasing for quite a long time, not waiting for anything or anyone, and he was genuinely startled when, after a while, he heard steps on the gravel inside, thinking at once it must be his uncle, and then he heard the rustle of branches cautiously drawn aside quite close to him, and caught sight of Catherine, dressed in dark colours or perhaps black, so that at first sight he couldn't distinguish her from the sombre background of the knotted vegetation; later on, however, he perceived her moving like dusk in the dusk, and he was no longer startled, for it seemed to him he'd known she would come here, but he said nothing, nor did he betray by the slightest sign that he was so close, but sat on in his corner on the base of the pedestal, quietly, though not deliberately hiding from her, and finally, when so much time had passed that it was too late for him to reveal his presence, embarrassed even to be watching her and wondering what she would think of him if she discovered him, he was surprised by the feeling which he had originally experienced in front of the monastery, and which had increased when they were sitting side by side in the pew, this feeling now died away, went out completely, perhaps even before she came, for now he felt completely cool, and he was surprised that this coolness was continuing, deepening inside himself, and he felt some undefined fear when he looked from his concealment at the woman sitting on the stone seat plunged in dusk, and thus in silence, leaning on the tabletop, she was thinking about something, but what surely was worst was that he could not in any way justify this new feeling; and perhaps he shivered or was numb and moved, wanting to change the position of his body, for a fragment of plaster he'd dislodged fell from a step to the floor and Catherine jumped up from the bench with a cry. He quietly said: 'It's I, Peter.'

She didn't reply at once, didn't reveal in any way that she had heard, though obviously she had, for, as though calmed by his words, she sat down again, leaning her arm on the table, and Peter caught in himself the desire to flee, but at once forgot it: he didn't know what Catherine was thinking, nor what she was waiting for, if indeed she were waiting at all, nor why she said nothing, and that was the worst of it, that intensified the still undefined fear (of what? of whom?) which had dominated him earlier and now shook him like a fever, and suddenly he wanted to put an end to it. He went towards her, conquering the weakness which was flowing through his body, afraid that if he prolonged the moment during which the distance from the spot where he was to the spot where she was sitting was marked, this weakness would overcome him entirely and, with his head full of vague suppositions which he didn't want and even feared to define more clearly, he finally stopped behind her (the stooping outline of her back was barely apparent in the gloom) and he cautiously put one hand on her arm, saying in a whisper: 'Don't be afraid, it's I,' startled that it was a whisper, for after all he didn't have to hide from anyone, and besides there was no one else in the vicinity, again in a whisper he asked: 'What's the matter? Are you crying?' for he felt her arm tremble under his hand as if something like a sob were welling up within her, and then at once that incomprehensible feeling of ill-defined fear disappeared somewhere without a trace, she rose violently from the seat and, turning her face to him (all in one movement: raising her body to a vertical position and the turn, with a movement too quick for the eye), but without dislodging his hand from her arm, she stood silent and as if she wanted to look into his eyes through the obscurity, her silence conveyed something of the sort, an amazed incredulity that it was he and no one else who was standing by her, emphasized still more by that shiver which was flowing from her to his hand, so that it was communicated to him too, and in which he sensed a sob suppressed by force, and unable to endure this, nor able to speak, he then reached to her face and fleetingly let his finger tips touch her brow, cheeks, eyelids (they were shut tight, dry), her cheeks again (they were dry too), and her lips, when he touched them, or so it seemed to him, were opening and closing as though she were gasping for air or wanted to say something, but had lost her voice, and they too were parched and burning, and he at once understood that she wasn't crying at all, and he regained his voice, but only said in a stifled whisper: 'I thought something had happened to you. That you were crying,' and she: 'You disappeared somewhere and I've been looking for you all afternoon. But I knew I'd find you,' also in a whisper, as if she didn't want anyone to hear them, while he: 'Yes, I was by the lake,' and she: 'But I thought... Oh, nothing. I was so afraid, foolishly,' and he: 'I didn't think about him at all,' for he at once understood what she had feared, and she: 'I knew I'd find you,' still in that insistent whisper, 'because if I hadn't, I'd have left already. I couldn't have stood this any longer,' with uncompromising certainty in her voice, so that he then, perceiving simultaneously that he still had his hand on her face and that the muscles of her cheeks were working under his finger tips as she whispered, he whispered: 'But it was you who told me not to think about him. For I wanted one day to be good, as in the past,' and she replied: 'Yes, it was I. I'm glad you didn't think.' She raised her hands and took his hand in hers, then without deliberation pressed it flat against her breasts so that he felt how rapidly they were rising and falling, and for the first time too, the entire naked woman, although she was dressed from top to toe, covered up so completely that he couldn't see an inch of her body, yet he felt it, had already felt it, across the rising and falling breathing of her breasts, even then he didn't know what it might signify, and whether, if he finally ever saw it, it would satisfy his knowledge, and Catherine, her reply barely audible, as though it were now insufficient, added firmly: 'Let it be good to the end,' and—obviously already divining this sublime, burning electric shock full of stupefaction which had seized him at the moment when she had whispered the last phrase—in a voice not much louder than a whisper, said: 'Let's go away from here,' just like that, with a passionate and expiring lowering of the voice: 'Let's go away from here,' perhaps even twice, and: 'Do you remember how once we used to go to the stream in the evenings? How the moon shone? How we bathed by the rock cliffs?' as if quite irrelevantly, and leading him towards the drive without letting his hand go from hers, continually in that passionate whisper which stifled everything else, then, in the drive, where he saw her face in the nocturnal after-glow, full of fever, excitement, her eyes gleaming and determined: 'I couldn't have stood this any longer. If I hadn't found you, I'd have left at once,' as if the mortal fear that she might not have found him was now transformed into delighted joy that she nevertheless had: 'Let's go, let's go at once, Peter.'

But when he awoke in the morning Paul was standing over him. Out of those crevices gleaming in the heavy bedrock of sleep, gleaming for a moment to reveal the misshapen fragments of reality surrounding him, for a moment he wrested himself back into the depths of the fluid miasma of dreams and memories which sleep granted him and of all those incidents which sleep confirmed or prolonged into infinity; he shut his eyes again stubbornly and turned back to the wall, so as to fall once again into all that which he wished would endure forever, but the crevices refused to close, they slowly opened wider and wider, and the daylight began washing at their edges, so soon they became finer than the eyelids with which he tried to veil himself. So he woke up for good, and his cousin Paul was standing over him. Perhaps he'd tugged at his arm or had even said something, for he retained a feeling of pressure on his skin, and discovered in himself the impression that he'd previously heard someone's voice coming from outside, and flowing towards him, into that sleepy obfuscation, but when he opened his eyes Paul only asked gruffly: 'Well, then?' then he too said: 'Well then?' without thinking at all, in the same tone of voice as Paul, and he sat up in bed.

They looked at one another as if with a touch of surprise, and as if they weren't prepared for the meeting, although in fact this could only be true of Peter, mindful as he was of the squabble yesterday on the terrace at table, and now startled, while Paul had surely come with some definite aim, Peter thought, as he looked fully awake at his cousin, and he also thought that perhaps he already guessed or even knew, but no, he couldn't know, how could he, no one could have seen anything, although the moon had been shining brightly at the time, and this calmed him, and it also amused him, Heaven knows why; his cousin seemed wretched and pitiful as he stood over him, and he blinked, but Peter couldn't achieve any sympathy for him just then, because if one is rich, then the poor often cause only laughter. But Paul must have sensed this touch of dislike in Peter's look, or perhaps that brief glimmer of laughter had irritated him, for he sat down on the edge of the bed and announced point-blank: 'Gavryluk arranged a massacre of the people at Stochek. I didn't want to tell you point-blank, but still . . .' he paused, for Peter had said 'Fool!' even before he'd thought at all of what Paul had so unceremoniously announced; he was certain this wasn't why he'd come, and it wasn't for this that he'd wakened him, he was hitting back at the contemptuous and unfriendly smile with which he'd greeted him, but he immediately stopped considering this and repeated in his thoughts, involuntarily: Gavryluk, massacre, Stochek, trying to catch the sound of these words and to understand what they meant; finally he uttered them aloud and Paul impetuously said: 'It happened last night. Our partisans had quarters there. It was a good village of ours, well located, no doubt you remember. They shot everyone they captured down to the last man. None of our men managed to get to their help,' and Peter, quietly: 'Why are you telling me this, Paul?' and Paul, startled by the question: 'What do you mean—why? He's your brother, after all.' This phrase sounded too slow in the silence which had fallen, and for a moment evidently Paul didn't think he'd said too much, why should he worry about telling Peter what he knew anyway; then he nervously said: 'Excuse me, I didn't want to upset you—it slipped out. But . . .' 'But what?' Peter asked, still in this quietly watchful tone of voice, and then Paul: 'But you're the only one in the family to count on in case of need. The only man among old people,' and Peter: 'Is that why you came here today?' mockingly and somewhat challenging, 'was that why?' 'Does it matter why? I brought Catherine a letter from abroad, if you must know. An entirely different matter. And then I wanted to discuss Gavryluk. Yes, I wanted to discuss him with you,' said Paul, furious and annoyed perhaps at himself.

Peter looked attentively at his cousin without speaking, and not until he realized that Paul was expecting another question did he ask: 'What do you expect me to do?' and, as he asked it, he heard the tone of voice he was using and suddenly realized the atmosphere which had prevailed between them from the moment he woke and sat up in bed (could it be an echo of the previous day's squabble?) and he again heard all his own questions and answers, distinctly sensing in them that watching and waiting for something which his cousin—so it appeared to him—hadn't yet said, although later he understood that the something had already been there in the phrase, 'He's your brother, after all,' and that from the start Paul had made him in a way responsible for the incidents at Stochek, certainly not on purpose, but he'd done it; however, before he understood this a good few minutes passed, during which Paul tried to explain elaborately that in fact he didn't expect anything of him, and he, Peter, heard with growing distaste and anger that it was nothing really, for what after all could be done to a band of brigands large in number and supported by the German authorities who assured them immunity, and that he'd simply wanted to share the catastrophic news with him, Peter, nothing more, every decent man would help the Polish partisans in any case. 'We do too,' Paul admitted, 'and so do all of your people. Mikolai Fiodorovich supplies them with as much food as possible. For only they are capable of handling the Ukrainian bands,' and then what would have to be done in order to help them still more efficiently, that closer contacts would be useful, particularly with Laudanski's unit (this name was uttered for the first time, although it seemed familiar to Peter), and that he, Peter, since he'd come and if he wanted to stay in Chupryn, might be useful too, all he expected of him was to be useful somehow, it was his duty after all, and then Peter, having grasped that involuntary allusion of his cousin, interrupted: 'On account of Gavryluk? Because he's my brother?' and Paul in confusion: 'Don't talk nonsense. Are you dreaming or what? Because you're a Pole. Isn't that enough?' 'Big words,' said Peter ironically to this, 'you always tended to use big words. But while you're about it, don't forget to mention that he's my family's bastard. But never mind,' and then quite dryly: 'If you need me, I'm at your disposal. However, I must know what I'm to do. For you still haven't gone beyond generalities. It seems to me that even you yourself don't know much. That your contact with the partisans only amounts to supplying them with food,' and again, after a pause for breath: 'As for Gavryluk, that's another matter. It's a matter between him and my family, or rather the reverse. And it certainly won't be solved by the help of Polish partisans. I think I'll be able to handle it myself, sooner or later,' and Paul, staring in surprise: 'What are you talking about, Peter?' and Peter: 'About Gavryluk, obviously.' 'Well yes, but what the devil do you want to do? After all, you can't hunt him down by yourself. Nicholas told me of some such plan of yours. It's foolish.' 'Not as foolish as it may seem. Never mind about anyone else, he'll want to talk to me. I think I can get to him,' said Peter firmly, but Paul: 'Don't be a fool,' and Peter: 'You may call me a fool, but have any of you thought of anything better?' to which Paul, red in the face, replied: 'You're a puppy! I wanted to treat you like a grown man, but I see you're still only a puppy. Your grandfather should be warned to watch you before someone hits you over the head,' and then again, as before, Peter quietly said: 'Go away, Paul. Please go away,' fearing that if his cousin didn't obey something would happen and dissolve forever the memory of their former friendship, but Paul rose without speaking and moved to the door, and although he turned back once, his hand already on the doorknob, and moved his lips as though he wanted to explain something, he merely shrugged and said not a word.

His footsteps in the corridor had died away before Peter cooled off and a silence fell, and then, when he finally calmed down, it was too late to call his cousin back and start the conversation again, without bias. He thought regretfully that this second squabble had been entirely without reason, after all Paul couldn't burden him with the responsibility for Gavryluk, perhaps this hadn't been his intention at all, but he, Peter, had grown unnecessarily excited, and he felt something like dregs of bitterness left over after the conversation, although he tried to evaluate it coolly, and he felt he wouldn't be able to get rid of those bitter dregs before he did . . . oh, nothing! he shrugged, better not think of what he ought to do, especially while Catherine was at Chupryn, let it all be as it had been yesterday, and although later, while he was dressing, he remembered Paul's mentioning some plan he'd made with Nick (he was surprised, surely they'd made no plans, he didn't recall any), he thrust the thought aside as quickly as possible. It came back to him much later, when, after failing to find Catherine, he learned the contents of the letter from abroad her cousin had brought to her, and Nick, as it turned out, had left for Krzysztopol, but even then, when he'd been left alone after Paul's exit, he'd thrust it aside and the dream which he'd had—although he washed, dressed, ate breakfast, moving about all the time—this dream he'd just dreamed enveloped him again and filled him with something unknown and pleasurable. But he had to waken from it.

It happened of course after lunch, for the immutable order of the day in the house at Chupryn didn't permit Mikolai Fiodorovich to come down to the drawing-room on the first floor any sooner. It was already quite hot, so that even strolls in the drive had ceased to be pleasant, and Peter, after meeting his uncle in the valley of the stream immersed in a sleepy, sweet confusion from which he didn't at all want to tear himself away, had returned through the park, looking around for Catherine; but no, there wasn't even a trace of her. His uncle carrying his fishing tackle soon caught up with him halfway, for it was too hot for him too, and he suggested showing him a few old, very interesting (he insisted) letters he'd unearthed while dusting papers in the attic, no doubt the property of the previous owners: Peter agreed to look at them, and they decided to go the library. There Demoiselle Spang joined them, also taking refuge indoors from the sun (her skin was yellow, unhealthy, and she was evidently in a bad temper), and to Peter's remark that a storm was certainly brewing, for this positively Asiatic weather couldn't last long, she replied quite sharply that it had already started, and she told him what Paul had told her about the massacre at Stochek, and that it would be best to go back to K. as quickly as possible, to which Peter replied that he knew, he'd also talked to his cousin, but as for returning, it was out of the question, minimizing her obviously increasing uneasiness—then his uncle asked about Catherine. Peter replied that he himself was wondering: 'I haven't seen her today,' he said quite calmly, with no ulterior thoughts or suspicions, and his uncle: 'I saw Paul in the distance as his horses were crossing the bridge. It seemed to me that a woman was sitting beside him,' and Peter: 'What? That's impossible. She came for several days!' and he quickened his step indignantly, to which his uncle said: 'No doubt I was only seeing things. But I thought that Catherine couldn't drive between Gleb and Chupryn as the fancy took her, or take solitary trips to town. Indeed it's nonsense.' 'Of course,' Peter seized on his words at once but without slowing down, so that his uncle and Demoiselle could hardly keep up with him. And then they saw his grandfather in the open window of the drawing-room; seeing them approach, he waved. They went into the house by the small gallery and from there direct to him. Still none of them had guessed anything, and they were talking as they walked, but when they were in the drawing-room and looked at him, they froze and there fell a moment of silence, brought about by the anguish on his grandfather's face; perhaps Mikolai Fiodorovich was still wondering how to tell them what he had to tell, and what he later said without unnecessary comments. Two or three hours must have passed since he'd known (probably at the time when he, Peter, had been quarrelling with his cousin), and he'd managed to prepare himself for the attitude he was to adopt, so Peter at once thought, as they'd plunged into that compact, thick silence, and he realized (or it seemed to him he did), in one flash of awareness he realized, or rather had a premonition why his grandfather had summoned them.

First Mikolai Fiodorovich motioned them to sit down (although this movement might also have been meaningless), with one of those indifferent, commanding gestures of his in which a sharper observer than Peter might have guessed blind helplessness, but they didn't sit down; and very likely he at once asked whether they wouldn't like something to drink, but Peter waited only a moment, until he'd said this, and he also had a premonition of what he would say, quite definitely what, and how he'd adapt himself to it and he surely felt right away, as soon as his grandfather had leaned out of the window and summoned them when he saw them approaching the house, certainly already at the moment when they'd entered the quiet of the drawing-room; and he twice had to ask his questions or whatever they were, some phrases or other, commonplace and introductory, to the conversation—whether they'd like something to drink—before Peter heard, upon hearing, however, he didn't understand anyway, for he turned aside and saw Demoiselle and his uncle looking, not at his grandfather, but at him and for a moment he held their gaze, trying to catch whether something was going to appear in their eyes which would help him to conclude whether they'd known in advance, or were only masking themselves from him, or whether they'd only now guessed that Mikolai Fiodorovich had summoned them all together, but no, it wasn't possible to read anything in their eyes; and he felt it all beginning again, as he had experienced it two days earlier, when first his throat had contracted as though an iron band had been clamped around his neck, and then the entire contents of his stomach had risen into his throat and for a second or two there had been no breath in his lungs, but he suddenly thought that, come what might, he wouldn't push it away, he'd long since stopped being a child (although only a few days earlier he'd known nothing about it) and had become a man, and he felt pride expanding in him like the wave of a violent explosion, and he at once met his grandfather's gaze, in whose eyes was reflected, Heaven knows why, an expression of dismay and bitter disappointment, and his grandfather, now sitting in a chair, said: 'Catherine has gone home. She had a letter from the Red Cross. It contained news of her husband,' and at once he felt again that wave of violent and unrestrained pride which he knew as the taste of his manhood, for it disposed of the pincers catching his neck, and he was able to look straight and openly into his grandfather's eyes as he awaited his words, which, as it seemed to him, were condemning him, and the wave collapsed, just as suddenly as it had previously risen.

He stood motionless in the centre of the drawing-room, thinking with a sort of relief: So it wasn't what I feared that concerned him, he doesn't know anything, nor does my uncle, nor Demoiselle, he also thought or rather simply repeated his grandfather's words in his mind, mechanically and without engaging his feelings: '... It contained news of her husband ...' and before that fragmentary phrase had made its way into the depths of his consciousness he had a roaring emptiness in his head, as though compressed air were being pumped into it under strong pressure, for a moment as brief as the twinkling of an eye, but in the end that phrase was there at the very bottom of his skull where it was at once transformed into a logical and terribly clear thought, or even into a series of thoughts simultaneously: Alexei ... so he's alive ... Oh God ... so he's alive ... Catherine isn't alone ... and then he shouted: 'It's impossible! It's not true!' and his grandfather, betraying uneasiness: 'What isn't?'; later however, evidently understanding Peter's implied intention and outburst, he said: 'Unfortunately it's true. They found him in one of the mass graves the German newspapers wrote about recently. His body has already been identified. The Swiss Red Cross are investigating the crime, so we can believe the news. He was lying there among the bodies of thousands of other officers,' and Peter said nothing, unable for the moment to put two and two together in that confusion of contradictory feelings which had suddenly overcome him (for only a moment earlier he'd seen Catherine at the side of her husband whose real existence he had discounted since he'd left with his mobilization order on the day before the war broke out, and then had disappeared into the brief confusion of September, leaving behind only the hated and painful recollections of those scenes in which he and Catherine had been the protagonists and which he, Peter, had watched; but again now he caught sight of him at her side with terrible clarity, materialized into a living body, whereas in the next fragment of a second his grandfather's words had deprived that outline of any signs of life, and he now perceived him in the form of something which only very roughly recalled him, something not at all human, but rather an object, a thing that was hideously disintegrating and stinking of decay, a thing cast on a heap of other things, associated with them by the past torment they had shared before dying), and Demoiselle asked whether Grandfather was sure of what he said, after all Polish prisoners from the Kozhelsk camp had managed to inform their relatives by official postcards of their location as early as '39, but nothing had come from Alexei, so was it possible to state with one hundred per cent certainty that he'd been among them, to which Grandfather: 'Need only officers from the Kozhelsk camp lie in that wood near Katyn? Not from other camps too? And in any case where's the proof that they were all able to send cards from there to their families? And even if they did, need every card have reached its destination? No, there isn't the slightest doubt. In any case, they'll also find the victims' identity papers,' and as though he'd started choking with helpless, empty anger, shame, and disgust, muttering: 'Monstrous, my God, how monstrous, defenceless prisoners!' he wiped his neck then his brow with one hand, and although his eyes were still cold, faded, and penetrating, they seemed to be afloat, as it were, in watery scum, so that this pain of his seized Peter too, and immediately that identical shame which his grandfather must have been feeling penetrated to his very marrow, for he too had a part of the blood of this man in his veins, so he went to him and put one hand on his arm with a gesture that was almost protective, so as to give him strength and comfort him, if that were at all possible, although his grandfather didn't even notice. In the end, however, as though he were forcing himself to speak, he quietly said: 'It's not us. We no longer exist. There are no Russians. There is only their memory. It's the Soviets. This massacre is not on our consciences.' He rose and then Peter—for his grandfather in rising had jerked his hand from his arm—suddenly liberated from that cordial bond which he'd felt between them for a moment and from the need of charging him with even half an ounce of his own strength, moved back so as to see him better. He broke into a brief, sharp, cruel laugh which changed at once into convulsive coughing though it was still a laugh that bubbled from his throat like spittle, and it echoed in the silence of the drawing-room as though it were inside a barrel, and stifled even those suddenly indrawn, suppressed breaths of theirs, and when it finally diminished to violent silence it seemed that it was returning yet again as an echo, but then it really was the end. Peter was standing by himself in the centre of the drawing-room as if he'd drawn back a moment earlier when his grandfather rose from the chair; under his look full of incredulity, amazement, and passionate disappointment, he stood confused, but erect and already quite certain that, apart from the bonds of blood and memories of their earlier understanding, nothing linked them now, their paths had separated widely, and withstanding that look of his grandfather's with cold tranquillity, even feeling that he could withstand it forever, he said, trying to clear his voice of any kind of emotion so that it sounded indifferent, spilling the words through his teeth slowly, word by word, though without pause or breath: 'Grandfather, you've found a fine and convenient explanation. If someone commits bestial murders, then they are Germans and Soviets. The Russians weren't present at this for there aren't any. An excellent classification, I must say, I can only congratulate you. It's the same with Gavryluk. If he kills people, then he doesn't belong to our family, he's merely a Ukrainian. We're pure—what am I saying?—we're holy,' and before his grandfather could shout at him to stop, he turned away and was outside the door. His grandfather's shout didn't reach him until much later, as he was walking away into the depths of the hall, it had evidently poured through the open door into the wider expanse and as it found no obstacle, it at once expanded, even rose up and then came back, sinking a little and growing weak, and it caught up with Peter from the front, as though his grandfather hadn't shouted to him from behind, in the drawing-room, but directly into his face, except that it was already weak, like a child's plea, not like the shout of a man accustomed to unquestioned obedience and domination over other people, so it was incapable of turning Peter from his path or even of awakening the shadow of hesitation in him, as he walked on without looking back across the hall and then upstairs to his room. Then he was in his room and after a number of quite automatic gestures which didn't engage his consciousness for a moment, he had packed and then was sitting on the terrace at the rear of the house drinking the tea which Fiodorchuk, on seeing him come down, had brought, and he was waiting for the horses which he'd ordered to be harnessed, and when Fiodorchuk came back and informed him the old gentleman didn't want him to leave the house, he nodded to him and went on, as before, drinking the unsweetened tea; he stared at the park with a calm, cold gaze which, however, saw nothing, listening to its dead, afternoon silence in which only the tuneless voice of Julia the Second was audible as she weeded by the wall: 'I lost my coral beads . . . red . . . cherry-red . . .' and then he was already on his way. He left the park behind, like a huge unbridled stain of reddened vegetation spreading murderously on the white cliffs of the ravine, and the lichenous steppe on the other side, above which glided a solitary hawk of serpentine shape looking for carrion, and the road stretched out and wound in a friable, dry heat as exhausting as despair.

III

FINALLY A PALE EVENING CAME ON, GLOWING with blue. When Peter had reached the summit of the hill from which Krzysztopol was quite visible in the Sert valley, he heard single shots behind him. Someone ran across the overgrown cemetery on the far side of the slope, then into a field of lupins; the tiny figure of a woman, and three smaller figures, those of children, right behind her; they were certainly panting for breath, but there was not enough wind to carry the sound of their breathing very far. Bandera's men jumped over the fence, stopped and reloaded their rifles without haste, then set off in the direction of the fleeing figures; meanwhile the woman's eyes sought some hiding place but found none, for the ground down below was too flat, and she went on dragging the children after her through the dew, and evidently one got hit, it began stumbling, so the men shouted to her that no matter what, she wouldn't get away from them, she mustn't exasperate them unnecessarily, and they at once moved out of the cemetery with long strides through the yellow, hot lupins which impressed their scent in the sky, and across which she'd just run, and soon he heard the woman's single shriek suddenly rending the silence like an accusation, and that was all Peter heard and saw at first when he left the road and cut across a valley as fast as possible, before he got to the outskirts of the township and despair began coming over him in case he should not get there by nightfall and find Nick, feeling he was already trapped within this tired body of his, and he was hungry and thirsty, and felt as if he had no legs.

Meanwhile the evening extinguished the heat. Peter made an effort to hurry. A roadside cross with Christ nailed to it, a wreath on His cracked brow, gazing at the last swallows in depths of blue, and greenfinches chattering on the telegraph wires, calm trees and a patrol of gendarmes marching from the direction of the bridge, marking their way with a cloud of dust. Then a deserted street. The shutters fastened, although here and there above the roofs thin smoke rose vertically. The warm bricks of the walls were plastered with various German notices in two or three languages, and posters. Behind Farnasik's oil mill a few workmen sat on a bench with women, talking quietly and chewing sunflower seeds. The curfew hour was near. Then behind a barrier the maze of little streets of the ghetto, strewn with smashed doors and shop fronts. Batory Street parallel to the barbed wire. A beggar at one of the gates had spread a newspaper on the ground and was eating crusts of bread and pies. The increasingly sleepy hum of flies. The tramp of patrols. Involuntarily Peter quickened his step. His fear was stupid and absurd, but he couldn't control it. Then he started running. The street by the railway station already. And finally in the shadow behind a dilapidated tenement, a path beaten across grass to a porch behind the broken-down façade. He stopped to draw breath; he was shivering. He read the notice: 'Joinery, repair of holy images, devotional articles.' He went up the steps. There was no light or sound. He pulled the iron handle, the bell didn't sound, and he opened the door. He went slowly down a long stone-vaulted passage which stank of human urine and cats. Beyond, he saw the yard, empty and dark, with a heap of barbed wire in the middle, and when he touched the wall and moved his hand along it as he walked, he could feel bullet holes. The doors at the sides were half open and blank. Then he saw no more, he heard only a brief crash on the back of his head, but without feeling it, and collapsed without pain to the ground.

The darkness stretched into infinity. The smell of resin and oil paint wafted into his face. Finally something gleamed along with voices which spoke as though from underground: 'So how many didn't I tell you there was five of them altogether along with the Bahnschutz or without never mind what are you talking about reckon with them six at once as he was watching through binoculars certainly me what my butt drenched in sweat eyes full then as they fired if you'd seen their hands six of them you say up to the elbows in blood and the women fled along the valley in blood up to their elbows and you what me I go to these five fellows quiet say I quiet you might have let them get closer wise after the event I fired off the entire magazine sure thing what sure thing right close up I wish to God I'd never done it with her no ceremony with her you're a fool she's a spy that was a short burst well quiet nothing's certain so they say and then perhaps the women turned left Turczyc was standing there what were you waiting for God only knows how was I to know he was in Hajnovka after all he was waiting for you to help him ah shut up you damnation I say shut up fighting the likes of them shut up in any case you didn't know anything about Turczyc under oath he didn't ask then the women ran into the marsh it was hard to get in there I tell you those bandits were firing along the highway the bastards were always in sight who was Turczyc I tell you after all and it was he got them with that gun of his and then made a good end to it quiet now someone is asleep here.' And the voices moved away like the ebbing wave of a tide, or perhaps they died down completely, and the darkness again moved up somewhere into infinity, but afterwards (Peter found it difficult to find any measure for the time which was passing) a narrow, misty crevice opened up and he saw Nick's curly head in it. Trying to raise himself higher he heard his own voice, blunted against the soft edge of sleep, as this voice asked a question, neither quietly nor loudly, without any kind of emphasis: 'Where have you been, Nicholas? It's dawn already. I've been looking for you all day. It wasn't until I got to Hajnovka that they told me you were here,' and Nick, without turning, so that he continued to see only the massive back of his head: 'Go to sleep. You've had a bad time. You'd better sleep it off. You'll make it. And in the meantime one thing and another will be done here,' in a voice not his own at all, but someone else's, in the depths, however, at once another voice which might have been an old woman's voice for it creaked like an unoiled door, muttered: 'No rest anywhere, no time to breathe, you could wish you were dead. Not even room for a quiet prayer. Oh no, you won't find salvation. If you pestered God a whole year, you wouldn't get it. It's impossible while you're on the go and shooting all the time. It's all wasted,' and that voice which belonged to Nick but was, as it were, not his, so strange did it seem: 'Sleep, Mother. Dawn is still a long way off, you'll rest. Then a long journey,' whereupon this woman said: 'Well, of course,

I'll rest my bones awhile. But afterwards it will have to start again. Tomorrow Gavryluk's men are setting off for Hanch-Chach. This injustice won't be wiped out till the world ends,' slowly, getting each word out one by one and with difficulty, so that Peter didn't hear them all, only those uttered more precisely, as they fell into the depths of this soft flood of his sleep. Then, however, it was surely already dawn.

An uncertain pale grey light crept through the cracks in the shutters, the room was entirely empty, and those people who had been near him, if they really had been, must have left while he was asleep or lying unconscious, and finally he began recalling that he'd walked from Hajnovka to Krzysztopol, until in Krzysztopol he found Station Street, and later down a long stone corridor in this house where a notice had said: 'Joinery, repair of holy images, devotional articles' until suddenly he'd been hit on the back of the head. So that's how it was, he remembered, I was knocked out unawares, that's what happened, but that was all, he remembered no more, his thoughts stretched out like rubber, incapable of precision, and this began tormenting him still more, no, he could not remember. He tried to change position, to stretch or at least turn over on his side, but he couldn't even move, something was pressing him down to the ground, although he wasn't tied, he could feel his arms hanging loose and free at his sides, nor was he sleeping, for indeed he could see he was lying in some room unknown to him, something like the interior of a woodshed or junk store; in the gloom the warm dust rose in clouds, and dust of rotten wood dried his throat; behind a table, a sort of joiner's bench, a tall peasant-style clock stood in the corner, stern and dumb as an ancestor, and carved wooden crosses were hanging on the walls; as he looked around, trying to force his gaze through the gloom that was still tenacious though brightening at the window, he felt his head swimming once more, and his thoughts again stretched out with growing effort like rubber, but one of them finally reminded him of a phrase overheard earlier, yesterday, that tomorrow Gavryluk's men were moving on Hanch-Chach, and at once he started racking his brains over this, he couldn't locate that name in his mind, it sounded foreign but at the same time familiar; but then he remembered that it was no doubt one of the settlements south of Krzysztopol, inhabited for the most part by Bessarabians, and finally yes, he finally had that image before his eyes, even more clearly than he'd expected it to appear: he and his father were driving along the road to Sudy, which went to one side of Hanch-Chach, situated among gardens full of red peppers, with a clay pit filled with stagnant yellow water, and plantings of eggplants and melons, and later the Sudy estate, a noisy evening after the shoot, he recalled his father was a young man then, and he a boy, pleased at his first shoot, proud of the old gun obtained from his grandfather, but before this colourful image could develop details it suddenly drew back into oblivion, and the next one must have gone back to some entirely different day, although it too showed idyllic scenery similar to Sudy, but his father in black and white was seated at a square table by the glowing fireplace, his high, pale hawk's face meditating over a game of chess. This image too didn't last very long, and in the next one that face was leaning towards Peter from between the rustling stems of grey marsh vegetation in a damp, grey, cold dawn, and it said: 'Don't worry. You must shoot snipe by smell, not sight. It's not an easy prey,' and it smiled, and he: 'Who's that by the campfire, Father? That Ruthenian,' and his father: 'Gavryluk? Oh, nobody in particular. Don't worry,' and the face smiled at him once again, and although Peter wanted to ask something else, still having before his eyes the narrow, evil smile of that unknown adolescent, he didn't ask, and fell asleep: before he managed to say anything, he fell asleep in the middle of that wise, tranquillizing, almost apologetic smile of his father, without having been able to find out anything from him about Gavryluk, and now—still with the hoarse, senile voice in his ears of that woman who wasn't anywhere about but who must have been there recently, for how else could her voice have penetrated so deeply into his memory—he knew that Gavryluk's men were setting out tomorrow for Hanch-Chach, he at once guessed their purpose, and with those half-swooning thoughts stretching like rubber, he turned with insistence to his father's face, evoked a moment before from the dark of oblivion, he listened with fearful attention to the voice of his own heart, trying to catch one or another of its unusual throbs, a sign which would command him to condemn him, but no, it was beating regularly, patiently counting the passing seconds, nothing more, and his father's face was smiling at him, unaltered, with that tranquillizing, somewhat sad smile, perhaps apologetic because he too was feeling sad, he couldn't bring himself to condemn him. The heart is often the most honest judge, it passes sentence and that's all, often on the basis of some gesture or other, some look, smile, a thought only, so he guided himself in precisely this way, and now passed judgment, exonerating him, though the sorrow remained, and then the silence surrounding him on all sides broke, as it were, into two, and began vibrating with human voices.

The room was still empty, no one had come in, and this forced him to reject his previous thoughts and to concentrate his attention so as to understand where the voices were coming from, and whom they belonged to, for this was how he heard them: they hadn't increased gradually, but had been uttered suddenly, as though halfway through a phrase, in the middle of a question, as if he'd been sleeping previously and had only just overheard them, now that he'd woken up, and a good deal of time passed before he realized they weren't illusory at all, but were coming from behind a partition. One spoke quite monotonously, the voice dripped into the darkness like porridge, a sweetened substance, treacherous, ambiguous, unfriendly, in it there vibrated as it were a note of concealed suspicion, and the other voice too, as it interrupted something on its own behalf; Peter soon caught the same tone in it, as though both voices were groping for one another, greasily and clammily, trying to catch and interlock with one another but continually escaping, and as time passed they began to entangle his too, interweaving it or perhaps having already interwoven it with their treacherous vibrations; a circle was whirling tightly around that uncomprehended vortex, that's precisely what it was, and he, Peter, was there inside it along with those voices which, when he closed his eyes, dripped slowly into the blackness under his eyelids from a distance: 'You talk as though you weren't one of us.' 'Nonsense, I was only trying to find some way out.' 'There wasn't anything to try, if the rifle was left.' 'That's all you know. I tell you there was no need to knock off those few bandits. Sebyla could have made an exchange, and Witalis's wife could have acted as go-between. It would have cost the lives of a few men, but the people in Stochek could have been saved.' 'Nothing could be done. Witalis's wife is spying for both sides. She'd have taken the money, but you wouldn't have been able to save the people at Stochek, they'd already have been dead a good few hours.' 'Not by that time. Pertz said they were counting on us.' 'Maybe, but that was a day or two earlier. And when they found us behind the rubbish heap of the settlement near Lishek, it must already have been the end for the people at Stochek.' 'Don't talk nonsense! No doubt that's the way you wanted it to be.' 'It's you who're talking nonsense. That night, the glare was reflected in the sky as though from an open stove. I wouldn't have helped them at all by starting negotiations. Anyway, if we hadn't killed them when they found us, our hiding place would have been discovered.' 'As if the hiding place matters!' 'We'd have had to take to the woods, but that settlement seemed as good as any place for these days.' 'That's not at all the way it was. Gavryluk's men didn't kill off the people at Stochek until dawn, and in the evening the glare was over Ospych, I remember perfectly, because I was patrolling close to the edge of the forest and saw it. You wasted an opportunity.' 'I wouldn't say it was ours that was wasted.' 'Then whose was it? Maybe you'd enlighten me? What I'm worried about aren't those few scoundrels, but the fact that the beginning of our end is starting. People will remember we didn't rescue the men at Stochek, and that they can't count on us.' 'You're looking at it all from the wrong angle. There was a spy among us, and he reported on the men at Stochek and said they were supplying us with food. And he also reported on other people who are on our side. Accurately—name, village, farm.' 'He reported, or still is reporting?' 'What's the difference. At Tokarchyk's interrogation by the auxiliary police, they read him the report from the first word to the last, and he recognized the handwriting.' 'That's an easy explanation.' 'It's not easy, but it's a fact. Before he lost consciousness, he whispered something to Pertz when they were taking him to the cell from interrogation, but Pertz didn't catch what he said, that's the worst of it. This is why people are turning away from us, because one of us is informing.' 'Nonsense!' 'You know very well, perhaps better than I do, that it isn't so.' 'I only know what other people are saying.' 'And this is precisely what they're saying,' and then through footsteps which suddenly sounded close to, he heard the voices behind the partition break off, and at once the violent blaze of a lamp like a knife stroke penetrated through the open door into the interior of the room and stopped for a moment in the air flecked by silver dust. The steps approached, and the light circled all around the room, so that in the beam creeping like a fiery snake Peter saw the joiner's bench and a basketful of rubbish and the chair and the crucifixes on the walls, himself remaining still in concealment, but when the light went out, someone nearby asked: 'This him?' and another, standing farther away, replied: 'That's him,' so the first said: 'Don't be afraid of me' to Peter who was silent, thinking that after all they'd seen him because they'd spoken to him, and the other: 'Who are you?' so then Peter: 'And you?' then the other quickly but not threateningly: 'You'll find out right away if you resist. You are to answer when I ask you a question,' but then the other, farther away, exclaimed: 'Calm down, Laudanski, I know him. He's the young fellow from Chupryn. Nicholas Fiodorchuk has vouched for him,' and Peter: 'I was just looking for him when they hit me on the head,' so the first man: 'Young man, you shouldn't have come creeping about on your own. It might have been still worse,' and he, letting this comment pass: 'Where's Nick? I'd like to see him,' to which the other: 'Well, all right, all right. Can you walk? There's nothing wrong with you, surely,' taking Peter by the arm and setting him on his feet, and Peter: 'No, probably not. I slept all night and I'm not getting anywhere. Where is he?' and the other: 'You'll see him pretty soon,' and then the other who was standing in the background and had scarcely spoken: 'I'll take him, it's my duty. I'm glad to be able to help you, sir,' and the first: 'Don't use such big words—"duty." Go to the track and check. The young man doesn't know what he's looking for and he'll get hit on the head again. Because he's Nicholas's friend is a poor reason for that. In future you must be careful, for the fellows work fast,' and immediately Peter realized it was already light. He was in the yard, he recognized it, that same pile of barbed wire was lying in the middle as in the evening, all was bathed in the pale, grey, clear gleam of dawn, and blinded he rubbed his eyes while the man who had brought him out disappeared, so that for a moment he was alone and had time to look about the place: the building stood among the burned-out skeletons of small houses, and beyond the disastrous wall where they had surprised him the day before he could see into the street opposite, at the side of which a cart with straw was standing. When, hearing a noise from the direction of the shed, he looked around, he again saw some man or other, but not the same man as before; he had a small, foxy face and his eyes were swimming with drowsiness. He watched him squeeze through the door which wouldn't open fully, as though someone inside were holding it, and when he finally pushed it angrily, it shuddered and stopped moving; he stood by it and, evidently not wanting to come nearer, said to Peter halfway across the yard: 'Nicholas has gone off already. They've gone into the forest near Hanch-Chach to stop Gavryluk's men.'

Returning through the passage towards the street, Peter looked back a few times and saw the man standing there at the door of the shed, watching him as before. Even after asking the man sitting in a cart whether he could go with him, and he'd climbed up, he saw him still staring with an expressionless and meaningless gaze. The man on the box, without even moving his head, asked: 'Nick wasn't there?' and, recognizing him as the man who'd come into the room with the lamp, Peter replied, remembering the name and that he'd already heard it before: 'No, he wasn't. He's gone to Hanch-Chach,' and the man briefly: 'We'll be there in an hour,' and he whipped up the horse.

They drove along a worn path in a beechwood in the sour and bitter smell of the moist brushwood of the year before mixed with lichenous fungus, and when the beechwood gave way to spruce thickets which were alarmingly silent and lifeless after the accompaniment of bird song, the hum of beetles in the tall whortleberries and the hiss of dung beetles scuttling into the undergrowth in alarm from the wheels, just as smoke on the sea announces the approach of a ship to land, so the brown curves of a roof projecting above the tops of the trees and bushes and a short chimney pot revealed to them a forester's hut, which Laudanski, on the box, had mentioned earlier in a querulous voice. The horse's hoofs emitted a friable echo as they came into contact with the sand of the track that was overgrown with thin grass, but the noise didn't resound, it was at once absorbed by stiflingly hot air that lay mellow along the earth's surface, and was quite thick higher up, motionless, not breathed on by the wind, and a falcon, circling high up in a southerly direction where a new, black, and dense barrier of forest rose, seemed nothing more than the soundless mirage of the heat.

After the night passed in a closed room, Peter slowly

relaxed, rocked by the regular trot of the horse and the swinging motion of the cart. In the pure light of day, the bent shoulders of the man's back, which was turned to him, first approached then moved away, according to whether he opened or closed his eyes, and words fell unbelievably slowly and uncertainly from some quite unreal attitude: 'You were still a schoolboy. No doubt it was the first time you'd ridden far afield, for your mother telephoned all around the district in alarm. We were harvesting, it was your holidays. Not looking at me, but continually watching the road from Chupryn, you began telling me you were thirteen already, although you looked much younger and certainly weren't more than ten, that your name was Peter, and that you'd come from town to the Cherestvienskis. You said a lot of nice things about that absurd Russian whom no one in the neighbouring farms liked because he kept himself apart from them. But I still didn't know he was your grandfather. You spoke of him as if he were some national hero, and we Podolians didn't have anything much against the Russians in those days, so I listened: this zone was once Austrian, not like now; after what they did to us in '39 and '40 nobody likes them. You were a funny boy. Are you a Pole or a Ruthenian, you asked me. A Pole, I said, from the Tartar landed gentry, the Laudanskis; I rent Ospych from the Sanguski family. I know him, you said then, he's a Lithuanian prince. What do you mean—Lithuanian? I replied. Except that no one ever sets eyes on him, he lives in France all the time. My father knows him, you told me. And I know your grandfather, said I, for I'd finally guessed you were the old man's grandson. He's a strange man, that father of yours, I told you then, in '22 when you settled here he'd ride around the district like a madman, he used to stop his horse on hilltops and weep. Then he would dismount at the crossroad inns, drink a lot, and weep again. The Russians drink like fish, people are used to it, but to think that such a big man should weep for no reason—they never saw anything like it. Then you told me: Leave my father out of this, he's not a bad man, only he can't find a place for himself in the world. You'd cry too if you were he, and then you covered your face from the sun with your cap as though you wanted to sleep, letting me know that the interview was over. Well, I went back to the men harvesting nearby, and you had a good sleep under a tree until evening, when one of the old man's servants found you and took you home. You've probably forgotten our meeting, eh?' but clearer and more real to Peter than Laudanski's chatter which was rising and falling as though in time with the cart's jolting were the bursts of gunfire that came from a great distance as they approached the forester's hut, which perhaps Laudanski could hear too and that was why, in his desire to turn Peter's attention away, and not to think of them himself, he was chattering on without much relevance, unnerved by something that was happening on the far side of the forest, even in those longer intervals of silence which expanded between the bursts of gunfire, filled only with the heavy hoofbeats of the horse and the rolling of the wheels, and Peter thought: My God, what's happening? Where are we going? What in the world am I doing in this forest? What's it got to do with me? He himself didn't know what concern it was of his. Was this supposed to be a journey on the track of Gavryluk, which he would sooner or later have to start? What shall I do when I come across him? All his thoughts asked questions, none gave a reply. And under their outer layer, a stream of other thoughts was incessantly wearing a path: What's happening to Catherine now? She didn't even have time to say good-bye. For him, that evening between Sunday and Monday had been something extraordinary and important (so that he couldn't collect all its cherished moments into one thought, and his memory, trying to recall the whole, racked his brain entirely in vain), but for her, for her, had that evening meant nothing? Or perhaps despair for her husband had caused her to forget. She had long thought Alexei killed in battle, although she never said so very plainly, but could some hope have lived on in her all the same? Could it be that she regretted what had happened, was reproaching herself for weakness? He was still filled with incomprehensible, insane excitement, and yet he knew nothing. Why did he have to think of her all the time? Why was he so determined to find Nick? How was he to help him? After all Nick was no longer the same Nick he had been years ago. That one single day away from the house had proved to him conclusively that his former friend already belonged to all those strange people of whom he, Peter, had sometimes heard vague rumours, making up for himself stupid pictures as of people in some spine-chilling adventure story, whereas upon meeting them they were nothing like it, they had smelled of manure, of the terror of trapped animals, of blood and the desire for revenge. Nick was one of them. Was that his, Peter's destiny too? But no reply was forthcoming, meanwhile the horse drew up and stopped, and then Peter raised his eyelids which were stuck together with heat and looked around prepared for anything.

The man whom he already called Laudanski in his thoughts was just getting clumsily off the cart, frowning. Smoke was rising from the chimney of the hut, scattering sparks as though someone inside were burning hay in a stove, the smell of horses and of freshly crushed cherries hung in the air, straw scattered by boots was strewn over the ground: no one came out to meet them.

Inside, there wasn't a living soul either, a lot of straw was lying about as though a number of men had just passed the night here, and a musty, goatlike stench of unwashed bodies and wretched food still lurked in the corners. In the fire-blackened walls stuck rusty nails, on one was hanging a rusty angle gauge and a plane without a blade, a fire was blazing in the stove, and although Laudanski shouted several times: 'Kurdiak, where the devil have you got to?' no one appeared until, after pushing aside the straw with one foot, he lifted a floorboard and crept into the cellar. Peter overheard a stifled conversation preceded by a sort of heavy thumping: 'Where've they gone they've gone will you tell me or won't you I don't know where I'll tell you O Jesus tell me then no farther than two furlongs it'll be when I don't know speak up yes sir it was early in the morning and the bandits went that way too to Hanch-Chach it was certainly a *provocateur* how so sir one of them said so where's Kurdiak how should I know where you are so I ran away from the truck don't talk sir I know nothing,' and then again that heavy thumping and Peter staggered against the wall, he was stifled by the overheated stench of the hut and by the general lack of air, by the lack of what our lungs need even when they have air in them, and then Laudanski scrambled out of the cellar wiping his forehead and groaning heavily. But it was better later on, when they'd gone outdoors again into the sunlight which was washing all the treetops in its high, direct stream and was gleaming on the black hide of the horse that was impatiently shaking off the flies, and they drove into the forest, a good way off the road between the trees, and there, in the undergrowth, Laudanski tied the reins, pulled a rifle from under the seat, and said to Peter with panting breath: 'Well, let's go. The young man is looking for something he hasn't lost and the devil only knows what he'll find now,' and after a moment: 'What did you have to see Nicholas about that was so important it made you come out of the Chupryn fortress into the wide world?' but before Peter could think of an answer he had walked away into a thicket so he had to run in order not to lose him, and then Laudanski asked no more, as if he had completely forgotten him, until finally the trees thinned a little and later they were at the very edge of the forest.

The edge of the forest fell away sharply, perpendicularly, into a valley, and now they could hear that firing, which they'd been hearing for half an hour at least, or three quarters, immediately in front of them as suddenly as if a soundproof curtain had been raised on their arrival. And at once they caught sight of the village in the bottom of the valley in red, leaping flames. Screaming shadows of people were running about in the orchards God knows where to, the bitter stench of burning and those shrieks reached the place where they were standing. On the paths and at the edges of fields machine guns were slicing at the legs of people in flight, they fell over, hid wherever they could, the more stupefied among them were trying to let cattle out of the barns, pigs, goats, horses, and were seizing whatever they could from under the sizzling rafters and ceilings that were falling in with dull explosions, under the machine-gun fire again, which was unceasingly and precisely hacking through the village with bullets. The drunken yelling of Germans and Ukrainians was audible, and then Peter heard nothing more than Laudanski breathing. He was drawing great gasps of air into his lungs and letting them out slowly, as if constricting them by force so as not to deprive himself of them all at once, so that they were like sighs, or something close to sighs, although they were not sighs at all, but finally that strange breathing of his broke off entirely as suddenly as it had begun. He slipped the rifle off his shoulder and took aim, but the bullet that was to be fired didn't join in with the shots of those others either then or later. Not until after a while, having nudged Peter with the muzzle, did he say: 'Get up,' as though from the bottom of a very slimy pit, 'Our men didn't make it,' and a good long time passed as he stood like this, leaning forward and saying nothing, but he was again breathing in loud, deep sighs, not heavily, but whistling rather, and with a sort of childish whimpering, he kept breathing, that was all, until finally: 'Hear that?' he asked, 'What's happened?' said Peter in reply, dully, almost voicelessly, and Laudanski: 'Get ready to join in! Our men are attacking from the direction of Sudy. At least some of the people will be saved. They're cutting off the killers, do you see? We must go around the valley, to join them. There's a long ride ahead of us,' and then they turned away and didn't look back again, and once more there was a silence, perhaps there really was, for that soundproof curtain fell as soon as they'd turned away from the valley into the forest.

He wouldn't forget this for a long time: the steep sides of the valley, the village enveloped in flames, and the shriek: for a long time or not at all. Especially that shriek, which was single and yet collective, blending into one, mounting, great, as high as Heaven, cutting into this sky as though into a hole, shattering it by force so as to fly up higher if there was anything still *higher* which might hear and listen, and even if there wasn't, then to leave at least a trace in that rarefied air in the furthest heights where—if nothing else—at least there were the wandering shades of their dead fathers and grandfathers, yes, undoubtedly; and the insistent thought: Gavryluk, it was he who did this, nagging irascibly, attacking (although it wasn't at all a new thought, since he'd already known everything for several days, had often experienced the thought, but it was one thing to know and something else to see, when this same thought took on a different meaning), and the thought, filled with shock, amazement, despair and hopelessness, kept returning as though with every individual movement of the cart rushing uphill over the roots that grew across the path and with every single word uttered from time to time by Laudanski. But later that image and shriek sank into him somewhere deeper, and there was only this track along which they were driving at a crazy gallop in dullness and stupefaction.

First they drove between two close walls of trees, later when these thinned out, along a dusty, sunny vista which led them by the hilltops swelling high over the district, and, still more exhausting, dog-tiring, insane, among softly splattering shots whenever the wood on the left thinned and they immediately came into the field of vision of the German-Ukrainian bands, and amidst silence when the wall of the forest closed again even though only for a moment and in which Laudanski, without turning back so as not to lose control of the wildly foaming horse he was spurring on, and without even turning his head so as to look at him, Peter, as he lay in the back on a few loose, crumpled bundles of hay in the bottom of the cart, in that total stupefaction of his; as if taking advantage of this silence, he kept telling him things briefly or asking questions in a mild, sad, almost sleepy voice (so that the silence couldn't be total even once, so he might satiate himself in it to the point of tranquillity), and he asked and told him these things not because he wanted to learn anything or communicate some knowledge of his own to him, but so that Peter shouldn't forget his constant presence, that he was on guard, was surely guiding this ramshackle rig which threatened to disintegrate at any moment, and that he would drive it out of this accursed district to a place where they would finally join up with their own men, for although the voice sounded mild and sleepy to him, Peter felt almost unconsciously that there was at the back of it some horrible tension of all the nerves, muscles, tendons, an attention that was directed not to him, Peter, at all, but to what was happening around them: to the forest, the path, the horse, and that he was constantly rushing ahead to what might happen or would happen, although in a voice that was mildly sleepy, sad, and almost inaudible he asked: 'You know Gavryluk?' to which Peter perhaps at once, but most probably not until the next interval of silence, replied: 'I don't know,' without even reluctance or the desire to delude him with a lie, for he really didn't know, although quite recently he'd still had the impression that he knew all the time and then (startled by Laudanski's question), he suddenly realized that he'd never been too sure whether he knew Gavryluk, although he'd seen him two or three times, and after a moment it even seemed to him that it had never occurred to him that he had had such a conviction, quite the contrary. I don't really know him at all, I know nothing about him which might approximate the truth, it's as though those meetings had never existed, for they've left in me no more than a blurred impression of something, something which can't be named, he suddenly realized, bringing those thoughts formed into clear phrases to the surface of this stupefaction and numbness of his, which were like a collapse into lethargy but permitted him to capture images and voices from outside, although these were stifled, distant, and as if drowned out by the expanse stretching into infinity; he emerged once again to the surface, though he made no effort, nor did he shift in the bottom of the cart where, half lying, half seated, he'd only just replied to Laudanski: 'I don't know,' and although this emergence and staying on the surface of the abyss of his own stupefaction did not last for long, he at least gained enough time to draw some sort of conclusions from those few clear and startling thoughts; for if he did not know Gavryluk at all, but had based his opinion on him on those misty impressions that were fading with the course of the years, and on incomplete accounts by third persons, then his judgment, opinion, view, couldn't have much value and meaning. He realized that by exculpating himself and his father along with his entire family he had been too rash and biased a judge, for although their shared guilt, or that of his father only, was too common an occurrence to be called guilt, a pre-marital romance between the lord of the manor and a peasant girl, culminating in the birth of a child, was only a *phenomenon* but not guilt in the eyes of the world in which it had happened, and could not have led to a different solution, in view of the social position of the pair, the half-feudal system prevailing, and all the factors which encouraged the hermetic sealing of social classes, allowing a narrow margin of moral tolerance to just such an episode while defining its limits in advance, yet it was undoubtedly guilt for me not to know through what spectacles to look at it: at the same time he realized that the ultimate cause of everything that had followed later, that had developed into such grievous results, was that sin of impurity (he didn't know what else to call it and although he'd never been very religious, particularly not of late, he rebelled against his family's simplification of things), and then the fact that the boy conceived in that ephemeral union had grown up with a sense of his own humiliation, of not belonging either to his mother's class or to his father's, for material help from the Cherestvienskis (which he might well regard as payment for his mother's shame) only emphasized this not belonging, and so the complex of illegitimacy took deep and permanent root in him and undoubtedly found added fuel in the national separation between his mother's class and his father's, a separation which set the servile class—his mother—and the master class—his father—against one another in constant conflict; all this only reinforced in him that illegitimacy complex, which might have become the main or perhaps even the only force from which he drew his hatred, and in his desire to liberate himself from his complex he had, in the end, to scale these various dividing walls and barriers, had to destroy them and also the people who'd erected them, or who by their very existence personified them—Peter realized this (although his uncle had explained it to him a few days ago, it had needed those last days for him to be able to think it over and he now realized it with terrible clarity, in mature reflection), still maintaining himself with difficulty on the surface of his momentary clarity but already fearing that at any moment he might sink, despite his efforts to avoid it, into the quagmire as before, and suddenly he heard Laudanski say: 'He was close to all of you,' to which he ambiguously replied: 'It may have seemed so, but I rather doubt whether my grandfather knows him at all well,' for when Laudanski's words reached him through the clatter of the fast-moving cart but before he'd decided to answer him, it occurred to him that his grandfather didn't know Gavryluk any better than he did. For at the time when he had followed him into his study and found him there with a book, his grandfather had told him that it was none of their concern, that these people on whose heels he was at present following would settle accounts with the bandits, that it was up to the various local Polish partisans, his grandfather said this holding the book he wasn't reading upside down and sitting motionless in his chair as if expecting him, Peter, to say something that would force him to take a stand or to change his reasoning, but he, Peter, hadn't said anything of the sort then, he couldn't, it hadn't happened to him as it did now that he was suddenly seeing the Gavryluk case in a rather different light. His grandfather couldn't have known Gavryluk, or hadn't wanted to betray to Peter that he did or—and here Peter was not playing a guessing game but basing himself only on what his grandfather had said—he had to accept the premise that he didn't know Gavryluk, for if he had, he wouldn't have wanted to pass off the settlement of this matter to other people, he'd have warned him that first and foremost the bandits were after them, the Cherestvienskis, that they were their primary target (they and their class), and everything Gavryluk was doing was taking place, as it were, in the family circle, and these crimes of his, these devastations, the burning of villages, hanging of people, all this wretched collaboration with the occupying forces, was only a by-product, as it were, of that fundamental settlement with them which was part of his illegitimacy complex, and he said, this time without hesitation or ambiguity in his voice: 'No, Grandfather doesn't know him. But I . . .' 'What about you? You said you didn't know him,' Laudanski interrupted, to which he: 'I think I'm on the right track now for getting to know him. I'm slowly guessing that what troubles him most is that he's what he is,' but Laudanski: 'Well, better for you to guess late than never,' with sorrow difficult to explain and tolerance in his voice, and then he felt he could no longer endure the tension to which he had been forcing himself for a good while so as to stay in this sort of relative equilibrium of consciousness and to keep himself on the surface of his own stupefaction, which was again overwhelming him with growing force; and having only said: 'This won't have any effect on what the bandits do. On me, at most,' he was already back (still half lying half sitting in the bottom of the cart without moving at all) below that dividing line above which was sobriety and the ability to think logically, in the depths of this befouled flood, misty and nauseating as though revolted by its own nullity, from which the ceaseless clatter of the gallop, the thundering of the horse, the noise of the cart rattled by its motion, and all Laudanski's next words turned back as though reflected. And at once his memory, going back still further, began unveiling that evening by the stream at Chupryn, rather late in the evening or perhaps night, but so bright with moonlight that it resembled day, and how, in the transparent living silver like mercury he'd lain with Catherine in the grass above the cliff, and Catherine had said at a certain moment, raising her head from his shoulder: 'You're very young. I'm afraid for you,' but he did not yet realize what she meant; it was after the time when, in the glittering spray of water raised by the stream shattering against the rocks scattered over its entire surface, in the spray which sprinkled all the flood waters below, he'd swum after her to the sandy, empty bank on the other side, and she had fled away from him, cutting the surface with long swishing movements of her arms and legs, and she'd laughed aloud, though not at all mockingly, until he finally caught up with her on that cool, sandy bank, for perhaps she hadn't been fleeing at all, perhaps she'd wanted to be caught as quickly as possible, and amidst the ceaseless whispering of the waters moved by the current she'd whispered: 'I'm afraid for you. You're so young,' in that full light of the moon and the thin glitter of stars in the motionless summer air, when he suddenly felt heat flow over him as if he'd stopped naked in front of a fire, for it was something which had never yet happened before, or even existed, nor had there existed in him even an approximate notion of what might exist in precisely such a way, but now it did, and every moment of it had lasted whole ages in expectancy, amazement, wonder, fear, joy, and silence, and Catherine's whisper, perhaps defensive, or perhaps only aggressive: 'I'm afraid for you. You're so young,' meant nothing, judged nothing, was indifferent and not connected with anything, for what he saw, felt, and wanted, knowing already then for sure that he wanted this, after ridding himself long ago of his previous fear, only this had any meaning at that moment, so that when she repeated the same phrase later—when they were lying side by side above the cliff, in damp, warm grass that was noisy and alive with crickets and beetles, where they'd often used to sit together when they were still small—in the same whisper as before, although there was in it a tone of concentrated solemnity (he didn't hear this tone until later), still not understanding what was the matter with her and even believing that Catherine was only instinctively repeating a thought of an hour earlier, or two hours, or perhaps years earlier, for it seemed to him that from the moment when he'd caught up with her on the bank to the moment when, raising her head from his chest, she again whispered: 'I'm afraid for you. You're so young,' whole years had passed, he said: 'You're young too. Does it mean anything that I'm five years younger?' so then she, moving his head slightly with her right hand as though she wanted to draw it still closer to herself, placing her left hand flat on his chest and then hiding her face on his chest so that he felt the spreading softness of her hair like silk momentarily touching his skin, and her warm breath, she said not loudly, in brief, shallow gasps: 'That's not what I meant at all. Not who's older or who's younger. And certainly not about myself. Only that you're different from Paul, different from what Alexei was, and from all the other men in our families.' Dumbfounded by the very sound of the names she'd uttered, but at once, as if unconsciously, he envisaged some dark, unguessable, cruel sphere of her secret associations which were independent of him, hideous, repelling him by their strangeness, burning his body like a white-hot iron—associations which, however, he didn't want to penetrate into, not wanting to destroy this unrepeatable moment in the full moonlight and thin glitter of the stars that was still continuing—he at once rejected the thought of them (of these associations) and now also stopped thinking about them before he'd really begun, and again plunged into his memory, so that he succeeded in catching the last clause of the last phrase she'd uttered: '. . . from all the other men in our families.' He asked: 'What do you mean by that?' alarmed for the first time, for in asking the question but without yet hearing an answer, hearing all the time that previous, earlier phrase, he caught that tone of concentrated solemnity which had certainly not been in Catherine's voice when she'd spoken of his youth on the sandy bank where he'd caught up with her and seized her, but which had been there when she said more or less the same thing again (without, however, repeating it, for it meant something else), there on the steep slope above the cliff, with her head on his chest, although when he finally heard that tone it immediately seemed to him that he'd also heard it before, but not until then did he pay special attention to it, it made him ponder and unnerved him as a result of that disastrous combination of names he hadn't expected to hear from her, at least not on this particular night, and then Catherine, as if sensing his sudden uneasiness, said: 'You've been living away from all of them. You're not sufficiently prepared for what you may meet here. For you, this was only a childhood idyll, holidays, Easter and Christmas, sleigh rides, riding and shooting, trips, secrets and gossip by the fire, legends told by nurserymaids, historical fairy tales of glory and knightly battles, a country of scents, sunshine, and dark halls lit by wax candles and full of portraits whose names spoke of faded yet still enduring power. But all this is untrue. And now you're a man and I don't know whether you're finding enough courage in yourself—for the fairy tale is ended—to lift up the real image and not lose yourself in the unhappy chaos of this region. Your youthfulness is too blind, not resistant to it all.' 'You talk like Uncle Theodore. As though you'd conspired together,' he said to this, with a slight smile, but at once very clearly hearing that half his smile was mixed with some harsh dissonance, for she was no longer resting her head on his chest, or rather was still keeping it there (so that he felt its entire weight), but not as before, with her face close so that suddenly he missed her breath on his skin (her mouth was at the level of his heart, and because of the pressing weight of her head he could hear that characteristic, dull, unsleeping beat inside people which was, perhaps, the beat of his own heart, but might equally well have been the beat of a pulse in her temple); she was looking straight at him, he saw her eyes reflecting all the nocturnal glow, she was gazing almost inquiringly and forcefully, although she spoke not much louder than a whisper, as if—without moving her lips—she weren't speaking at all but was only thinking, and he in some way known only to himself and for the first time that night in a tested way, succeeded in hearing these thoughts of hers and could translate them into the language of sounds: 'I can't explain any more clearly to you. In fact I don't even know what I mean when I say I'm afraid for you. On account of Gavryluk, perhaps? For what if he wants to kill you? All he's concerned with is us. One day the Germans will let him come here, not in secret as he did when they murdered Madame Irène. A wolf's instinct lurks in him deep under the influence of that smattering of culture which you all gave him, and now blood has been shed, it has revealed itself in blood. I myself don't know what he wants. All of them—Paul, my father-in-law, your family, the various neighbours—all know what they want. They want to survive. They say it's essential to fight the Germans and Ukrainians as much as possible until the war ends and we'll be on top again. But will it ever end? And shall we really be on top? They say the only thing that must be prevented is to have them sole survivors on the scorched earth, for it is our common property, and then we shall somehow cope with them. For only we Poles can give the Ukrainians more than they've had so far, only we can slowly raise them higher, no one from outside could. And I say so too. By day. For at night, when one can see the red glare of fires in the distance and it seems that people's screams carry further, then I cannot drive other thoughts out of my head. Sometimes I'd like to go away from here, to escape. To be anywhere but only with my own people, where there's only one enemy, and he can be recognized easily. This is no place for you, Peter. You haven't the resistance the men here have. Now I feel that you don't want to go back to K., and will get involved in all this. Even if you don't want to, you'll have to get involved. For Gavryluk will soon find out you're here and will try to kill you. And so will you. I know you'll try to do the same. I'm afraid. Peter, let's go away. Let's not lose our last chance. It's getting worse from month to month. Let's go to K. together, Peter,' and she rose on her hands, looking at him, and then again she leaned over, face touched face, and he meanwhile slowly turned his head aside, for he couldn't bear Catherine to seek his eyes so insistently, and, after glancing into the moon-soaked night, into that silvery pure infinity, in which, not far beyond the ravine, amidst the flourishing gardens Chupryn village slept in a vigilant, silent dream; as a child he had run there to play with Ukrainian boys, now however the language in which they'd once communicated so well and cordially had ceased to be understandable at all, and was of no use; it seemed to him that he could see at a distance which normally the eye doesn't reach, in some misty, unearthly gleam that was spying on him with thousands of unknown eyes—hearing everything, seeing, calling ceaselessly and crying in Ukrainian: 'We'll meet again,' so that both he and his family should hear it and not know the soothing tranquillity of sleep—the mixed, mongrel villages of Olejniki and the Ukrainian Uchty and Krasiche and Sarny and Hajnovka in which, with rifles hidden under their beds, those various Pavluks, Gresiuks, Michaleks, and Ivans were sleeping, and if it were not for that one look into the beloved, painful, and also hateful distance, he would undoubtedly have agreed with Catherine, but the glance couldn't be withdrawn and there was only a long, unhappy moment of silence, and then Catherine, who'd already understood that he wasn't going to reply to her, said in an extinguished voice: 'I know, I'm weak, perhaps foolish. I won't say such things to you again. But sometimes I've had as much as I can endure of this dying all day long, this dying in the evenings, and then how long the night is, though one always has to smile and keep up appearances. Only dawn will liberate me from this horrible feeling. Everyone here is so wise! They'll save the world, or mercilessly condemn it to destruction. But it has nothing to do with me, nothing! I want to have my own life. Well, but what can you know about it? You're too young. It's no concern of yours, after all, to get me out of this abyss. All the more so since you have your own worries. But it just adds to my fears. For you too may go under through that patriotic wisdom of theirs. And then it'll be too late when you remember what I said to you. Gavryluk will come here, that's certain,' and together with her falling silent, not at all suddenly, for her voice ebbed away from her, as it were, dying slowly, directly on his chest, he wanted to say something to cancel out everything she had said and to turn them back again towards that extraordinary moment when he'd caught up with her on the sandy bank, and even earlier, for that desire had been growing within him when her voice was still sounding in the night's silence, as if it were beyond her words and independent of them, or despite them, but he at once thought that for that moment to be able to return, he would have to overcome her revolt and even that feeling of loneliness which—he sensed—grew up in her as she spoke, and he'd remained so stubbornly silent, to overcome and erase it from her memory; but he'd said nothing of the sort, nor did he make any gesture to remind her of that moment or to awaken everything in her again, he couldn't, he dared not, though all the time he kept his hand on her hip, stroking it caressingly but, as it were, in a reflex action, without thinking, having understood only that he had missed the possibility of holding on to this common property of theirs—even if it were only an illusory moment in the surrounding reality—that he had missed holding on to it only until dawn, if not forever, that by his silence he had thrust Catherine into a loneliness from which she wished to tear herself, to escape, perhaps by confiding first of all in him, admitting it to him, unveiling it, that loneliness which had been building up in her layer by layer for a long time; and the silence went on, besides, it was already dawn, the branches of the nearby trees stood stiff and black against the background of a sky that was changing to ultramarine, the metallic gleam of the moon was already entirely cold, corpse-like, and Catherine's last phrase (in which the name of Gavryluk had sounded too clearly to be disregarded and thrust aside) returned as if by a magnified echo into the very centre of their silence, and now that he'd woken up, although he hadn't been alseep, though he felt it would have done him good to have just one brief moment of deep, complete sleep, except that he wouldn't be able to fall asleep in the rhythm of the insane ride and noise of the cart which sounded even louder than it had done before. He understood, as soon as he began to come back to reality, that it was sounding not only with the memory of that name, spoken aloud perhaps several times by Laudanski, it resounded and didn't die away, staying on the very edge of the precipice of his stupefied awareness, torturing his pride, his self-confidence, arousing anger and hatred but at the same time revealing to him his own weakness, his lack of orientation in the situation in which he'd found himself, and he understood that he'd not matured enough to make decisions, that he was still unfledged as a man, something Catherine had defined merely by

'You're too young,' but in that feeling of humiliating weakness he sensed at the same time some future strength (that name, the sound of that name, still resounding), it unveiled yet again and brought closer to his awareness that night, the stream, the sandy bank and the woman who, in the marvellous and mysterious way which has been known to all women from the dawn of humanity, yet which is always new and fresh, had conceived a man in him, although she'd not yet taught him to be one. But he'd already woken up for good, it was as though his memory suddenly grew bewildered, he felt his own sobriety as a sort of awakening into nullity, disagreeable and unstable, though it happened too late for him to be able to join in Laudanski's monologue in which the name of Gavryluk had appeared so often; but although his memory was in a state of bewilderment, he drew from it (as a result of the memory which it returned to him), in this sudden sobriety, not only Catherine but him too, Gavryluk, both of them, as though linked by some fatal thread of destiny, and he drew it into the bright afternoon on this forest road over which the hot and dust-filled air lay motionless, and even the premonition that he would no longer be able to think of her or him separately, that they'd both become an integral part of his experiences, of his passions, his destiny, almost the air which he'd always have to breathe, and it was completely obvious, so that Laudanski, whether or not he knew the truth about Gavryluk, about him, Peter, about his family, about Catherine and all their mutual relationships, said, as if referring to his, Peter's thoughts or complementing them: 'So now surely you understand why he didn't come out on top under Soviet rule?' in a voice clear but wooden, in which there was no feeling, and he himself at once uttered the response: 'For then he might only have been some Pole or Ukrainian or other, who'd been trapped by Soviet visions of their Red paradise. And yet he isn't just someone or other. He's half gentleman, half peasant. He gets all his pride from one blood, and also all his belief that he's someone destined to rule, someone better than the environment in which he had to grow up, and from the other blood he gets his belief that the land he lives on is his mother's inheritance, that her forefathers ploughed this land every spring, so that it belongs to him. A disastrous combination!' and then the wood had come to an end.

They were galloping along narrow paths over ploughed fields and marshland, the opening of the valley stretching, so Peter guessed, no doubt from Hanch-Chach itself as far as Sudy, and again the shriek was in the air. However, it wasn't the same shriek Peter had heard an hour or two ago over the burning village, for in this present shriek the crying of children dominated, while the adults, bent and silent, were walking along the road as though asleep, driving before them young cattle saved from the massacre and carrying all kinds of superfluous objects; and when, after slowing down a little, to pass by the groups going God knows where, Laudanski asked about his own men, they opened their mouths and only moved their lips, as if they wanted to say many things in reply but couldn't utter a single rational sound.

The voices, as if covered with a thick layer of earth, merged into one uninterrupted monologue. Amidst the trunks of tall, strong pine trees overgrown with bluish everlasting beards of moss and fungus, rose the juniper-bitter smoke of bonfires lit by the refugees; partisans mingled with them, hastily brought together by a cooked meal, and Laudanski was dozing on the ground, grinding his teeth in his sleep as if working his jaws over something insoluble. Above him, a horse was snuffling in its nose-bag, and the sun, having completed a semicircle, was sinking over the forest. Still earlier, Peter had asked here and there whether anyone had seen Nicholas Fiodorchuk, but whether they knew him or not, they disposed of Peter with small talk and then in turn asked him who he was, but he didn't reply, and they let him alone; it was evident that the fact he'd come with Laudanski satisfied them, so it was not proper or worth while to ask, and still later, before Laudanski woke up, he began wondering what he'd really been concerned about when he left home two days ago, in what or whom he was interested, for if he finally encountered Nicholas, he'd have to tell him; however, he was unable to squeeze anything but a vague recollection of a squabble with his grandfather and a handful of vague intentions out of his dull and aching head, as though some sickness were racking him or something inside his head had suddenly broken down, with which he hadn't yet been able to come to terms. He would gladly have lain down flat on his back and slept for at least a few hours, so as finally to dispel this pale nightmare from beneath his eyelids, and for some clear thoughts to be reborn in him, but he couldn't, for it was as though his weariness were itself the greatest enemy of sleep. He continued to look without seeing anything. In the host of voices that were submerging him a terror sounded for which he had no name. Terror, despair, and stubborn resolution also animated the movements and attitude of all these people in their rags and footwear worn down by their march as they now prepared for another march to some place to which he, Peter, was in no hurry to go to. There was neither moderation nor an end to resignation. The sort of irresistible desire which had recently torn him away from home had now gone out, for these people whom he saw all around him were alien to him, still quite alien, and it didn't seem at all as simple as he'd formerly supposed to form bonds with them, to get close to them, to blend into one thing with them, so as to subjugate his own purposes and his own aim to their aim, somehow to erase himself within their collective purpose, and it even seemed hostile to him. When he thought back, it was as if he'd never been in Chupryn, had never enjoyed anything or loved anything, had not been attached to anything, to any values it would have been worth while suffering for, and also that he'd never had enough sleep or food. Only hatred, growing steadily, losing its frames and outlines, becoming impersonal, overcame him entirely, so there was no way to expel it from his chest. He felt alone, and as though left behind in a desert. He could see himself as from a great distance, like a man absorbed by the desert air of this wilderness brooded over by hatred, stifled with passions, bursting with heat, which looked just like those regions of Asia Minor when his uncle visited them in his talks, though less rocky and of a different colour, and that solitary man who had halted there in the immeasurable distance was suffering from the cold despite the burning sun everywhere, and was looking around helplessly; no return, no way ahead. What had once excited him, had mobilized him, that awareness of the necessity of settling his family accounts with Gavryluk, which it had seemed his duty to do and which his nearest relatives were expecting of him despite their hidden anxious intent to postpone the moment of execution or even to imbue him with discouragement, just that, although quite recently it had burned in his chest with a great flame, now was scattered over, as it were, with a layer of ashes, and execution was still further off than it had been in Chupryn. And then, when Laudanski shook himself free of his doze, got up from the ground, when the brass of the sun had melted into the heath colour of early dusk, and the grass again began to sound with cicadas and move with manifold throngs of beetles and crickets, he was sufficiently tired to agree to anything. The nightmare under his eylids seemed to have grown tense, swollen, it was thrusting his eyes into the depths of their sockets, and when Laudanski came up, he leaned over and touched his arm, and was perhaps even shaking him to bring him back to his senses, but he obviously guessed his agony, for he said: 'It looks to me as though you've had enough. If I didn't know that you've already run away from home more than once, I'd think this was the first time. But it seems to me you've had enough for now,' but when Peter didn't reply, for he was trying to force something like a smile out of himself and on to the surface of his face, though of course nothing came out of it, he added: 'Our life is like chopping down trees in an old forest, you see? You must really harden yourself. But you've had a taste of it now, you'll be back,' and Peter, trying with all his might to get closer to him out of that distance, asked: 'Where?' 'Here. With us,' said Laudanski quite firmly, and he had a voice that was deceptively reminiscent to Peter of his father's voice as now he spoke to Peter across the empty space which separated them, startlingly similar as he repeated: 'Here. With us,' to which Peter, almost amazed, said: 'Not . . . ?' and he stated: 'Not no—but yes. But time is needed for that,' pressing his fingers into his arm until it hurt, 'There's no point in looking for young Fiodorchuk. I've known since this morning you wouldn't find him. But I thought to myself it wouldn't do any harm if you saw some of these things for yourself. For there's not much use in the way all of you sit protected behind the walls of Chupryn, as if in some fortress or other. Very little use, I tell you. Something more ought to be done by the Cherestvienskis on account of Gavryluk, I think,' and it was now really as if he were his father, for he'd once said to him, in this voice that was half firm, half melancholy but cruel, just as he now said through the lips of the robust giant: 'Now you must think over what you have to think over, don't get upset, you'll have time for everything,' and he passed his hand over the back of Peter's neck, and Peter turned to stone and was stunned by the effect of this touch which was like his father's, he was caressing with an almost embarrassed gesture a child who had grown up in his absence but who still needed a secret, fond, protective caress, then he asked in the same voice as before, alien yet familiar: 'Where shall I send you? For you won't get to Chupryn by a direct road either on foot or riding. Those Ukrainians and the SS are devastating the region towards Nikorycha and our men have their hands full with them. Maybe to Gleb, eh? Old Mrs. Woynovich, if I remember rightly, is your aunt or something like that, isn't she?' 'Yes, my aunt,' said Peter to this in total submission. 'Well, all right, my men will get you there somehow. And think of me sometimes, for we probably shan't meet again for a while,' and he pressed his hand on his arm, and was gone. The soothing, protective touch of his hand stretching into the limitless waste that surrounded Peter had gone, so had his voice, which had calmly given him *time*, had offered him the best of all good things now—time to consider his own capacities, to collect himself, and for a cool consideration of his plans, this time which hitherto no one had offered him, or so it seemed to him, not even his uncle, for they all wanted either to protect him for what he ought to do in future or had silently pushed him towards it—and while Laudanski's voice, resounding for a moment in his ears like the voice of his father resurrected from oblivion, had offered him just that time which he most needed, and then, after a moment, not the faintest recollection remained of that touch on his arm and that voice, and the previous sensation of wandering in a desert had returned, somewhere there in its depths lingered a feeling that he wouldn't be alone when he came to grips with himself, which after all was only a question of the time which he'd acquired.

And then, with four men he didn't know (who didn't pay much attention to him, and were settling some complicated matters of their own between themselves), he walked or rather dragged himself in a dull, half-conscious silence through the forest, and he was completely blinded in this crowded darkness of a night without walls. His companions had no faces or names or surnames, and spoke in low voices: 'Don't you know what happened? Gavryluk's bandits came into the very centre of the village and a Gestapo column stopped us. What's that you're saying? To get at them, we'd have had to throw fifty or so grenades. And where were you? On the hill behind the Jewish cemetery. Couldn't you get there? They were firing machine guns for a half hour. No one expected that affairs would take such a turn until the last moment. How many did they get, d'you know? About twenty men. They killed three on the road in the forest. Something ought to be done. Nothing doing, because it's happened again beyond Nikorycha. Well, but surely you'll fight them? That remains to be seen. It's too bad Kapitanchyk wasn't here, he'd have told you they'd been warned in advance. That's impossible! Your ambush near Ospych and now the fact that they came with the Gestapo surely means something. That German, the one they caught, knew we'd be coming from the cemetery. Please don't suggest such ideas to me. It all depends how one looks at it. First, we'll have to cut off the hands of the people who employ Gavryluk. Their villages ought to go up in smoke in compensation for ours. Well, smoke doesn't solve everything. If it goes on much longer, they will slaughter us all. It can't be worse than it is, I'm telling you. It's not worth shit. We don't know their hiding place, nor they ours. Either we attack somewhere or they do, and it'll go on like this indefinitely. It's time to put an end to Gavryluk once and for all. When Kapitanchyk joins Laudanski perhaps they'll be able to act together. When we get there I'll just drop down, I'm so worn out,' thus monotonously, always the same, as though they were a buzzing swarm of insects, they talked and talked, constantly circling around the same matters, as if there were no others and there never would be, condemned to them forever by some catastrophic fate.

The night sky stretched black and silver, like a bubble scattered with glittering, finely ground salt. His thoughts, groping in the darkness, threw brief rays of light which flared up at irregular intervals to reveal certain persons and places, his chaotic memories were drawing back, summoning up half-forgotten events while familiar people and relatives flitted by in packed images, as well as the whole blood-spattered history of this land that was filled with an uproar of groans and curses, all seen across the indifferent whispering of the forest and the rustle of mosses scorched by the heat of the day crumbling underfoot as he dragged himself along behind these four men of Laudanski's, not knowing, not wondering, not even trying to wonder where they were going, on through a forest extending into infinity, then across fields when the forest finally came to an end, along some disused road from which, behind a wide glare, could be seen a wide valley full of mist like a grey island, and a bridge across which they crawled, at short distances behind one another, a bridge near a mill from which could be heard, after they'd dragged themselves across, a shout in their direction, for evidently they had been seen, and it wasn't a friendly shout, but how could they see in this darkness as thick as felt who was a friend and who an enemy, it was a man's shout, and immediately after it a shot, but only one, the bullet whizzed over their heads as if from a catapult, and the noise was drowned as soon as it sounded in the clatter of the mill wheel and the howling of dogs, though the man who had fired didn't let them off the chain; in any case they were already far away and greedily gasping for breath, waiting a moment in the undergrowth, then again Peter was walking, dragging himself behind these four men of Laudanski's through another forest, then more fields, and still farther, endlessly, so that even his thoughts took on the shapes of a long, rough road, along which he would drag himself into the darkness from one dawn to the next behind these unknown men with whom he was linked by nothing but belonging to the same species, but at some time, finally, when the time given to him had passed, something would have to link him with them, and he would drag along this road continually hearing their monotonously buzzing voices, circling everlastingly around these same matters which they couldn't tear themselves away from or drop, yes, he would drag himself in this way to the end of his tether as he was now dragging himself to the point of choking, he was walking, and then, when both the next forest and next fields ended, through a village, still following them, and even when he lay down in a stable on the outskirts of this village and lay there motionless like a tree trunk on dried-up, sharp reeds in a stable between harnesses hanging by chains from the ceiling, where only the regular breathing of horses and their brief, cautious neighing were to be heard, he dragged on through his sleep, walking after Laudanski's men down that rough, unending road, although he didn't stir once he'd lain down on the reeds, he could still hear their voices buzz on as before, and he didn't even stop when he saw the face of his cousin Paul through the mist, even that face of Paul's, furious, flushed with blood, which was for a time only an uneven, wide opening edged with a narrow, ugly band of red full of a roaring which was trying to shout down those other voices buzzing monotonously in his ears, it shouted above his head: 'You puppy! You damned puppy! Nicholas Fiodorchuk has been turning half the county upside down looking for you! Do you want to get into Gavryluk's hands?' even that face which emerged suddenly from the dull torrent of his sleep, was unable to stop him, for he was still walking, dragging after Laudanski's men through fields, through the forest and on, on, although he could already see quite clearly the motionless, shabby walls of the stable, the narrow windows in lead-framed panes, and he could see that the wandering shadows of darkness on the walls were like great unreal birds, and he could even smell the odours of darkness, earth, vegetation and summer flowing from outside the windows into the stuffiness of horse sweat and the ammoniac stench of their excreta, nevertheless he went on walking, dragging along that road although in reality he now was moving, he even got up and blindly took a few steps, for suddenly there were no shabby walls with narrow windows, he was surrounded by air vibrating with cicadas and then Paul, who was evidently stepping just behind him, pushed him and he staggered and fell helplessly on his back, like a beetle. But just then he finally stopped in his wanderings, and everything at once stopped around him and within him too.

The close, thick darkness hitherto surrounding him, in which small crevices had only now and then opened, brightened from end to end. He saw the sky above him, bloodily torn apart by the first summery gleam, and Paul standing there looking down at him from a height, enlarged, distended, his long lanky legs in black riding boots with tops in which his torso was artificially stuck somewhere high up, and he saw that Paul appeared to be startled by what had happened, as if he hadn't fore-seen the strength of his own arm giving the blow, nor his, Peter's weakness, and he saw he was waiting to see whether he, Peter, would rise by his own power or whether he would call for help; and, standing over him so, he had to suppress his earlier shouting, to stifle it, evidently he realized it was useless and that nothing would penetrate to the man lying there, for he now said nothing and his whole face grimaced with a mixture of feelings difficult to describe, over which irritated embar-rassment prevailed, as if now that he'd hit him he didn't want to retreat from his position of strength in relation to Peter, but was at the same time startled by what he'd done, and this was accompanied by a sort of shame. In the end Peter raised himself from the ground, his cousin took a step back to give him room, waiting to see whether he'd throw himself at him, but no, Peter did nothing of the sort, merely stood still, quietly and calmly, asking indifferently: 'What do you want? Why have you come?' with total indifference, for now that he'd rid himself of that road and was no longer walking or dragging himself in a sort of hypnotic trance after the men, it was a matter of total indifference to him what happened, he'd left the decision to Paul (this was what Paul had been shouting at him in the stable, after leaning over to him out of his own sleep, and that brutal shove in the middle of his chest, after which he'd fallen to the ground, moving away from his own thoughts entirely). Then Paul, as if he'd finally decided what part to play, said in a voice which betrayed controlled fury, a sort of long-standing grudge, suspicion, and impatience (as if Peter had also said something a moment before): 'Shut up, right? I don't want to hear any of your damn' chatter. I didn't think you were such a fool as to fall into the clutches of that fellow,' and then—for Peter was standing quite motionless in his sudden silence and tranquillity—he hurled at him: 'Come on,' walking off in the direction of the road where a cart harnessed to two horses was standing, which Peter hadn't noticed before, not turning even once to see whether Peter had heard and was following him.

The cart dragged along joltingly by the horses dispelled the thickness of the greyly shining air; the miles of deserted country road quickly passed by. The wheels ground gently into the soft sand, stifling the sound of the impatiently trotting hoofs, raising Peter higher and higher above the threshold of sleep which, apart from the spectral impression of a journey to nowhere, had left behind in him only a vague image of Catherine, more unclear even than that of the journey, although he didn't recall thinking he was going to her when he'd dragged himself after Laudanski's men; however, this unending journey to nowhere had been erased in the light of awakening, while Catherine's image remained, evidently it had been impressed into his awareness without his having to exert very much will power. He was sitting to the right of his cousin, as soft as a rag doll discarded by children at play, and he was listening to the saw-like voices of insects aroused in the roadside grass of the ditches; it was a matter of total indifference to him what happened or where they were driving to, until he caught sight, above some yellow smoke in the distance which was rising in spirals over an island of intensely green trees, of the flapping wings of a flock of doves surging into flight, and he realized that the smoke was coming from the kitchen chimney of the manor at Gleb.

Paul had spoken to him only three times: once, when they stopped by the cart, he'd said: 'Get up,' when they drove off he'd said: 'I expected something different of you,' and when they drove up to the porch of the manor: 'Get out,' he said, getting out first himself, and waiting for him. When Peter jumped down to the gravel which grated under his boots somehow strangely and too loudly in the morning tranquillity, he looked automatically at the clock over the porch: it showed a quarter to four. Without speaking he went after his cousin.

They passed through the front hall, up the stairs, down a corridor on the second floor without meeting anyone on the way, and then Paul stopped at a door half hidden by a curtain, opened it and, moving aside, spoke to him, not loudly, the first words in this house: 'Go in,' and when Peter went inside he closed the door after him. Peter then heard, at the same time as the door handle turned, the noise of a key in the lock, then the departing footsteps of his cousin until they died away.

He stood against the door, without at once recognizing the room, although he had often spent the night in it when he used to drive over to the Woynovich family. Tarnished gilt and faded silks were reflected in the richly ornamented rococo mirrors, there was scarcely a yard or so of space between the closely packed pieces of furniture (little tables, a spinet, a bureau, silk armchairs, chandeliers, wall brackets and pictures, all seemed to be heaped one on top of the other, as though some catastrophic flood had washed them out of ruins, piled them up, and then, when the water finally receded, they'd come to rest in this very room), creating an unpleasant impression that depressed him. A cheap photograph fifty years old or more, in a *fin-de-siècle* frame, of a ballet dancer raising puffy, lavishly pleated skirts to show drawers fastened amidst lace and cambric below the knee, and who seemed to be winking her eye at him ironically, was the only other note of that ornate interior. But he finally recognized it all, of course. So here he was again where he'd never expected to return, nor wanted to, between the walls of the room which in the past had heard his childish weeping, and had seen all his dumb helplessness in those hot evenings and nights in July and August 1939 which brought no coolness; he'd come here a few times from Chupryn to stay and had been able to picture another room located a floor below, where his grown-up, masculine, handsome, and proud cousin Alexei was holding in his arms his young, newly-wed wife who only a few months before had been his, Peter's, contemporary in games and who, it seemed, no one could take away from him, but whom Alexei had taken and was holding in his arms there, only a floor below, not caring much about his solitude or even aware of it; between these walls, which had also seen his joy when Alexei had to leave one day, though they hadn't seen his feelings of shock, uncertainty, sorrow, and pity when he learned that after the Soviet invasion Alexei had vanished like a stone dropped into water, and he'd sought fearfully for a sign of grief for him in that beloved face (please forgive me, Alexei, I didn't intend to steal her from you, but she belonged to me from the very start, although she didn't know it); between walls which had hardly been appropriate for imagined and genuine farewells where, or so it seemed to him, he need only close his eyes tight for them to be populated with figures—his grandmother with a tiny smile of hope in her face, his grandfather (I'd like at least you to be spared from the conflagration and to bear witness for all of us by your existence), his uncle with his grey eyes like those in old icons gazing at everything and nothing, bearing the limitless grief caused by his own encounter with oblivion, Paul (don't pretend to be Daphnis, you fool, it's time you came to grips with your family's affairs), Alexei, Nick, a big stalwart man with fair hair and strong, flat face, yes, it was Laudanski (we deserve something more from you all, young man, I'm counting on you), his father, his mother (I loved him, but he was always a stranger to me, don't tell him so, Peter), and Julia the Second, and Catherine, and they would all lean over him and utter disordered questions, like water from the coldest of springs and streams, which has a fiercely sobering power, perhaps they'd forgive him if he were ever guilty of anything—here he was again between these walls, and he thought in a sort of premonition that it was for the last time and then, not thinking at all, not coming to any decisions any more, he went like a dummy to a pouf in a corner and sat down on it. Time was passing, it was passing faster and faster while he, looking back into the past, saw in his dull, futile weariness a human figure entirely different from himself, an entirely different Peter Cherestvienski, who was no longer able to arouse in himself that slight interest which a faded photograph of the past can arouse, and he went on sitting there just as he'd sat down, leaning rather to one side, uncomfortably, because it didn't occur to him to sit in any other way, without even feeling hungry or thirsty, and he listened almost without knowing it to the tiny echoes of this house as they seeped into the room under the door, through the windows, through invisible cracks in the walls, through all the pores of wood and plaster, and suddenly he became aware of a crystallizing thought: If something doesn't happen now, at once, right away, it never will. Nothing happened.

He opened his eyes. In the silence of the house, which was never real silence but merely the silence of human beings, for the walls, floors, and objects inside it were living intensely, somewhere, far off, a thin and penetrating sound vibrated. Perhaps it had been in the air for a long time and Peter had already heard it before and had automatically associated it with that living silence which surrounded him and which he'd grown used to as he heard it or even without hearing it at all, but now he suddenly heard it in reality, or his senses grew sharp, as it were, and disconnected this vibrating, thin, penetrating sound from all that combination of sounds which belonged to the dead world of objects and connected it instead with the silence of human beings which this single sound at once destroyed utterly. When he listened intently, he realized that the sound seemed to be slowly increasing to the utmost limits of the source that uttered it, then hurried steps sounded somewhere below, then again quick and light on the stairs leading from below to the second floor, then quite close, not isolated or separated from but rather as though within that penetrating sound all the time.

Peter breathed heavily. He heard his breath and suddenly caught the sound of something else, or rather, while hearing it all the time, he caught that high, penetrating, thin sound changing into something more comprehensible than before: into a shrieking, which was now quite close, and stifled only by the wall. But it still seemed to him that he must have been listening to it for a very long time before he realized that the shrieking was a woman's shrieking, and he at once saw the door begin to shudder from blows, before he realized that he could also hear them, those heavily thumping, furious blows, as though someone were drumming with little fists on the wood in a rhythm to match her own shrieking, and then everything suddenly broke off. In the depths of the corridor, a new sound penetrated to him, steps, slow and springy, certainly those of a man, and, 'You snake, you've killed him,' he heard the phrase shrieked with furious despair in a voice that made him realize that earlier too he'd been hearing Catherine, and another phrase, or rather several phrases, were uttered in Paul's voice: 'I love him more than you do. Like a brother. He's my only friend and I don't want him to get as deep into this as I am. I want to spare him that,' and then the iron click of the key turned in the lock. Catherine was already standing on the threshold with her hair loose about her pale face, flushed patches on her cheeks, breathing fast and staring into the pinkish gloom of the interior, leaning forward as if she were getting ready to jump but lacked the strength to breach the threshold, while Paul's face was thoughtful, no, it was devoid, rather, of any expression, his hand still suspended helplessly on the doorknob was narrow, long, and pale as the hand of a corpse frozen to the bone, a piece of dead flesh still not torn from the frame, but then it came alive, moved as Catherine finally crossed the threshold and ran, tore inside, and this was precisely the moment when the white hand of his cousin moved to press the metal of the doorknob, and it closed the door behind the woman.

A sudden silence fell and then at once Catherine whispered: 'Oh God, Pete, what have you done?' as she rushed to the pouf on which he was sitting without having stirred from the moment the door closed, as if nothing were happening, and catching his arm: 'My dearest boy, after all, I can't be with you, you must understand. Why did you run away?' she whispered close to his mouth, weeping and accusing him, and then Peter, although he hadn't thought of it at all, and in any case her proximity, her despair and sobbing hadn't given him time to think, said: 'That wasn't why. That wasn't why at all,' without even admitting into his awareness her surprise at his own words (surprise like an electric shock, like the thrust of steel into a living body), for at once, as he said that that wasn't why, he realized that this island on which he'd found himself was no island of salvation and that that sweet period of careless boyhood, of innocence, simplicity, and poetry had long since died, and although perhaps he'd already been aware of this for a few days, he summed up at this moment, like a flash of lightning, what had happened to those plans of his, and he understood to the core that, since nothing could rescue that time, nothing or no one, he'd been deluding himself in vain, now indeed he wouldn't even want the island, he'd have rejected any magic formula able to bring it back, had it been offered to him, and he saw ahead a cold grey expanse that stretched a long way, already growing alive with people, and it was as though a salty wave of the sea tide had engulfed him, then thrown him up on a shore and left him naked on the sand. He knew now that he must go away.

He longed to touch Catherine once again, to feel her pulse once more, alive and throbbing under her temples, but already she had moved away. He was too tired to pursue her, to seize her, as he'd meant to a moment earlier. A steel-grey haze of weariness veiled everything from him and in addition it had grown bright and hot around him, not dark, as is usual in rooms crowded with furniture where the windows are covered with velvet curtains. He rose with an effort and tried to pursue the shape of Catherine which was escaping him, becoming blurred in the haze; he felt a childish sensation of fear lest cruel fate might take her from him forever, but the room and then the corridor too, and even the stairs, melted quickly away into that steel-grey haze, and soon began to yield, to open up some depths as bottomless as an abyss before him. One brief moment more, and the walls of the manor suddenly turned black, in the window frames he could see naked sky and white clouds billowing across it. Of the manor house only a skeleton full of air was left, and then, thinking indistinctly: It's too bad I wasn't able to touch her once more, to hold her in my arms, he thought that now he really must be on his way without hesitation, for this, he'd discovered, was a place which only people at the limits of their lives visited, or people who have disappeared from the world's surface forever and are not mortal at all, for if even a part of them lives on in the memories of others, they too live, but he ought to have left as soon as possible if he didn't want to surrender to them (the dead are as alone as the living—they demand support), and if he didn't want to surrender to the arms that were reaching out for him. This was why, without turning back, he crossed the square next to something reminiscent of a station with railway lines, and entered a path leading upwards.

The sun was blindingly bright, but everything—the clump of trees which he soon left behind, and the path, and the rock walls of the valley and the entire valley, deserted from end to end, and the distant mountain peaks—all was plunged into and covered with a dense, stifling, intolerable haze which veiled his eyes as well and deprived him of the power to think. He tried to collect his strength and take quicker steps as he climbed the hillside, but the road was becoming longer and was lost in this strange haze, and the gusts of wind were too feeble to dispel it, they died down too soon. It was still day, and it seemed to Peter that noon hadn't passed yet, but finally the barely visible mountain chain began to blaze white, and he realized he was approaching the place from which he'd started his journey. He soon caught sight of the two chestnut trees suspended over the precipice as if they got there by accident, scattered with whiteness that seemed to blaze rather than flower, and the freshly tarred road which was so black that when he shut his eyes, parched with the heat, he still saw it for a moment beneath his eyelids, like a deep crevice of shade cut into a sea of fire. But then he was already standing on the light-brown, naked terrace of a rock fault in front of the half-ruined wall of an inn, or perhaps shelter, under the cruel sun, by a wall which gave no shade at all, and somewhere, under the eaves which gave no shade either, was the old countrywoman sitting as before, when he'd been here earlier before going down into the valley, she was motionless as before, dressed in black, shielding herself from the heat with a black kerchief, stiff in meditation, silent. The dog, just as before, was sleeping, stretched flat as a corpse by the foundation of the fence encircling the inn, and in the burning and dead silence, as before, not a voice spoke. Looking at the old woman, Peter wondered whether it had really been from here that he'd gone down into the valley, or whether he'd gone anywhere at all, and whether anything had changed and time hadn't moved a step forward, or was it that it only seemed to him he'd travelled a long way going somewhere, and had discovered once again that which the passage of time had enveloped. But he couldn't give himself a rational or adequate answer to this question, he was too tired. Dead-tired. After experiencing the boundless, destructive, but at the same time fortifying flow of time, as enduring as only earth, air, fire, and water can be, undefeated and elemental time, he found in himself the conviction that he must not yield or surrender to its flow which moved into the past and future, but that he should harness it in any way he could and should try, in that future sombrely opening up before him, consciously to carry over whatever was worth preserving of the past, so that it should endure. And to endure.